J. D. DAVIES

The Cursed SHORE

CANELO

First published in the United Kingdom in 2024 by

Canelo
Unit 9, 5th Floor
Cargo Works, 1-2 Hatfields
London SE1 9PG
United Kingdom

Copyright © J. D. Davies 2024

The moral right of J. D. Davies to be identified as the creator of this work has been asserted in accordance with the Copyright, Designs and Patents Act, 1988.

All rights reserved. No part of this publication may be reproduced or transmitted in any form or by any means, electronic or mechanical, including photocopy, recording, or any information storage and retrieval system, without permission in writing from the publisher.

A CIP catalogue record for this book is available from the British Library.

Print ISBN 978 1 80436 605 9
Ebook ISBN 978 1 80436 611 0

This book is a work of fiction. Names, characters, businesses, organizations, places and events are either the product of the author's imagination or are used fictitiously. Any resemblance to actual persons, living or dead, events or locales is entirely coincidental.

Cover design by Patrick Knowles

Look for more great books at www.canelo.co

Printed and bound in Great Britain by Clays Ltd, Elcograf S.p.A.

For Rowan

Far its rocky knoll descried
Saint Michael's chapel cuts the sky.
I climbed; —beneath me, bright and wide,
Lay the lone coast of Brittany.

Bright in the sunset, weird and still,
It lay beside the Atlantic wave,
As if the wizard Merlin's will
Yet charmed it from his forest grave.

Behind me on their grassy sweep,
Bearded with lichen, scrawled and gray,
The giant stones of Carnac sleep.
In the mild evening of the May…

And there across the watery way,
See, low above the tide at flood.
The sickle-sweep of Quiberou bay
Whose beach once ran with loyal blood!

He longed for it, —pressed on! — In vain.
At the Straits failed that spirit brave.
The South was parent of his pain,
The South is mistress of his grave.

        Matthew Arnold, Stanzas Composed at Carnac

PROLOGUE

27 JUNE 1795

All around him, the dead giants of stone were stirring.

When he touched them, they still seemed no more than rocks. Unmoving, unseeing; the same they had been all his life. For hundreds, perhaps thousands, of lives before his. But today, as the thick summer mist spun its cloak around them and around him, he would willingly swear an oath that the standing stones of Carnac were coming to life. They were becoming flesh and blood again, the giants rising from their graves. He tried to tell himself it was the mist, only the mist, creating the impression the stones were living, breathing, moving. It couldn't be anything else, could it?

But even if the giants were coming to life, the game still had to be played. It still had to be won.

'*Unan, daou, tri, pevar, pemp...*' One, two, three, four, five...

'*...eizh warn ugent, nav warn ugent, tregont!*' Twenty-eight, twenty-nine, thirty.

He opened his eyes, looked around to check that the nearest standing stones were not really sprouting limbs and tearing themselves out of the soil of Brittany, then shouted with all the force his ten-year-old lungs could muster, 'Ready or not, here I come!'

Thierry Kervran ran toward the closest stones, checking behind each. There was no sign of his quarry, not even in the hollow under a stone that had been pulled down years before to clear a path for a horse and plough. He ran down one line of stones, then up another. The lines were much longer, but surely Vincent couldn't have run any further during a count of thirty? Thierry zigzagged through the stones, one part of him still hunting Vincent Radoux, the other evading any newly resurrected giants that might be pursuing him.

Vincent said they weren't giants. He said they were King Arthur's knights, turned to stone by Morgayne the Sorceress after the Battle of Camlann. But what did Vincent know? His father had been guillotined the autumn before last for being a traitor to the Republic, a royalist and a believer in the old religion, so perverse ideas ran in the Radoux family. Melanie scoffed at both of them, saying the stones were just stones. Sometimes he didn't know why they still played with Melanie.

Thierry checked the ruined charcoal-burner's hut on the far side of the furthest stones. Nothing. Vincent had vanished. What if a giant had risen up and swallowed him? Or, in the impossible event that Vincent's theory about the stones was correct, what if Morgayne had snatched him away to her lair in the Forest of Broceliande?

Thierry stopped running, put his hands on his knees and tried to breathe more slowly. Perhaps if he stayed still and listened, he might hear Vincent's mocking laughter in the distance, giving him a sense of where he was.

The mist seemed to be clearing slowly. There were glimpses of sunshine over to the east. And there were voices, very faint, very far away, from somewhere in the direction of Carnac village. Voices he recognised, calling his name.

'Thierry! Thierry, where are you?'

Vincent calling out in Breton, Melanie in French. Melanie had disappeared somewhere before the game began. She was always doing that. Girls were very strange beasts, Thierry had decided on his last birthday.

'You've spoiled the game!' Thierry shouted as he ran toward them.

'Forget your stupid game!' bawled Melanie, her voice as commanding and unchallengeable as ever even though she was the same age as Vincent and Thierry. 'Come and see this! Come and see what I've just seen!'

He could see his friends now, their outlines wraith-like in the mist. But before he reached them, they both turned and began to run toward the village.

'See what?' shouted Thierry as he struggled to keep up with them.

'You just wait! It'll be worth it!'

Melanie was easily outpacing the two boys. The only sister of five older brothers, children of a father who had been killed fighting for the Army of the North, she had grown up having to compete for every crumb and race for every prize. As he drew level with Vincent, Thierry glanced across to his friend.

'What's she seen that's so important?'

'Dunno, she didn't say.'

'Why do we always do what she tells us?'

Vincent shrugged.

'She's Melanie. Of course we do what she tells us.'

A familiar hill rose out of the mist ahead of them. Everyone in Carnac knew the hill wasn't natural, and Vincent was convinced it covered the tomb of King

Arthur himself. Melanie was already halfway up it, intent on reaching the small, ruined chapel that crowned its summit. In the olden time before the revolution, the time that the children could now barely remember, the time of priests and kings, it had been called the Chapel of Saint-Michel. The local *sans-culottes* tore it to pieces a couple of years earlier when the news of the sometime queen Marie Antoinette's execution reached Carnac. Now it was an empty, roofless shell, but on a clear day it was possible to see far out to sea, all the way over to Belle-Île and beyond.

Melanie was leaning against the whitewashed wall of the chapel, grinning at her two breathless friends as they finally made the summit.

'You're snails,' she said mockingly. 'I should be the one they call up for the Army of Italy or the Marine Nationale in a few years' time, not you two.'

Thierry ignored the barb.

'So what have you brought us to see?' he snapped.

She said nothing, but pointed to the south, toward the sea. The mist was clearing more rapidly over Quiberon than it was from the higher ground above Carnac, the ground where the ancient stones stood. Thierry took in the familiar sights – the impossibly thin strip of land that stretched out like a crooked finger far into the sea, the flat promontory of Quiberon at the end of it, the ramparts of Fort Sans-Culotte at Penthièvre with the large *Tricolore* flying from it. But today there was a new sight in the bay.

'Sixty-five,' said Vincent under his breath, 'sixty-six—'

'Sixty-nine or seventy,' said Melanie. 'I've already counted them. Nine warships, I think, the rest merchantmen.'

'Transports,' said Vincent. 'See the boats pulling away from them, making for the beaches?'

'What's it mean?' asked Thierry. 'Is it the Lorient squadron, bringing in a new army against the Chouans and the Vendéeans?'

The children were silent for a few moments, staring hard at the spectacle out in the bay. But despite the lingering mist and the distance between them and the multitude of boats heading for the shore, they were able to make out the preponderant colour worn by the disembarking troops. It was certainly not blue, the uniform of the French Republic's armies. It was red, a colour associated by every Frenchman, woman and child with one power alone. Then a slight breeze that would shortly dispel the last of the morning mist ruffled the grass on the summit of the great mound of Saint-Michel, the ensigns on a few of the ships in the bay began to stir, and Melanie pointed at a ship distinguished by a long narrow white pennant flying from its foremast.

'No,' she said, the matter no longer in doubt. 'It's the English. The English are invading France.'

PART ONE

FIVE MONTHS EARLIER

CHAPTER ONE

Lord Wilden stepped through his front door and immediately lost his balance. Only the exemplary reactions of Daniel, the new footman, in stretching out an arm that Wilden's flailing hand managed to grasp saved him from an undignified landing upon his aristocratic arse. The blizzard, now several hours old, was in full spate once again, howling down Hill Street from the direction of Hyde Park. The ground beneath Wilden's feet, where fresh snow concealed the previous day's fall, now compacted into ice, was treacherous beyond measure. He thanked Daniel profusely, then once again considered the wisdom of his decisions not to command the saddling of his horse nor to order his coach brought round from the mews behind the house. He had more of a care for his servants than for himself, making him something of a rarity among the peerage of England, and he would not compel them to venture out on such a night as this. The truth was that if he could, he too would not have ventured through his door at all. He would much prefer to be seated before his fire, a glass of claret in his hand, reading the dispatches from the commanders of the fleet in the Mediterranean and his agents in Paris, Saint Petersburg, Madrid and elsewhere.

For sure, it was not a night to be walking the streets of Mayfair. Perhaps the only saving grace was that the snowstorm would also discourage the footpads, the ding coves and the scores of other criminal vermin who haunted the environs of Westminster. Nor would the harlots and strumpets be parading their wares in these conditions. So Wilden pulled his cloak tighter around him, pulled down his tricorn until it was very nearly over his eyes, bowed his head against the relentless snow, and set off to meet the man who had summoned him.

He skirted Shepherd Market, crossed Piccadilly – quieter than usual, for few Hackneys and even fewer lone riders were abroad – and made his way into Green Park, struggling with every step he took. The wind and the depth of the virgin snow made progress difficult, and the lights of the clubhouses adjacent to the park were tempting, but Wilden trudged his way onward. He would not do this for anyone else, except the king, he decided. Not for Earl Spencer, First Lord of the Admiralty, and his superior within that august department. Certainly not for the Prince of Wales, that worthless clodpole, nor for any of his scapegrace brothers. No, Edward Pardew, fifth Baron Wilden of Alveley Hall in the County of Shropshire, would not have placed one toe outside his warm if spartan rooms in Hill Street were it not for the two initials at the bottom of the short note that had arrived earlier that evening.

On toward Horse Guards, where candles burned in many of the windows and several unfortunate soldiers, presumably the men who had drawn the short straws, were engaged in the Sisyphean task of attempting to clear snow from the parade ground. A sentry on the gate leading to Whitehall challenged him, but a sergeant emerged from the warmth of the adjacent guardroom, reprimanded the guard for his impertinence, and saluted Wilden as he passed. Down Whitehall, and finally his destination was in sight. No challenge from the solitary sentry here, who came to attention immediately. Wilden smiled to himself. With his cloak pulled up and his hat pulled down, only a fraction of his face could be seen. Wilden could have been anyone, a swindler or even an assassin intent on murdering the occupant of the building he now entered. Somehow, he doubted that Monsieur Robespierre had been guarded so sketchily in his days of pomp and power before the guillotine took his head. But the single shivering sentry at the door of the most powerful man in the country was undoubtedly truer to the English way.

A footman helped him out of his cloak, took that garment and his hat, and gave him entirely superfluous directions. Wilden had been in the house often and knew the way. Several more footmen and a handful of scurrying clerks inclined their heads respectfully as he passed. The final one saw him approach down a narrow corridor, knocked on the door at its end, heard a response from within, and turned the handle to admit him.

Wilden stepped into a dark room lit by an impossibly small number of candles. Most of them were on or around the desk that faced him, behind which sat a slight, pale fellow in a black gown. The man seemed not to see Wilden, his attention still fixed on the paper before him.

Wilden coughed and addressed the man who had summoned him.

'Prime Minister.'

William Pitt, first lord of the Treasury and Prime Minister of Great Britain and her empire, finally put down the paper, rubbed his eyes, and looked directly at his guest.

'My lord. My apologies for bringing you out on such a night as this.'

'A splendid excuse for a pleasant walk, Prime Minister.'

'You *walked*? In this? From *Mayfair*? Good God, Ned, have you taken leave of your senses?'

'It seemed the most efficient and expeditious way of responding to your summons.'

Pitt shook his head.

'Sometimes I despair of you, Ned Wilden. Walking from Hill Street to Downing Street on such a night as this. Swimming in the Serpentine, I'm told, even at this time of year. *For your health*, or so you're said to claim. Remember, my lord, we still have that wager in the Brooks's betting book. The one that says I'll outlive you, the sum to be paid from the loser's estate by his executors.'

Pitt's confidence in winning the wager seemed as unassailable as it had been the day it was made, despite the evidence to the contrary. For one thing, an almost empty decanter of port stood close to Pitt's left hand. Wilden had it on good authority that the prime minister, plagued by ill health throughout his life, had once been advised by a doctor that a bottle of port a day would be a capital and infallible cure for his many ailments. Pitt was a highly intelligent man who had been admitted to the University of Cambridge when he was only thirteen, but his logic could sometimes go astonishingly awry. For instance, he extrapolated from that single doctor's opinion that an even greater dosage of the medication in question could only have an even more beneficial effect, so the House of Commons was one of the very few places where the prime minister could be seen more than a few inches from the reassuring companionship of a bottle or two of the Kingdom of Portugal's finest export.

Pitt made a gesture that Ned Wilden interpreted as an invitation to take one of the two uncomfortable chairs in front of the prime minister's desk.

'Excuse me a moment while I complete my perusal of the latest dispatches from Vienna,' said Pitt, returning to the paper in his hand.

The clock in the corner of the room had one of the loudest ticks Wilden had ever heard. It was a gross and gaudy timepiece, out of kilter with both its surroundings and its owner, but it had been a present from the king on the tenth anniversary of Pitt's taking office at the tender age of twenty-four, such a miraculous elevation being somewhat easier when one's father had been prime minister before. Wilden thought the clock was probably a gesture of gratitude for sparing His Majesty the ordeal of selecting a new prime minister every few months, as had been the case during several intervals in his reign.

Wilden and Pitt had much in common. Both were relatively young men, the prime minister thirty-five and the lord of the Admiralty only a little younger. Both devoted themselves to their work with a singlemindedness unfashionable for their age. Neither had ever married. It would have been an exaggeration to say that they liked each other, but on the very rare occasions when Lord Wilden was ever in his cups, he sometimes thought of William Pitt as the brother he never had. But he knew the prime minister would never have allowed himself such a foolish, sentimental thought. Even so, perhaps in some way they were kindred spirits, and that was why the prime minister sometimes entrusted Wilden with secrets and tasks that he would not have dreamed of confiding to one of the jovial, red-faced, back-slapping fellows of the *ton*. Wilden already knew that this would be one of those occasions.

At length, Pitt put down the paper he had been reading and rubbed his eyes once again.

'Damn Austrians,' he sighed, 'too many archdukes – can't keep track of 'em all. But the emperor is steady, thank God. Unwavering. Steadfast. So, we have no worries on that score, Ned.'

Wilden knew that Pitt spent most of his waking hours trying to keep together the fragile coalition that opposed republican France. The Spanish were wavering – when were they not? – but everything hinged on the Austrians, who provided the bulk of the armies opposing the atheist French fanatics who had guillotined their king, queen, countless members of their nobility and so many others, innocents of all ranks and conditions. But the Emperor Francis had good reason to be unwavering and steadfast. After all, Marie Antoinette had been his sister.

'Good news indeed, Prime Minister.'

'Capital, in fact. Glass of port, Ned?'

'Thank you, but no, Prime Minister. A little early for me. Perhaps some snuff, though?'

Pitt pushed the snuffbox across the desk with one hand, draining what was left in the decanter of port into his hand with the other.

'So, Ned, the notion of an expedition to Brittany. You've cast an eye over the proposal?'

'As you commanded, Prime Minister.'

Wilden took a pinch of snuff and inhaled loudly through both nostrils.

'Your thoughts, then?'

Wilden sighed. He had many thoughts on the documents he had perused over the previous few days, not all of which were likely to be welcome to the prime minister. But nothing ventured, and so forth. Well, so be it.

'On paper it seems eminently sensible as a proposal, sir. Bridport's and Cornwallis's fleet to cover an expeditionary force, the inshore squadron to be commanded by Sir John Borlase Warren, a capital fellow. The army to consist primarily of the French royalist *emigré* regiments, with several of our regiments of the line in reserve and to be deployed only if essential. That army to establish a bridgehead on the shores of Quiberon Bay, then combine with the extant irregular royalist forces in the west of France, namely the Chouans and the Vendéeans. An army totalling some three hundred thousand men in all, or so our exiled French friends assure us, the first objective of this mighty combined royalist army to be the capture of the enemy's dockyard at Lorient. As I say, Prime Minister, eminently sensible. Eminently achievable. On paper.'

'I'm waiting, Ned.'

'Waiting, sir?'

'Waiting for the "but". Of all those who serve government in capacities of state, I can always depend on you most of all for the killing "buts".'

Wilden took a deep breath. Unlike some of their colleagues in government, the prime minister was not averse to hearing contrary opinions. But Ned Wilden knew there was only so much contrariness that even William Pitt could tolerate.

'Well, Prime Minister, as I see it the French royalists are divided into factions who hate each other almost as vehemently as they hate the republicans. There are those who favour the constitutional model that England has, and that France possessed briefly before the reign of terror took hold. But then there are those who wish for the restoration of the monarchy as it was before the revolution began, the king holding absolute and arbitrary power, and all the rest of it. This faction is led by the late king's younger brother, the Count of Artois.'

Pitt smiled tightly and took another sip of his port. He was usually the man who lectured his ministers in the blindingly obvious, but he did not object to being on the receiving end for once.

'And as we both know, Ned, the count is a man not entirely brookable to English sensibilities.'

Wilden nodded. It was a common jest in the clubrooms of Pall Mall and Saint James's that the Count of Artois' notion of a Sunday well spent was to sit through a four-hour mass, then order and witness the mass execution of a few thousand republicans, followed by an invigorating hour or two of self-flagellation.

'As you say, Prime Minister. To make matters worse, both factions place much reliance on the Chouans. But my agents in Brittany inform me that the Chouan army remains unworthy of the name, despite all the assurances to the contrary from our exiled French friends. I would describe them as no more than a ragtag collection of loosely federated peasant mobs with no real leadership, few weapons and almost as little love for the English or the *emigrés* as they have for the republicans. Taken in the round, then, I would advise against the commitment of English ships, gold and perhaps soldiers in a cause where the aims are imprecise and our allies so inconstant.'

Pitt leaned forward and steepled his fingers.

'Thank you for your frankness, my lord. Your familiar and welcome frankness. But here we cross from your world into mine, and mine has certain, ah, complexities that we also need to consider.'

'Complexities, sir?'

'Just so. For instance, the *emigrés* in London are very influential and very vocal. They have what one might describe as undue influence within the Houses of Parliament. Should they be so inclined, they could make life difficult for the ministry. Very difficult indeed, if truth be told, and as you know our position is already fragile enough. But there is an even greater complexity, and that, my lord, resides in Kew Palace.'

'The king,' said Wilden.

Pitt nodded, then took another sip of port.

'His Majesty is an enthusiast for this expedition. "Landing in Brittany, Mister Pitt, what what!" he says to me at our every audience. "Take Lorient, a triumphant march through Brittany, dish the murderers in Paris, at the very least divert enough of their armies to weaken the other fronts. A capital scheme, Mister Pitt, most capital!" Who am I to deny the will of the Lord's anointed, Ned? His Majesty has convinced himself that if all goes in our favour, this expedition will be the means to put the Bourbons back on the throne and extirpate the canker of revolution from the whole of Europe, England included. I think he would not listen favourably to your discourse of the divisions and weaknesses of our royalist allies.'

Wilden nodded sympathetically. He had ample personal experience of the peccadilloes of King George the Third and did not envy Pitt his task of mollifying the unpredictable monarch.

'Then the expedition will go ahead?'

'Oh, it will go ahead eventually, once the spring comes, once the French royalists can assemble sufficient force, once Bridport can be persuaded to leave the blockade of Brest long enough to escort the armada to

Brittany. But it occurs both to His Majesty and myself that the delicate elements you outlined so succinctly, my lord, demand certain, ah, *special arrangements,* if we may call them that. We have an idea in mind… In His Majesty's opinion, and mine, though, all these considerations also demand the presence of an Englishman of some standing – to smooth over quarrels among the French, say, or between them and our own commanders. A man with a perfect understanding of the issues involved. A man who knows my mind and that of His Majesty.'

It was the coldest day of the winter, and Pitt's room was not warm. Even so, Wilden was aware that he was beginning to sweat. There was a tightness in his heart, and he prayed he was not suffering the beginnings of an apoplexy.

'You wish me to go with the expedition, Prime Minister?'

'Who better, Ned? And if it prevails, you might be the first Englishman to ride into a liberated Lorient. Who knows, eh, if the scheme succeeds beyond any of our wildest dreams then you may be the first to enter free Paris!'

Wilden's wildest dreams were actually taking him in other directions. They conjured up visions of oncoming republican hordes and of his mangled body lying in a rancid Breton ditch. They brought forward the image of his French cousin, Philippe Kermorvant, Vicomte de Saint-Victor, a naval captain, whose estate lay somewhere in Brittany. What if he should become his kinsman's prisoner, just as Philippe had once been his? Remote possibilities, wild thoughts indeed, but there was one terrible certainty underpinning Pitt's so-reasonable words.

'But, Prime Minister,' said Wilden, 'surely that means I will need to be aboard a ship to cross to France. I will actually have to be at sea.'

'My dear Wilden,' said Pitt, 'you are a lord of the Admiralty. Surely there is no better place for you to be?'

'A civil lord, Prime Minister, and the most junior of them—'

'Damn it, Ned, *I need you there*. England needs you there. This could be the winning of the war, the return of a king to France, everything we have worked for and dreamed of these last years. I don't trust the French royalists one jot. Yes, I trust Lord Bridport, Cornwallis, Warren, all of them on our side, but I would trust them better still, and even be less wary of our French allies, if my own eyes were upon them every hour of every day. That cannot be, so I must send in my stead a man I would trust with my life. Besides, Ned, the expedition will take several months to assemble, and it will only be able to cross in the summer. Who knows what may happen in that time, eh? The French might surrender long before you can get your feet wet. So don't look as though you've seen your father's ghost, my lord, and at least join me for one toast before you venture back out into the blizzard.'

Without waiting for a reply, Pitt poured a glass for Wilden and refilled his own, leaving the decanter empty. Wilden knew that not many moments would pass before the prime minister summoned a footman to refill it.

'Damnation to those twin hydras of atheism and republicanism, Ned Wilden! *Vive le roi Louis! Vive le roi George!*'

Wilden raised his glass and repeated the toast, but his thoughts were frantic and far away. They were on the high seas, and on the hostile shore of France.

CHAPTER TWO

From a jumble of old mould-infested documents and journals written by Leonore Kermorvant at different times, discovered in the muniment room of the Chateau de Brechelean, Brittany

I am not the sort of woman who keeps a journal.

Journals are for simpering English spinsters in country vicarages. They are for the likes of my neighbour Sandrine Cadoudal, who records every minute of every day of the unremittingly tedious life she lives with her sister. I think she fancies herself a new Madame de Sévigné or Madame Desmoulins, but a small boy using a slate to scribble down what he did at school that day is a superior diarist to poor Sandrine. She used to read me lengthy passages from her journal, which she records in a flowing hand, written up daily in large and expensive leather-bound volumes, but that was before she shunned me for denouncing my husband to the Jacobins, thus causing his death upon the guillotine. Being spared the ordeal of the elder Cadoudal's vapid thoughts was one of the consolations of our falling out irrevocably when she denounced me as a Jezebel who had whored with my husband's brother. I have not spoken to her since, and count it one of the great mercies of my life.

My late husband, Alexandre, was a brute when in drink, which became nearly every waking hour. I do not entirely blame him for this, for his manhood had been mutilated and rendered impotent in a hunting accident, and no man, let alone a proud and vigorous man, can easily come to terms with such a loss. Moreover, he was a covert royalist, facilitating meetings of those sympathetic to the Chouan rebels and joining in their intrigues against the Republic. In an act driven by spite, jealousy and blatant self-interest he denounced his legitimate half-brother, Philippe, the Vicomte de Saint-Victor, the lawful owner of the estate Alexandre had thought of as his own. I fully expect to receive judgement for my sin in sending my husband to his death to save the life of his brother, but I will not look for it nor accept it from the likes of Sandrine Cadoudal.

Philippe, brought up in the land that now calls itself the United States of America, had come to France, his exiled father's homeland, in the hope of gaining a commission in the Republic's navy. In this he succeeded, although his first command ended in defeat by a British warship and captivity on a prison hulk, from which he escaped. He obtained a second command, this time in the Mediterranean, but was relieved of this in circumstances he has been reluctant to speak about. He inhabits Brechelean, the chateau of his ancestors, as do I, Leonore, widow of Alexandre Kermorvant. But contrary to Sandrine Cadoudal's suspicions, we live in different wings. We see each other only at mealtimes, and avoid the unanswered question that lies between us. The question of feelings.

He spends as much time as he can away from the chateau. He rides out to the far corners of his land, meeting the tenants and planning improvements. He goes to Paris to solicit for a new command in the Marine Nationale. And now he has gone to Rennes in response to an invitation from a merchant of that place, the substance of which he has not revealed to me. He says he is unlikely to return to the chateau for weeks, perhaps months.

Someone with a suspicious inclination — someone like, say, Sandrine Cadoudal — might incline to the opinion that Philippe

Kermorvant, Vicomte de Saint-Victor, my brother-in-law, is trying to avoid me.

So why have I chosen to begin a journal on this day, of all days? Until last year in France, such an act might well have been a path to the guillotine, providing evidence the agents of the Committee of Public Safety could bring against any citizen of the Republic to justify sending them to that inexorable fate. But the Terror has abated since the fall last year of Robespierre and the more fanatical Jacobins who followed him, and France is a little more her normal self. That is what I thought until today, when I witnessed a battle.

—

'That's gunfire, Citizeness. We should turn back, get to safety in the chateau.'

Dear Roman, always protective of his mistress. Two years ago, he was no more than a starving child beggar on the streets of Brest, where Philippe found him and his friend Olivier, and took them into the service of the Kermorvants. Now the two of them are the indispensable pillars upon which the entire estate of Brechelean stands. Olivier proved to be not only literate but the possessor of previously unsuspected clerical skills and relieved me of much of the drudgery of letter-writing and ledger-tallying. Roman took to riding a horse as if he was born to it, developing into an indefatigable apprentice estate manager for whom no problem on a tenant's property was too small. He also continues to insist upon the earnest republican form of address, 'Citizeness', at a time when almost every living creature in France has reverted to the time-honoured 'Madame' and 'Mademoiselle'.

But he is undoubtedly right about the sound of gunfire coming from beyond the ridge ahead. Not a few poachers with shotguns, for certain. I hear the sounds of successive fusillades of what can only be several hundred muskets accompanied by orders shouted in both French and Breton, the cries of wounded men as they are struck, the frantic whinnying of panicking horses.

'A quick look, Roman,' I say. 'No more than that. When is there ever a chance to witness the making of history?'

Before he can reply and try once more to discourage me, I spur my horse forward, leaving him no choice but to follow. We gallop along the lane leading to the ridge, the cacophony of battle growing ever louder. I know even as I ride that my curiosity is folly. We might be mistaken for enemy scouts and shot on sight. I might be captured and ravaged by an entire army. But I have read of so many battles of history, of Alexander and Hannibal and Caesar, of the great Condé and Turenne, that the opportunity to witness one makes me abandon all sense.

As we ride higher, the trees become denser and the road narrower. Large, strangely shaped rocks are strewn across the landscape as though giants have played marbles with them. One or both armies could have pickets in the forest, and we would be easy targets for them. But we encounter nobody and emerge into a clearing that gives a good view of the broad, partly wooded valley below.

The troops of the Republic, marked out by their blue uniforms and the Tricolours that fly in their vanguard, are advancing in good order from the west end of the valley, pausing every few strides to fire into the Chouan ranks opposing them. The Chouans wear no uniforms, only the familiar rough clothes of Breton peasants, but many of them wear white cockades in their round hats or else bear badges of the Sacred Heart on their goat-skin jackets, the symbols of their loyalty to their so-called king. Most of them are clustered around the ruined mill to the east, men in makeshift uniforms and none, all fighting under the white flags of the royalist cause. The Chouans, perhaps five hundred of them, are falling back in the face of the Blue advance. The

Republican troops are undoubtedly better disciplined, their fire more co-ordinated than that of their opponents. A few Chouans are turning and running for the cover of the woods at the far end of the valley.

There is death in abundance. I see a Chouan who could have been no older than Roman rise from behind a pile of rubble that had once been one of the walls of the mill, take aim, and perish as a red fountain bursts from his head before he can press his trigger. An old sergeant of the Blue troops takes a shot in the belly but continues to exhort his men to advance, only falling to the ground and bleeding out his life when his men are past him and running for the mill. The first few republicans are already engaged in hand-to-hand combat with the Chouan rearguard, and I see a fat, bewhiskered Chouan stabbed by three or four bayonets as successive assailants come up to him.

'Mistress,' says Roman urgently, taking hold of the reins of my horse, 'it's not safe! For pity's sake, Citizeness—'

The sight of what happens next silences him. The Chouans seem to be in full retreat, abandoning the mill and running for their lives toward the woods behind. The exultant Blues are themselves breaking into a run, ignoring the frantic orders from their officers to hold their lines and keep their discipline. The first of them are already at the ruined mill when loud whoops, cries of 'Vive le roi!' and a chorus of horses' hooves come from the trees. The first of the concealed Chouan cavalry emerge onto the open ground, four or five dozen horsemen in good order, riding hard for the Blues ahead of them. Blues who have no cavalry of their own.

If I was a true lady, one of the sort who peopled elegant Parisian salons in the time of the ancien régime, I would turn away rather than watch the slaughter in the valley below. Oh yes, it is horrible beyond description. It is truly something that no human being should ever witness, let alone be a part of.

No one, certainly no well-bred chatelaine, should see horsemen bringing their swords down in great sweeping arcs to sever arms from shoulders and heads from necks. None should ever witness men dying beneath hooves or bleeding to death from ugly slashes across their chests. The Blues, utterly surprised by the presence of enemy cavalry and the suddenness and ferocity of their charge, abandon all order and begin to run. A few of their officers try frantically to order their men into defensive squares, but there is no time or space to do so. I see a handful of horsemen brought down by bayonet thrusts into the flanks, shoulders or barrels of their steeds but otherwise the momentum is all with the Chouans. A brace of young Blue officers, surely no older than young Roman at my side or his friend Olivier, stand back to back as they discharge their pistols and wave their swords, trying desperately but vainly to kill an enemy or two before they themselves are cut down. A single stroke of the sword from one of the mounted Chouans slashes open the neck of one, then in the same action penetrates so deeply through the shoulder of the another that the blade must go straight to the heart.

My attention is drawn increasingly to this victorious rider, who boldly continues to ride up the valley cutting, slashing and exhorting his men to complete their victory. He is better dressed than all the others in the Chouan army, a silk shirt worn not under the rough goatshair jackets sported by most of the royalists but under a white tunic coat that could only have been part of an officer's uniform from the old royal army. He wears the common tricorn of the time, but it is adorned by both the white cockade of the royalist cause and a flamboyant ostrich feather, giving him the look of one of those dashing old chevaliers from the history books, the men who crushed Spain's invincible tercios *and conquered all before them in the days of the great Cardinal Richelieu. He is quite a young man, certainly little older than am I, and the glimpses I have of his face, albeit from a distance, suggested a rare beauty of features among the men of Brittany. He is clearly the general commanding the little Chouan army.*

He falls in the moment of victory, and I gasp aloud. He is struck by a random pistol shot, fired with no real aim by a Blue officer just before that doomed republican takes a fatal sword thrust from the Chouan through his right eye. The chevalier, for such is how I now think of him, slumps forward but remains in the saddle, still waving his sword to exhort his men. The Chouan troops run past him, some now crying out 'Montjoie! Saint Denis!', the traditional battle cry of the Bourbon armies, others singing the royal anthem, the 'Marche Henri Quatre'. The chevalier manages to urge his horse a few paces forward before he slumps to his right and falls from the saddle. Two of his men run immediately to attend him, but there is no sign of a surgeon seeing to any of the fallen Chouan troops, let alone to their victorious chief.

'It's over, Citizeness,' says Roman. 'We should leave now. The Blue troops are scattering into the woods all around. We must ride back to the chateau at once. Now, Citizeness! Madame Kermorvant!'

But the thought is already in my mind. It is insanity, and it might very well lead to my death. I am a loyal citizen of the Republic, whatever my dead husband might have been. I have no truck with the Chouans nor their so-called boy-king who languishes in the Temple Prison. The days of monarchs and prelates are done in France. Vive la République!

Yet I still take up my reins, and despite Roman's barely heard protests, I spur my horse down into the valley.

—

Leonore Kermorvant spurred her horse into a gallop, leaving her young attendant far in her wake. The shallow valley stretched ahead of her, the forest off to her right. Out here, close to the boundary of Brechelean land, she felt a freedom that was missing within the walls of the old chateau. Every stone of that ancient, crumbling fortress bore witness to the burden that weighed upon her. But out on the estate, the wind in her eyes and her hair, she could forget her guilt and her uncertain relationship with Philippe Kermorvant for a few precious minutes each day. Even as she rode down into the valley, though, she sensed that her impulsive decision to ride into the midst of the Chouan rebels, the sworn enemies of the Republic she believed in wholeheartedly, would only multiply her burden and compound her guilt.

CHAPTER THREE

From the papers of Leonore Kermorvant

A dozen or so Chouans surrounded Roman and I, their muskets pointing at us. Their leathery hands and faces, rough clothes and goatskins made them indistinguishable from ordinary Breton peasants, only the Sacred Hearts pinned to a few chests and sleeves betraying their loyalty. They studied me not as a potential enemy or even as an object of lust, but rather as though they were assessing the merits of a promising heifer.

'Prove you're not a Blue spy, madame,' said their apparent leader, a wiry youth whose worn but once expensive coat and breeches marked him out from the more roughly attired men around him. His delicate fingers, too, had never known labour in the fields or the forests. He spoke in Breton, but his accent was well-educated and his tone haughty, traits that became even more marked when he repeated his injunction in French. If there had been any lingering uncertainty of his loyalty, his use of madame instead of the republican form, 'citizeness', put the question beyond doubt.

'Would a Blue spy ride brazenly into the midst of your army?' I said in Breton.

He considered this. His men, meanwhile, boggled at the unexpected spectacle of a well-born lady who spoke the language of the peasantry.

'Then what are you, madame? One of those ghouls who takes pleasure from viewing the freshly dead and the maimed?'

Were there such people? It was a revelation to me, although since coming into the country I had learned never to be surprised by anything Brittany had to offer. But I had no time to debate the matter with this impertinent, pompous child-officer.

'I saw your leader fall,' I said impatiently. 'I have some small knowledge of physic and nursing. My home is also nearby, and I can provide a safe and comfortable place where he can recover, should there be a need for it.'

Some of the Chouans looked at each other and whispered among themselves. The officer seemed in two minds.

'Your name and that of your residence, madame?' he demanded, this time in French.

'I am the widow Kermorvant of the Chateau de Brechelean. My husband, Alexandre Kermorvant, was executed for his loyalty to the king.'

To refer to anyone as a king, and to call upon Alexandre's deluded and fatal allegiance to serve my own interests, stuck in the craw, but needs must. The young officer considered the information I had offered. Then, and without a word, he turned and walked over to the group of concerned men clustered around their fallen leader.

I fully expected Roman to berate me for offering the hospitality of the chateau to a rebel, but he seemed terrified into silence by the sight of so many gruff, hostile and ursine peasants aiming weapons directly at him. He avoided any contact with me by taking a sudden and inordinate interest in the wellbeing of his horse, leaving me with nothing to do but watch swarms of flies settling without distinction on the Blue and Chouan corpses that littered the valley.

At length the young officer returned, beckoned for us to dismount, and led us over to the place where the royalist leader lay. The fallen chevalier was a large, well-muscled man, his black hair flecked with grey, a crucifix hanging from his neck. He was conscious, stripped to the waist, very pale, and lying on a makeshift litter as an ugly-looking brute with a filthy face and hands attempted clumsily to stitch the vicious, bloody wound in his side while another peasant held a grubby cloth in pace to stem the bleeding as much as possible. Concerned Chouans, at least some of whom had to be officers, although it was impossible to tell from their clothing, stood at a respectful distance, murmuring among themselves.

'Madame Kermorvant,' said the Chouan leader in a pleasant, educated voice. 'I once had the honour of meeting your husband. He was a martyr for the cause of his king and the true France. You must have been very proud of him.' He frowned. 'But forgive me, madame, I neglect my manners. I am Colonel Georges Cozanet of the Catholic and Royal Army of France,'

'Colonel Cozanet,' I said, but as I uttered the words, resisting the urge to correct him regarding my feelings about Alexandre's treason against the Republic, the Chouan winced and stifled a yell of pain.

I stepped forward, gripped his shoulder and yelled at his would-be surgeon, 'Give me those, you clumsy droch!'

The man stared at me as if I, the refined woman who was calling him a cretin in his own language, was a being from another world, then grunted in barely intelligible Breton to Colonel Cozanet. The colonel murmured a reply, then the man handed me the needle and twine with which he had been stitching his commander.

'You should drink brandy,' I said to Colonel Cozanet.

'Later, perhaps, to celebrate our victory. But believe me when I say I am no stranger to pain, madame. I have learned to bear worse than this.'

The scars from old wounds on his torso bore witness to the truth of the remark.

I began to stitch. He grimaced, but kept his eyes fixed upon me.

'You have done this before,' he said, good-naturedly.

'I grew up in Côte d'Or in Burgundy,' I said. 'We were far from any town and any doctor. My mother was the healer and nurse for the village, as her mother had been before her. I was the oldest child, and I had four brothers who were always cutting themselves or breaking limbs. Several sisters, too, three of whose bastards I helped deliver. But I doubt if the old Académie royale de chirurgie would approve of my training or my experience, Colonel.'

'Then they would be the worse for it,' said Cozanet, smiling. 'You are infinitely superior to old Gourvennec, there, though he wouldn't pretend to be anything more than a village butcher. Our proper surgeon got himself killed a week ago, the damn fool, so poor Gourvennec has had to do his best since then. But when a king sits on the throne again, madame, I'll willingly vouch for you before any Académie royale.'

A flatterer. I had encountered enough of those in my life. But the Chouan colonel had a sincerity to him, as well as a stoicism that enabled him to bear the great pain that must have been pulsing through him. For the wound was a deep one, and I doubted if my clumsy skills with a needle, though superior to those of the butcher Gourvennec, would be sufficient to prevent him bleeding to death.

All around us, beyond the immediate circle gathered around Colonel Cozanet, the royalist troops were savouring their victory. Many were scavenging the clothes and weapons of the republican dead, others sitting where they could to smoke their pipes or drink from the leather flasks or animal skins they carried. A few songs started up, half-heartedly at first and then more lustily. I recognised some of the bawdier ballads often sung by the peasants on Brechelean land as they toiled in the fields.

Cozanet, too, was enjoying the sight of his men celebrating the fruits of their victory, but he suddenly seemed to remember something important and beckoned for the youthful officer who had first interrogated me to come to him.

'Yves,' he said, 'you need to make dispositions. Scouts, pickets, sentries, all need to be assigned.'

'I know, Colonel, but we've been awaiting your orders. Above all, do we stay here overnight or resume our march?'

'This ground can't be defended,' said Cozanet. 'We'll move to a position on the higher ground, make camp there, set off again in the morning—'

'Forgive the interruption of a mere woman,' I said as forcefully as I could, 'but you cannot remain in open country, Colonel. I know these lands, they offer you little protection against a sudden attack. But being on the march is also unthinkable in your condition, Breton roads could easily make your wound burst open again. You require complete rest, Colonel Cozanet, time for the wound to heal and for you to recover sufficient strength.'

Cozanet shook his head.

'Also unthinkable, Madame Kermorvant. We have a rendez-vous to keep. Convalescence is a luxury I cannot afford.'

'You can afford it, Colonel, for the price of shunning it will undoubtedly be your death. If you say you respect my skills as a surgeon and a nurse, then respect my word too. If you try to walk ten paces or lift yourself into a saddle, your only rendezvous will be with the grave.'

'She says she can accommodate you in her home, sir,' said Yves. 'She says it isn't far. And we have ample time to make the rendezvous.'

Cozanet lay back and took a deep breath.

'This is true, madame? Your home is near, and you're willing to nurse me there?'

'The Chateau de Brechelean is very close, Colonel. I willingly offer you my hospitality.'

He grimaced, perhaps from the severe pain he must still have felt, perhaps from his concern for the risk I would be running.

'It will be dangerous for you if the Blues return to these parts and discover you have been sheltering what they would call a traitor to their Republic, madame. Your generosity of spirit might very well lead you to the guillotine.'

'I saw my husband die on the guillotine, sir. I have no great fear of it.'

Cozanet nodded, and within an hour we were on the road to the chateau, the colonel recumbent on a litter that was moved as gently as possible by a troop of particularly burly Chouans.

I had spoken the truth when I said I had no great fear of the guillotine. I had no children to leave motherless and my family in Burgundy would probably not learn of my death for many months. Perhaps my brother-in-law Philippe would mourn me, but he was always distant, preoccupied and never seemed to notice me. He was also wedded to the sea, an implacable and jealous mistress that monopolised the favours of those in thrall to her. No, the one doubt that troubled my breast as we drew nearer to home was how Philippe might react if he discovered that I had offered the hospitality of his house to a man that he, a staunch republican and until recently a captain of the Marine Nationale, would undoubtedly regard as an enemy.

You are a good servant of the Republic, Leonore Kermorvant, I thought. This royalist colonel should be your enemy too. You should have nothing to do with him. You should contact the nearest Blue garrison to inform them of his whereabouts, and to insist that he has compelled you to accommodate him. Anything else is treason, and this is a war.

Yet as I looked down from my horse at the very pale but still manly features of the man lying on the litter, I found it impossible to think of him as my enemy.

CHAPTER FOUR

'Your decision, Monsieur le Vicomte? Captain Kermorvant?'

Philippe Kermorvant stared out of the window of the ornate and spacious first-floor room. The Heinrichs' town apartment faced the west front of the sometime cathedral of Rennes, the only part of the ancient structure still standing. The rest of it had fallen down years before, the elder Heinrich said, and rebuilding had restarted barely months before the storming of the Bastille, heralding an age when the faith that had once impelled men to build and fill such vast structures fell victim to a new set of beliefs. What remained of Rennes Cathedral still stood, a curious reminder of a France that seemed so far away in time and yet had perished only five or six years previously. A France that Philippe Kermorvant had never known. A France that his father's writings had done so much to destroy.

It was his father's name that had brought him here, to this room in Rennes, to be flattered and courted by the other two men in the room, father and son, both Swiss: the bald, bull-like Antoine Heinrich and his slender, elegantly attired son, Augustin. Despite looking and smelling more like a veteran prize fighter who had fought in several bouts too many and had been poured into clothes that were at once too small and too grand for him, Antoine Heinrich seemed to be a highly educated man and professed himself a great admirer of the works of that illustrious thinker and writer Edouard Kermorvant, Vicomte de Saint-Victor, the renowned Verité, Philippe's late father. It was plausible. The Swiss, a curious people in so many ways, had a liking for free-thinkers and those exiled from other lands, and Philippe knew his father had lived in their midst for some years after he was banished from France and before he went to America, where he met and married Philippe's English mother. So yes, he could understand why the Heinrichs, merchants engaged in several lucrative trades but clearly liberally inclined and intellectually curious men, might wish to meet with the son of Verité.

But to seek to employ him on the mission they had outlined over dinner the previous day? To offer him the command of a new corsair, a privateer, that they were setting out? Philippe was not convinced. The truth, as he had explained in straight language to his Swiss hosts, was that he still hoped to be restored to the Marine Nationale, to receive another command in the Republic's navy. He was now a sea-captain of considerable experience, having served in three navies and on merchant vessels. Since coming to France to offer his services to the navy of his fatherland, Philippe had commanded two frigates, fighting a losing battle in the first against a much more powerful British ship and winning the second against a larger Neapolitan man-of-war. It was a better record than most captains in the fledgling Marine Nationale could boast, and his experience of serving three different navies was surely unique in France. Philippe was confident his evident merits would, in the fullness of time—

He continued to elaborate his point, but he was under no illusion that his confidence sounded utterly hollow. Not even Philippe himself truly believed what he was saying. After all, if he was such an unusual and valuable asset to the French Republic, why was he in the apartment in Rennes at all? Why was he not somewhere in the Atlantic, commanding a frigate out of Brest or Lorient, or else serving in the Mediterranean or the Caribbean or the Indian Ocean? Heinrich *père* listened courteously, but his chubby fingers drumming on the arm of his chair suggested that he, too, did not believe a word of it.

'Of course, Captain. I understand entirely,' he said levelly when Philippe had finished. 'It would be the natural ambition of a man of honour like yourself. But if I may venture a thought, sir, I have it on very good authority that there are no vacancies in any of the Republic's ships. All the commands are filled. Of course, you know better than my son and I that vacancies can occur at any time. If there was to be a great battle, for example, and a dozen captains killed… or if the new ships on the stocks are competed rather more quickly than is the present expectation… or if the ministry in Paris changes again, and the adherents of this faction or that were to be purged… You will forgive my frankness, Monsieur le Vicomte, but Augustin and I are foreigners here, neutrals, so we may perhaps speak with a freedom to which you and your countrymen are unaccustomed.'

Philippe made no immediate answer. Everything Heinrich said was true, and the same thoughts had frequently crossed his mind in recent weeks. All his visits to Paris, all his calls at the Ministry of Marine, had borne no fruit. There was no sign of any of the changed circumstances that Antoine Heinrich outlined coming to pass. So why was Philippe still so reluctant to admit the attractiveness of the offer being made to him?

'Besides, Citizen,' said Augustin Heinrich, a seemingly diffident young man, in one of his rare forays into the conversation, 'it will surely redound greatly to your credit if your cruise in command of our corsair is a success, as it is sure to be. Surely such a triumph would bring your name to the attention of the minister of the Marine? And if it is as successful as we all hope, the prize profits for all of us will be significant.'

Philippe sat in silence for a few moments, then rose and walked to the window with the view of the cathedral. There was no doubt that it was a tempting offer. Antoine Heinrich was the *armateur*, or principal owner, of an eighteen-gun corsair fitting out at Concarneau, acting on behalf of a syndicate of co-owners who, he claimed, included members of the National Convention, judges and generals. Philippe could join these distinguished pillars of the Republic and own a share in the ship that he himself would captain. Heinrich *père* had explained the ship's mission succinctly, making it apparent that Philippe had been chosen to command it for rather more than the accident of his name and the respect that Antoine Heinrich felt for his father.

'Russia is coming into the war,' Heinrich had said. 'No doubt of it. I have it on quite impeccable authority that the Empress Catherine has signed a treaty with England and is sending a squadron to join their navy.'

Philippe had felt a pang of regret when Heinrich revealed this intelligence. Not so many years before he had commanded a frigate in the Russian navy, having volunteered his services to that nation after the war for the independence of the United States had ended and he had grown bored of service in merchant ships. He had discovered that the great seaman and hero of the American revolution, John Paul Jones, proposed to serve the Empress Catherine, so Philippe had gone along in his wake. Russia had given him a wife and son, both now dead, and some of the best friends he had ever made, men who would now become his enemies and whose ships he might face in battle.

'But against that,' Heinrich continued, 'we must weigh your Republic's astounding victory over the Netherlands. The transformation of that land into the newborn Batavian Republic, no less, resolute for the principles of liberty, and now a good friend to France. So put the two things together, Captain Kermorvant, and what do we have? A convenient base from which French ships may now prey upon England's Baltic trade, upon which their navy depends. So much timber, tar and pitch—'

'Masts,' said Augustin Heinrich.

'Masts indeed, and all the other trades of those waters. Russia's own sea-trades, all now fair game for the first bold corsair captain and first intrepid syndicate to send a well-armed ship into that sea. A sea that you know well, Monsieur le Vicomte. A sea that you sailed in the service of the Empress Catherine. You know the coasts and the harbours and the ships of the Baltic in a way that no other French captain does. So there you have it, my dear sir. A mission made for you. One that will make you rich, or even richer – I do not seek to pry into your account ledger, sir.' It was as well he did not, thought Philippe, for all he would have seen was an endless debit column and precious little credit. 'And it is also a mission that will weaken England, of course, once our other sea-wolves from Dunkirk and Saint-Malo follow our lead into the

Baltic. And that, Monsieur le Vicomte, is sure to bring your name to the attention of the minister of the Marine, especially as all the other distinguished shareholders in the voyage will be singing your praises into the ears of those in authority in the Republic. So, it is time for you to decide, Captain Kermorvant. Do you accept my offer? Do you accept the command of the ship that I propose to name *La Verité?*'

Oui.
Non.
Non.
Oui.

It should be a simple decision. Unlike many of his erstwhile comrades in the Marine Nationale, Philippe did not regard corsairs as being somehow beneath his dignity, for his first sea service had been aboard privateers set out by the newly independent State of Virginia very nearly twenty years before. Then again, the sums being offered by the Heinrichs, even before any profits from prizes were entered into the equation, would be both welcome and timely. The estate of Brechelean had suffered in the revolution and subsequent war, fields were untilled and the coffers empty, and many parts of the chateau were in urgent need of repair. The ancient building, the home of his ancestors for many generations, drained money as voraciously as a fleet under refit. Moreover, Heinrich was undoubtedly right; a successful corsair command could certainly bring a captain to the attention of the authorities. Had not some of France's most renowned admirals down the ages – Duguay-Trouin, Jean Bart, all the rest – started out as corsairs?

Oui, then. It could only be *oui*.

Yet there was still that invisible spectre screaming *non*. This sceptre was clad in the dress uniform of a captain in the Marine Nationale, and in the swirling mists and shadows behind it sailed a dozen or more men-of-war, the warships that Philippe might perhaps command in future and lead to glorious victories in the name of the Republic. Was a privateering expedition, especially one set out at the behest of a foreigner, really the best course to achieve that goal?

Then there was that foreigner himself. Belying his appearance, Antoine Heinrich could play the perfect gentleman and was undoubtedly a model host who could flatter and entice as well as the smoothest Parisian fop. The offer he had laid before his visitor was extraordinarily generous, and thus extraordinarily tempting. But Philippe could not bring himself to like the man. Heinrich dressed the part of a wealthy and respectable bourgeois, but Philippe felt there was something of the gutter about him. Certainly something of the smell of the gutter. The man was too presumptuous, too inquisitive about Philippe's personal affairs, too arrogant altogether. Could he really trust Antoine Heinrich and his superficial, insipid son?

So – *non*?

Philippe took a deep breath, aware that Heinrich *père et fils* were watching him, that their patience had its limits, and that he had to give them an answer before he left their apartment. It all hinged on the likelihood of him obtaining a new command in the Marine Nationale in the foreseeable future. No illusions now, no spectres of futures that might be unattainable, only cold logic and reason, as his father had demanded of him in every situation.

No formal reason had been given for Philippe's abrupt dismissal from the command of the frigate *Le Torrington* in the Toulon fleet. There had been no court-martial, no arrest on any charge. There had not even been a meeting with Admiral Pierre Martin, commander-in-chief of the fleet in the Mediterranean, merely a cursory note from the admiral informing Philippe that he was being relieved of his command with immediate effect. He had requested an interview with the admiral, but to no avail. He attempted to make contact with Jeanbon Saint-André, the *representant en mission* or envoy of the Committee of Public Safety, a man who had previously favoured Philippe and promoted his career, but Saint-André was away from Toulon with no indication of when, or even if, he would return.

Philippe only gained some inkling of the reasons for his apparent disgrace a few days later, on the night before he left Toulon. He dined with his friend François Parmentier, captain of the frigate *Forbin*, which had come into the dockyard for careening, repairs and revictualling. The *restaurant*, one of the first examples in Toulon of the new kind of eating place that had become all the rage in Paris, was nearly empty. Perhaps it was the weather, Frank Parmentier speculated, for Toulon was in the throes of a December snowstorm, or else perhaps the notoriously independent and contrarian Provençals were expressing their disdain for all things Parisian.

Parmentier had a knack of gleaning intelligence from a catholic and bewilderingly extensive array of informants ranging from cleaners to courtesans, and he unveiled his analysis of Philippe's downfall with the theatricality of a conjuror.

'There are two stories, but they're not mutually exclusive. The one concerns our old friend Fidelin.'

Rear-Admiral Sebastien Fidelin had been Admiral Martin's second in command until evidence unearthed accidentally by Philippe while his ship was in Malta raised suspicions that Fidelin might in fact be the English agent who was known to hold rank in the fleet. He had attempted to divert suspicion from himself by pointing the finger at Philippe instead, but Jeanbon Saint-André, then the government's all-powerful representative at Toulon, demonstrated his opinion on the matter by arranging for Fidelin to be transferred to a seemingly prestigious but remote command in the Caribbean.

'Fidelin hasn't gone quietly,' said Frank Parmentier. 'He was to join his new flagship at Lorient but managed to go there from Toulon by way of Paris, where he still has friends in the National Convention and on the Committee of Public Safety. I'm told that he's been trying to get me dismissed, too, for formally denouncing him as an English spy – based on your evidence, of course, but I was the one who spoke the words.'

Philippe considered Frank's intelligence. It was perfectly believable; Fidelin was a devious character. Philippe's colourful life story and English mother made him an inevitable target of whispers and suspicions. So yes, he could well believe what Frank Parmentier had told him.

'You said there was a second story.'

'Ah yes. That one. Well now, Monsieur le Vicomte, your time on Corsica has raised some eyebrows. Not your official mission, even if it proved futile, but what you did when you went back there a second time.'

In the previous year, an enigmatic young general of Corsican origin had sent Philippe to his native island to attempt to convince a rebel leader to declare for France in opposition to the offer of the Corsican crown to King George of England. The mission had been a failure, but not before Philippe had a torrid and troubling relationship with the rebel leader's passionate daughter, a relationship that complicated the tentative and unspoken feelings between him and his sister-in-law, Leonore. Before, too, an unexpected opportunity had arisen to avenge his lost wife and son.

'I had a formal warrant from Admiral Martin for a month's leave of absence,' said Philippe defensively.

'Of course you did. But nobody, the admiral included, thought you'd use that leave to go back to Corsica, a land by then under enemy occupation, and kill the Russian ambassador to the viceregal court.'

'The Russian ambassador who murdered my wife and son,' said Philippe.

'And in a duel,' said Parmentier. 'All very honourable no doubt, Monsieur le Vicomte. But that presented our rulers with a difficulty. Russia is sympathetic to France's enemies, but the old empress is still reluctant to join the war on their side. Her son, the imperial heir, is even more hesitant. So Paris and our diplomats in Saint Petersburg are making every effort to keep Russia out of the war against us. A captain of the Marine Nationale killing their ambassador, a personal friend of the heir, is hardly conducive to that end.'

If that had weighed in the decision to dismiss him, Philippe considered, it was now rendered academic by the intelligence of Russia's imminent entry into the war that Antoine Heinrich had announced earlier in their conversation. Besides, Vladimir Kyrilovich Bulgakov, the man who had killed Philippe's beloved Tasha and Ivan, had amply deserved to die. But there would still be men in Paris likely to take offence at what Philippe had done, and he had no doubt that Admiral Sebastien Fidelin and his friends would have been quick to use the story against the already suspect, half-English, perhaps far too foreign for the good of the Republic, Captain Philippe Kermorvant.

He turned back from the window, his decision made.

'Present me with the papers, Citizens, and I will sign them. I will captain your corsair.'

CHAPTER FIVE

From the papers of Leonore Kermorvant

Georges, for that was how I now addressed Colonel Cozanet, healed with astonishing celerity. It was no more than a day or two before he was sitting up in bed, despite my warnings that he was sure to reopen his wound. He was taking his first steps in a little over a week and managing short strolls in the gardens within a fortnight. I nursed him day and night while he was confined to bed, the necessary intimacy seemingly causing him more embarrassment than it did me. He constantly expressed his gratitude for my attentions, without which he said he was certain he would have died, and apologised incessantly for the inconvenience to which he was putting me and the household staff of the chateau. I reassured him that he need not berate himself on any of our accounts, but the truth was that I did not know what the servants thought of his presence. I had few concerns about the maids and footmen, local youths who had only been in our service for a few months and who had no idea of the identity of the sickly gentleman recuperating from unspecified injuries in the Blue Bedchamber. Jacques and Martha Penhouet, the ancient steward and housekeeper of the chateau, were sworn to secrecy, and I thought I could rely on their renowned discretion. Olivier and Roman were different cases, both highly intelligent youths who had grown up scratching a living on the streets of Brest, doing whatever was necessary to stay alive and find their next meal. I liked to believe that they were both fond of me and would not betray my secret to the authorities of the Republic. Whether they would do so to the Vicomte de Saint-Victor, their employer and saviour from lives of beggary, was rather more opaque.

My attempts to conceal the identity of my guest were aided by Georges's order to his troops to make camp well away from the chateau, so there would appear to be no necessary connection between the Chouan soldiers billeted nearby and the invalid lying within the walls of Brechelean. The young officer he had named as Yves, and who it transpired rejoiced in the title (but not the estate nor the income, all lost when his father and two elder brothers were guillotined) of the Marquis de Montargis, came to the chateau every few days for conference with his colonel and to receive orders for onward transmission, and I can imagine that his too-obviously aristocratic demeanour and youthful beauty set tongues wagging below stairs.

Those spring days when Georges was convalescing became a sort of idyll. The war was far away, the concerns of the estate that consumed me from day to day suddenly no more than trifles. At first I read to him, but as soon as he could sit up he insisted on reading for himself. He was a markedly intelligent man, the self-taught son of a blacksmith who had been promoted even through the stultifyingly rigid hierarchy of the old Armée Royale. He was familiar with the works of Voltaire, Diderot and even Verité, even though he disagreed vehemently with the philosophy of the sometime owner of the chateau in which he was a guest.

'That I should lie within the very walls that spawned Verité,' he said to me one day early in his recovery, when I was changing the dressing of his wound. 'Perhaps in his very bed. My confessor will be aghast. I fear for the penances he may impose.'

I laughed. In truth, Georges Cozanet made me laugh often. He had a charming and unaffected disposition, unlike so many Breton men, whose attitude to women was little different to that *which they employed to train dogs. He took an interest in his surroundings and in the wider world, again unlike so many of those I encountered regularly. I did not press him on matters of the war or politics, for there I knew we would disagree, but he devoured all the newssheets that came from Paris a week or two after their publication and the more local ones out of Rouen, Rennes and Nantes. Equally, he did not enquire too closely about Alexandre and his fate, nor about Philippe. He was that great rarity in Brittany, a courteous, intelligent and discreet man.*

I fear, however, that I am not an equally discreet woman. One morning a while later, when his recovery had progressed, we were walking in the old garden behind the chateau, the housekeeper, Martha Penhouet, at a discreet distance acting as chaperone. The dew was still upon the ground, the morning chorus of the songbirds in full spate. For once it was a still, warm, dry day, the sun giving promise of one of the first truly memorable days of the year. The garden was still laid out in the formal style of the last century, and Georges expressed great delight in its intricacy and old-fashioned patterns. He was waxing lyrical upon the garden being undoubtedly a relic of the famous age of Louis le Grand, King Louis the Fourteenth, a time when France had been at its greatest under an enlightened and benevolent monarch, when the glories of the morning brought on a kind of temporary madness in my heart.

'Tell me, Georges,' I said, the words coming before I could think better of them, 'do you have family?'

To this day, I remember the expression on his face. I remember my immediate sense of shame and mortification. Some, the likes of Sandrine Cadoudal, would probably say that at any time, it is not the sort of question a virtuous widow of quality ought to ask a man with whom she is barely acquainted. In those days, though, when the country was still racked by war and rebellion and the memories of the guillotine were so fresh, it was not a question that the French ever dared ask of each other.

I realised my mistake at once, but I could not unsay the words. But Georges, to his credit, answered the question directly and without any dissimulation.

'I had a wife and six children,' he said, the pain underlining every word. 'Three boys, three girls. I left them at home in La Bouillie. Then, one day, the Blue soldiers came. They raped my wife and daughters, shot my sons as they tried to fight, then burned the house and bayoneted the women. Appropriate revolutionary justice, the local representant en mission *said, for my so-called treason against the Republic. So, no, madame, I have no family.'*

I turned to look at him, but my eyes were too full of tears to see his face clearly. I touched his sleeve with my fingers.

'My heart bleeds for you, Georges.'

He looked away, and I knew that he, too, was weeping.

'Pain has been the lot of almost every man, woman and child in France these last three years, Leonore. My story is little different to ten thousand, one hundred thousand others. But that is why I continue to fight for the king – that no one in the years to come will have to know the pain we have known.'

I nodded, though even then and there, as we stood in the garden of Brechelean and silently expressed our respective griefs, I knew that whatever Georges Cozanet believed, the return of the Bourbon kings would not bring us all to some sort of Elysium. If they could work such miracles, surely the heads of Louis the Sixteenth and Marie Antoinette would still be on their shoulders.

We walked on, and Georges turned the subject to the impressive display of hydrangeas, then new to France but seemingly well suited to the difficult soil and unpredictable climate of the west of Brittany. He had a good understanding of horticulture born, he said, of the gardener at his local chateau being the boon drinking partner of his father. So we walked and talked, although in truth he did most of the talking. But as the sun rose higher and higher, I could not drive from my memory the fate of his family. The horror should have been unimaginable, but I found I could imagine it all too well. And among the terrors crowding my mind came a new thought, unlooked for and unwanted.

Georges had lost his wife and children. What he needed, even if he did not know it himself, was a new wife, a mother to give him new children.

Such were the insane, unthinkable flights of fancy that could be thought possible and attainable in France in those years of madness. Flights of folly, more like. To think such things even for a single second was to betray Philippe – but how could it be? I had no understanding of any kind with Philippe Kermorvant. Yet as Georges stooped down with only the slightest wince to inspect and praise another hydrangea, I thought of Philippe's face, his kindness and empathy, and I felt shame that I could also harbour thoughts about Georges Cozanet in the very same moment, the very same breath. They were feelings I had not known since the earliest days of my marriage to Alexandre, when he had been loving in every way and I had known real passion and love for him. I could not possibly be having those feelings again, not for two men at the same time. Before the revolution, in the time of the priests, I expect I would have been guilty of some sin or other.

No, Leonore. Colonel Georges Cozanet would be gone in days, back to the war that would probably kill him. But there was more than that. He was a royalist, a Chouan, a traitor to the Republic. He was an enemy of France, or at least of the sort of France in which I believed, and that made him my enemy too.

He rose, turned to me and opened his mouth to speak, but no words came. He was looking at something or someone behind me. I turned and looked down the barrel of a pistol aimed at Georges' head. A pistol held by Philippe, Vicomte de Saint-Victor, my brother-in-law.

'This is my land,' he said tersely. 'My chateau. You are a trespasser, Citizen, and you have invaded my home. By the laws of the Republic and even those of the old kingdom, I am entirely within my rights to shoot you dead.'

CHAPTER SIX

Philippe was aiming directly between Cozanet's eyes. The range was so close that he could not possibly miss, the abundant bushes and undergrowth that fringed the formal garden having concealed his approach until he was immediately behind Leonore and the Chouan general. Leonore gasped and swayed but did not faint. Cozanet, though, seemed unperturbed by Philippe's unexpected intervention.

'I presume I have the honour of being in the presence of the Vicomte de Saint-Victor,' he said, a slight note of amusement in his voice.

'You, Citizen, have no honour. You are a rebel. You are a traitor to the Republic.'

'Philippe—' said Leonore, but Philippe cut her off.

'I will choose to believe that this man has imposed himself on you, Citizeness, and that you have been forced to act against your will.'

'Philippe—'

Philippe seemed not to hear her. Instead his attention, and his aim, remained resolutely focused on Georges Cozanet.

'You have invaded my property, Citizen. You wage war against the people of France, and you have brought that war here, to my own land.'

Cozanet still had a wistful smile.

'Well, Monsieur le Vicomte, we could argue for many days and nights about which side has been waging war against the people – mine, that seeks to restore the rightful king and the rule of law, or yours, that has slaughtered thousands of the people of France upon the guillotine. But I suspect I would not change your mind, just as you will not change mine.'

'I do not seek to change your mind, sir. I seek to put a bullet in it.'

'Philippe!' snapped Leonore, seemingly recovered from the shock of Philippe's sudden appearance. 'I invited Colonel Cozanet here to heal his wounds. He did not coerce me in any way. None of what has happened here has been against my will. If you seek the guilty party who has brought a Chouan into your house, Captain, then put your bullet in me.'

Philippe's arm faltered, but only for a moment.

'We will talk of this later, Citizeness,' he said, 'after I have dispatched this traitor.'

Leonore, her hands clenched and her face reddening, seemed ready to argue the case with a furious riposte, but Cozanet forestalled her, merely by raising an eyebrow.

'Dispatch me, sir? And when will you do that?'

'Now, this very minute,' said Philippe angrily, taking a new aim.

'I think not, Monsieur le Vicomte,' said a new voice from behind Philippe.

He turned and stared at the two pistols in the hands of a youth he did not know. A dozen more men in peasant garb were emerging from the bushes on the south side of the garden. All were heavily armed.

'Relieve the vicomte of his pistol, Yves,' said Cozanet calmly.

On a nod from the Marquis de Montargis, one of the Chouans came forward and took Philippe's weapon from him.

'Now, sir,' said Cozanet, 'it is indeed your house and not my place to offer you hospitality within it, but I hope neither you nor Madame Kermorvant here will consider me impertinent if I propose we all go within and take a light repast?'

—

The three sat upon delicate Louis Quinze chairs in the west drawing room of the chateau. A couple of bearded Chouans guarded the doors, admitting only the aged housekeeper, Martha Penhouet, carrying a tray with a cafetière and three cups. It could have been a scene from any bourgeois drawing room in France.

'I compliment you on the quality of your coffee, Monsieur le Vicomte,' said Cozanet upon taking his first sip.

'I will take no compliments from you, Citizen,' Philippe hissed.

'No. I understand that.'

'So what is to be my fate? Summary execution? A sham court upon charges of treason to your so-called king?'

Leonore blanched at that.

'Georges—' she began.

'"Georges", madame?' said Philippe, glaring at her and nodding. 'Yes, I see how it all lies now.'

Leonore bristled and seemed about to launch into a furious denial of Philippe's implication, but Cozanet ignored the exchange. He put down the cup and stood, forestalling any intervention from Leonore. He walked to the window overlooking the garden they had just vacated, then turned back to address Philippe.

'You are undoubtedly a traitor to the kingdom, Monsieur le Vicomte, and the punishment for traitors is amply recorded in the annals of history. Quite apart from your command of two warships engaged in warfare against the king's enemies, those commands being a matter of public record, the papers I have perused in your study tell me that you have been offered command of a corsair designed to sail against the friends of the king at the behest of some wealthy foreigner, a Swiss. Multiple treasons, Monsieur le Vicomte, and irrefutable evidence in your own hand. But, of course, you also carry treason in your blood – your father's treason against his king and all the laws of God. The poisonous writings of Verité did much to spark the so-called revolution, so your execution would serve as a most instructive example, don't you think?'

Leonore was agitated. The good monarchist in her should have agreed with every word of Cozanet's brutal sentiments, *but this was Philippe.*

'Colonel Cozanet,' she said urgently, her voice raised and emphatic, 'I beg you, as the one who has tended your wounds – saved your life, perhaps – surely you cannot repay my mercies by killing one who is dear to me!'

Cozanet looked uncomfortable and took a deep breath.

'Your appeal has much weight, madame, but my primary duty is to Louis the Seventeenth, King of France, and his justice demands that this man should die.'

'The child you call your king is in the Temple prison,' she said defiantly. 'No judges sit in his name anywhere in France. You are the sole judge here, monsieur, and this man's fate rests with you alone.'

'Save your breath, Leonore,' said Philippe. 'He's the sole judge indeed, and I expect no mercy at his hands.'

'So be it,' said Cozanet, sitting once again and draining his coffee. 'I regret having to imprison you in your own house, Monsieur le Vicomte, but it's necessary while I consider my decision.'

'A pretence of consideration before the inevitable verdict? Very magnanimous of you, Citizen.'

Cozanet signalled to the two guards at the door. They came over, but Leonore stepped in front of them.

'Don't touch him! This is the Vicomte de Saint-Victor! His land, his chateau! How dare you—'

Cozanet grasped her arm to restrain her, but she turned sharply and slapped him hard with her free hand. For a moment, Leonore and the Chouan colonel stared furiously at each other.

'Always choose your battles, Leonore,' said Philippe. 'A warrior always recognises when the odds are against him. Against her, indeed. Choose your battle, and learn to accept when it's lost. When it's time to surrender.'

'Good advice, Monsieur le Vicomte,' said Cozanet. 'Advice worth following, madame.'

Philippe submitted himself to Cozanet's two Chouan guards. Leonore continued to protest and struggled against Cozanet's grip, but the Chouans roughly manhandled Philippe out of the room, along the principal corridor of the oldest part of the chateau, through the hall, then down into the great kitchen, disused for many years. A door at the far end opened into the wine cellar, and Philippe found himself pushed toward the racks of dusty vintages laid down by his father and even, in some cases, his grandfather. There were, he reflected, worse places in the Chateau de Brechelean for the Vicomte de Saint-Victor to spend his last hours on earth.

The key turned in the lock and the door of the wine cellar began to open. Philippe stood, determined to face his fate with courage. But no Chouans came through the door, no Colonel Georges Cozanet. Instead Olivier stood there, and immediately behind him was Leonore. Olivier inclined his head to both of them and withdrew.

'You are an unlikely executioner, madame,' said Philippe.

'There will be no execution, today or any day, even if your foolhardiness and pride sometimes deserve it, Philippe Kermorvant. Colonel Cozanet and his men have left.'

'Left?'

'You can inspect the chateau and the grounds, sir. Both are empty.'

Philippe could think of no adequate response. It was inconceivable. The civil war of the Blues and the Whites for the future of France was not characterised by mercy from one side to the other, and with or without even a sham of legal process, his hot-tempered folly in coming to the chateau at all should have ended in his death.

'It must be a ruse,' he said, his puzzlement evident in his voice.

'No ruse. Roman saw them off the land, the colonel at their head. They march west and will not return. But the colonel left a note for you, Citizen. It is upon the small table in the west drawing room.'

Still unable to credit her words, Philippe brushed past her without apology and took the spiral stairs two at a time, his boots echoing off the ancient stone.

Back through the kitchen, this time containing the familiar sight of Martha Penhouet with two of the young maids, curing a side of ham. The old woman gasped when she saw him and crossed herself. She tried to say something, but no words came, only tears. Philippe nodded to her, then strode through his house – still his house despite its defilement by the royalist rebels – until he reached the drawing room, where he sighted Cozanet's letter at once. It was unsealed, and he unfolded it as Leonore entered the room behind him.

Monsieur le Vicomte, it began.

> I have reached my verdict, and as you are reading these words you will now know what it is. In the name of the king I grant you mercy and release you.
>
> You are a fellow warrior, sir, and I do not doubt that you will either disbelieve my sincerity or, at best, find this choice of mine inexplicable. I expect I will have to account for it to higher authority, if only because my deputy, the Marquis de Montargis, vehemently opposes my decision. I expect him to denounce me, one of his many reasons for doing so being that, despite his youth, he believes his birth makes him better qualified for the command than a mere blacksmith's son. But whatever my fate at his hands and those of my superiors on earth, I am confident that when I come before the

throne of Heaven I can justify myself before the greatest judge of all, the one whom we must all face.

Perhaps you wish to learn my reasons for releasing you. In the first instance, it seems an ungentlemanly act to imprison a man in his own home, and perhaps to execute him within his own lands. Upon his own lawn, indeed. Above all, though, I may well owe my life to the kindness and nursing care of Madame Kermorvant, and I do not wish to cause that dear lady to bear the grief she would certainly endure if I were to impose the full rigour of the king's justice upon you. It was already time enough for me to leave and resume my duties, although I will never forget her compassion and sympathy. She knew what she was risking in inviting an enemy of your Republic into your home, but she displayed singularity and exemplary courage in taking that risk. She has pleaded your cause with passion, and in truth, sir, it is she who is responsible for the sparing of your life. During my time in your home, I have learned that this is not the first time she has done so. She is a paragon among women, Monsieur le Vicomte, and you are a fortunate man – although whether you realise this is not for me to say.

So I take my leave and pray that we never cross swords in times to come, for if we do I don't believe the same mercy will be extended again by either of us.

> I wish you joy of your freedom, sir, and success in your forthcoming voyage.
>
> Georges Cozanet
>
> Colonel in the service of the Catholic and Royal Army of France for His Most Christian Majesty King Louis the Seventeenth.

He read the note a second time, then placed it back on the table.

'Philippe—' said Leonore.

Philippe turned to face her.

'I do not want words from you, Citizeness. I will return to Concarneau tomorrow. Meanwhile we will eat apart and live apart. We will talk of what transpired here when I return from my voyage.'

'But that may be months away!' she protested.

'Then you will have months to think of what you can possibly say to me.'

He turned from her and left the room, leaving Leonore standing rigidly in the middle of the room, angrily forming the blistering rejoinder she would now have no opportunity to deliver.

PART TWO

CHAPTER SEVEN

Philippe looked forward from the quarterdeck of *La Verité*. The ship lay alongside a quay across from the *ville close* of Concarneau, the old fortified town on an island in the middle of the harbour. It was seven in the morning, the tide was flooding and the port was bustling. Fishing boats were heading out to sea, some bound for the inshore waters off Penmarch and the Île de Sein, others setting their courses further afield. Three luggers were struggling out into the teeth of the south-westerly breeze, laden with provisions for the Brest fleet. A corsair, newly returned from a successful cruise against Spanish coasters off the coast of Galicia, was heeled over for careening on the other side of the harbour. All of Philippe's attention, though, was on his new command. Throwing himself into her fitting out seemed the best way of expunging the memory of what had happened at the Chateau de Brechelean, so Philippe focused all his efforts on the familiar, comforting rituals of readying a ship for sea. He had just undertaken a detailed tour of inspection with the effusive Augustin Heinrich, acting as his father's deputy, and he was content with what he saw. He looked over the eighteen new twelve-pounder guns arrayed on the single gun deck, then up at the newly stepped masts. A few men were still in the rigging and on the deck making final adjustments, painting and polishing. From below came the sound of hammering as the carpenter and his crew completed some joinery in what would soon be Philippe's cabin. To all intents and purposes, though, the ship was complete. She rode high in the water, for she had yet to take in her stores and victuals. Many of these were piled high on the quayside awaiting available hands to load them into the hold. Eighty barrels of water were stacked alongside sixty of wine, five kegs of brandy and thirty barrels of salt beef, together with prodigious quantities of sardines, cod, ham, bacon, biscuits and other apparent necessities for the voyage. Philippe was convinced Antoine Heinrich had greatly overprovided, purchasing nearly enough to sustain a First Rate going on a long foreign voyage rather than a corsair the size of a small frigate destined for waters where there would always be friendly or neutral harbours available in which to revictual. He could only hope that such generous provision would not overload the hull and impede the corsair's sailing. For the moment, though, *La Verité* had the look and feel of a trim, well found and above all fast ship.

Antoine Heinrich had evidently not stinted in the amount he was willing to spend on the fitting out of the ship, and his son had proudly recited the amounts expended to Philippe during their tour. Eighteen thousand livres on provisions, thirty thousand to the crew in advance wages, another thirty thousand on the ordnance, a seemingly extravagant four thousand on the sails, a frankly incredible six hundred on an atlas… Philippe had already banked his own advance against anticipated prize money, an astonishing but very welcome five thousand livres. Antoine Heinrich should surely have named his corsair the *Croesus*, not *La Verité*.

Heinrich *fils* purred at Philippe's praise for the ship.

'The master shipwright's excelled himself, my father says,' grinned Heinrich, 'but then, we knew we were hiring the best, as we were with all the suppliers. Thirty years he's been building the best-found ships on the coast. The fastest, too. His name and reputation were bywords even as far away as Rennes.'

Philippe grunted in agreement. The privateer's fine lines had impressed him when he first saw them, and he reckoned *La Verité* would be able to sail closer to the wind than any other vessel he had sailed on, let alone commanded. But Breton shipwrights often built ships for very specific purposes where speed and sailing qualities were at a premium, notably smuggling expeditions to England where they needed to be able escape King George's revenue cutters.

'She'll be a shock for the Baltic traders,' said Philippe. 'And I'll wager she'll outsail anything the English or the Russians put out to escort their convoys.'

'So you're content with your command, Captain Kermorvant?'

'As to that, Citizen Heinrich, I'll reserve judgement until I've seen what sort of crew we can get, and how they perform on the proving voyage.'

Philippe began to have his questions answered during the next few days as volunteers for *La Verité* began to appear in Concarneau. It was remarkable how quickly word got around the maritime regions of Brittany and, indeed, far beyond too, of a new corsair fitting for sea with a wealthy owner who was offering astonishingly generous terms to volunteers and had victualled the ship in a remarkably bountiful manner. The Marine Nationale was meant to have first call on seamen's services, but the Bretons – and corsair crews were overwhelmingly Breton

– had a very different view of things. So by the final date allotted for volunteers to come forward, there was quite a jostling, swearing, unruly crowd of men on the quayside at Concarneau. Augustin Heinrich took on the task of entering the names of the men himself, sitting behind a small portable table on the quayside as men presented themselves before him. Philippe stood just behind him, assessing each man as they stepped forward in turn.

'Name and condition?' asked Heinrich for what had to be the thirtieth time that day. The man before him was slight and ugly, missing his right ear and most of his teeth.

'Le Polotec, Gwenc'hlan, Citizen. Caulker. Six years in the dockyard at Lorient, four on the slavers out of Nantes, three in coastal trades.'

Augustin Heinrich recorded the man's name in the rough copy of the muster book.

'Number one hundred and sixty-three,' said Heinrich. 'See the bosun yonder, show him your certificates and he'll assign you to a mess and a station. Next!'

Philippe looked at the remaining line, straggling alongside the quayside. Another thirty or forty men, enough to comfortably fill the remaining seventeen places among the nominal ship's complement of one hundred and eighty. Philippe was tempted to enter all of them. The Heinrichs, to whom money seemed no object, would surely not demur if more men were crammed into the hull, the more to man the prizes galore that *La Verité* would undoubtedly take during her northern cruise. Most of the men already entered were Bretons, as had been the case with Philippe's first command in the Marine Nationale, the frigate *Le Zephyr* in the Brest fleet. Quite how the remote, desolate west coast of Brittany could produce so many men for one privateer, let alone all her sisters sailing from Saint-Malo, Vannes, Nantes and elsewhere, despite the incessant demands for manpower of the Marine Nationale and the Republic's armies, was a mystery to confound both the priests of the old disposition and the philosophers of the new.

Perhaps a fifth to a quarter of those fetching up on the quayside at Concarneau were wearing red bonnets, one of the semi-official ways of showing republican sympathies. Such symbols were less prevalent by then, the month of Floreal in Year III of the Republican calendar, than they had been two years earlier at the peak of the Terror, when such empty gestures like a particular colour of bonnet or rosette could be all it took to save a man from the guillotine or consign him to it. But in the month that royalists and recidivists alike still called May 1795, public fervour for one side or the other in France's bitter civil war was less apparent, especially in places like Concarneau and the other Breton ports where the only ideology that mattered was the making of money.

Even some amply qualified and experienced officers had crawled out of the well-hidden nooks where they had somehow evaded the attention of the Republic's officials and naval officers. The gunner, a stout, unsmiling Provençal named Vuillermoz, had entered the old Marine Royale as long ago as the fifties and had served in the American war, where he had fought in several of the same engagements as Philippe. The sailing master, a Breton named Ar Braz, seemed equally competent despite his liking for the bottle. All that was well and good but Philippe still lacked a lieutenant for the voyage. Ar Braz would never do, for it would be courting disaster to have a lieutenant who was both a sot and a Breton who might be inclined to favour his own countrymen. Antoine Henrich had made some unsubtle hints about his son's suitability for the position, but Philippe resisted the notion and even threatened to resign the command if such a preposterous proposal was executed. Augustin Heinrich was capable enough with a quill but he was no seaman, having only been to sea as a passenger three or four times in his life. His father insisted on him going on the voyage of *La Verité* nonetheless, so Philippe was reconciled to taking Heinrich *fils* as a supernumerary. But if a competent lieutenant could not be found within the next two or three weeks, Philippe knew that he might have to concede the point and give the position to this youthful Swiss lubber.

The next man in the line of volunteers, a well-muscled fellow of forty or more with only three fingers on his right hand, stepped forward, offered the semblance of a salute to Philippe, then stood before Augustin Heinrich.

'Name and condition?'

'Dieter Teschow, your honour. Topman.'

'*Deutscher*?' demanded Philippe.

'Mecklenburger, your excellency. From Rostock.'

Philippe had a memory of a long, low coast, broken only by a very tall church steeple, seen from the deck of his first command, the Russian frigate *Strela*.

'You're a long way from Rostock, Herr Teschow. Your experience?'

'Fifteen years in the Baltic trade, Captain, then seven on the Atlantic out of Gothenburg and Amsterdam. I've got certificates from all the skippers I served under. Herr Heinrich, there, has them.'

Philippe nodded. He was intrigued to know how a Rostocker came to be in Concarneau in the far west of Brittany, volunteering for a corsair, but in a time of war and with a crew to be filled, it paid not to ask too many questions. Dieter Teschow had the look of a sturdy seaman, a man who could haul and draw, reef and steer, and as long as he had those skills he could be a Mahometan or an Eskino for all Philippe cared. Augustin Heinrich entered the German's name into the book, directed him to the boatswain, then beckoned a blond, bearded giant wearing a red bonnet to come forward. Philippe was reminded of pictures of the ancient Northmen who pillaged the shores of Europe in years gone by.

'Name and condition?' said Augustin Heinrich, although for once, he looked the man in the eye. The *armateur*'s son even seemed to smile faintly.

'Marcus Drever of Harray in the Orcades, master. Orkney, ye ken. If ye prefer, master.'

The man's identity, confidently spoken in broken and appallingly pronounced pidgin French, provoked chatter in the line behind him and among those already entered who were still within earshot.

'You're a Scot?' said Philippe. Marcus Drever gave a single nod. 'Yet you wear the *bonnet rouge* of revolution. You're a subject of King George, and yet you wish to sail against your own country. Against England. How is that so, Citizen?'

Marcus Drever kept his eyes to the ground, seemingly unwilling to meet Philippe's gaze.

'England isna my country, Citizen Captain,' he said slowly and gruffly, still avoiding Philippe's eyes. 'Not an England with kings and a tyrant like yon Billy Pitt, anyways. Liberty, equality, fraternity, *vive la République*, that's what I believe. Same goes for plenty of boys in Scotland, even a few braw lads in Orkney.'

Philippe knew that France and Scotland had been close allies in centuries gone by and that some Scots, even some

Englishmen, were friends to the ideals of the revolution and the republic they had spawned, despite the war. There had been talk of uprisings in Edinburgh, and Pitt's government had staged a series of exemplary trials before packing the ringleaders off to a new penal colony on the far side of the world. He had encountered foreign sailors among the crews of the two warships he had commanded for the Republic, but never one from King George's own realm. But there was something wrong about the way Marcus Drever's declaration of loyalty to the ideals of the Republic was spoken. The words were flat and passionless, almost as though the Scot was delivering a badly rehearsed speech from memory. Moreover, the red bonnet he wore was far too small for his head, suggesting it was not his own.

The possibility of Drever being some sort of British spy crossed Philippe's mind, but he immediately dismissed the thought. Surely no spy would speak so poorly or look so mean, and the likes of William Pitt and Philippe's own English cousin, the ascetic and emotionless spymaster Lord Wilden, could have no possible interest in the voyage of a single French corsair.

'Your experience, Marcus Drever?'

'I have his certificates here,' said Augustin Heinrich, waving a clutch of papers. 'Perfectly in order. Danzig to Leith and the return voyage many times, many other voyages in the Baltic and the North Sea. Mate on most of those voyages, sometimes master going coastwise. Master's mate I think, Captain.'

Heinrich's enthusiasm on behalf of this one man, a foreigner, struck Philippe as odd. He took the certificates and leafed through them. All perfectly in order as Heinrich *fils* said, and again, it was inconceivable that any spy would go to the trouble to forge ten or so different hands just to get a place on a mere corsair. That being so, only the eternal custom of the sea mattered.

'I decide on the warrant officers, Citizen Heinrich,' said Philippe, a little tetchily. '*Matelot* first class until he can be tried on the proving voyage.'

Heinrich inclined his head respectfully.

'As you say, Monsieur le Vicomte.'

Philippe did not catch the glance that passed between Heinrich and Drever, for his attention had been taken by a new arrival. The shape and gait of the vast man who emerged from behind the piles of chippings and walked down the line of volunteers to not a few grumblings and catcalls about queue jumping were very familiar. Unmistakeable, in fact. Philippe had last seen this huge figure in the aftermath of the battle when his command *Le Zephyr* was defeated and captured by the larger British frigate HMS *Chester*. He had not expected ever to set eyes on the man again.

The colossus halted before him and came to attention, seemingly oblivious to the stares and jeers from the Breton shipwrights and the corsairmen assembled on the quayside of Concarneau.

'Sometime Enseigne de Vaisseau Juan Ugarte reporting and volunteering to serve, *mon Capitaine*.'

The immense Basque broke into a broad grin, and Philippe knew he had his lieutenant for the voyage of *La Verité*.

CHAPTER EIGHT

The side party came to attention, the Marines presented arms, the boatswain piped the still, and Lord Wilden stepped onto the deck of HMS *Royal George*, the flagship of the Channel Fleet, lying a few leagues south-west of the Lizard. Ignoring the persistent drizzle, Wilden doffed his hat, first to the ensign as he knew naval men did, then to the sharp-faced old man in an admiral's uniform who stood before him. Alexander Hood, Admiral Lord Bridport, returned the salute.

'Welcome to the fleet, Lord Wilden. I trust you had a pleasant voyage from Falmouth?'

Bridport's tone and expression made it plain that the welcome was reluctantly offered and that pleasantness was the very last experience the admiral wished for his guest.

'Tolerable, my lord, tolerable,' said Wilden with an insouciance that he did not truly feel.

The fast cutter that had carried him from Carrick Roads to the fleet had indeed been a tolerable, even a pleasant experience. The same could not be said for the ten days of unseasonal summer gales that had kept him in Falmouth, forced to dine every night with the governor of Pendennis Castle, an ancient and painfully deaf general who was very nearly a hundred and had entered the army in the reign of Queen Anne. Nor had the previous weeks been much better, with much of the time consumed by interminable meetings with the French royalist officers who were to command the expedition and by witnessing the embarkation of their army at Lymington. The so-called Army of Brittany, the principal component of the equally so-called Catholic and Royal Army of His Majesty King Louis the Seventeenth, consisted of some four thousand men, formed from *emigré* units that had been scattered far and wide after the revolution in their native country. One regiment had come from Toulon to England by way of Corsica, where the standard of King George the Third still flew precariously, others had been drawn from Germany or the Austrian service, others still fleeing from the Netherlands before it fell to their republican enemies. But by the very nature of the sort of men they were, the kind who could find or buy a way out of France before the guillotine shaved their necks, the *emigré* army consisted overwhelmingly of men of noble birth, and thus of officers. To provide a rank and file for them to command, the ancient castles and prison hulks of England had been scoured for potential recruits from among the ranks of the French prisoners already taken in the war. Unsurprisingly to Wilden's mind, many men who had previously espoused the principals of Robespierre and the *sans-culottes* suddenly experienced miraculous conversions overnight, went to mass and proclaimed their undying love for the king. The prospect of freedom could work miracles indeed, even if the commanders of the expeditionary force elected to ignore the question of how their new recruits might behave when they set foot on French soil again, or faced the guns of their former comrades-in-arms. Lord Moira, who commanded the British reserve division that was only to deploy well after the French forces had established the bridgehead, was scathing on the subject of his allies, and Wilden concurred entirely with the general's assessment.

But all of that, all the politics, all the internecine squabbles of the French royalists, all the petty disputes over precedence, even the nagging thought at the back of his mind that he and Pitt and the royalist leaders might have made a calamitous mistake in their conception of the expedition – all of it paled in comparison with the prospect before him: the prospect of the notoriously contrary and irascible Lord Bridport, the admiral commanding Britain's Channel Fleet and the man bearing the responsibility of maintaining the blockade of Brest, one of the lynchpins of Britain's security. For if France's Brest fleet should escape its harbour, it could wreak untold havoc on Britain's Atlantic trade. So, the force that Bridport commanded was the senior and most prestigious fleet in the Royal Navy, her commander a man who had to bear an extraordinarily heavy burden of responsibility. Some men bore that burden lightly and uncomplainingly, but Alexander Hood, now in his seventieth year, was not such a man.

Bridport introduced his flag captain, Dommett, who in turn introduced Wilden to several of the nine lieutenants and some other officers of *Royal George*, a monstrous First Rate of one hundred guns, then led Wilden and his admiral to the great cabin at the stern. This *Royal George* was a new ship, the namesake of and replacement for the man-o'-war that had calamitously sunk at Spithead some twelve years earlier when the bottom simply fell off. Wilden remembered how the reports of her loss, and that of the admiral and some nine hundred souls, had even reached and caused profound grief among the villagers on his Shropshire estate. He did not quite understand why his predecessors at the Admiralty, in their infinite wisdom, had chosen to bestow exactly the same name on the successor of a ship that had perished so calamitously. But it was the ship named after the king, and therein, Wilden knew, probably lay the answer. George the Third would undoubtedly insist that one of the greatest of his flagships should be named after himself.

Shouts from the deck, the creaking of the timbers and a suddenly perceptible motion of the hull – several motions in several directions, all simultaneous – made Wilden aware both that the flagship was beginning to move and that his stomach was expressing its disquiet at the fact. This was an utterly alien world, for despite the high rank he held in the Admiralty, the fifth Baron Wilden could count on one hand the number of times in his life he had gone to sea. None of those aquatic excursions had ever lasted more than a few hours, but now he would be expected to endure several days of this floating purgatory in notoriously turbulent waters, surrounded by men who did not think as he did, whose lives were dictated by the mysterious and capricious whims of the wind and tide, and who spoke in an utterly impenetrable language that only vaguely resembled intelligible English. He would give every appearance of taking it in his stride, Ned Wilden told himself. He would not dishonour himself. He would learn from the experience. If only his stomach would be compliant in his aspirations.

Through the stern windows of the flagship, several other ships of the fleet could be seen manoeuvring to gain the best advantage of the wind, their black-and-gold colour schemes welcome relief from the uniform grey of the sea and sky. Captain Dommett poured wine, the three men toasted the king, then Bridport gestured for Wilden to sit. The flag captain made his excuses, saying he had to return to the business of the ship, and Wilden was left alone with Bridport.

The admiral was not known for social niceties or lengthy preambles.

'So Warren's finally got the French off their arses and out to sea?' said Bridport gruffly.

Wilden knew he needed to reply, but the combined effect of the wine, the sea-swell and the ever-increasing motion of the ship made him gulp a couple of large breaths before he dared attempt to speak.

'That is my understanding, sir. The expeditionary squadron sailed from Lymington on the twelfth and should rendezvous with you in the next day or two.'

'Damn fool business,' snorted Bridport. 'I know Quiberon – I had the old *Minerva*, frigate of Thirty-Two, in the battle off there back in fifty-nine, when we fought under old Hawke. Bad shore, too much foul ground. That peninsula – why, my lord, it's no more than a feeble spit of land. An entire army could be trapped there by two men and their dog. The whole of Brittany ain't much better. It would be like the French landing in Cornwall and expecting to take London from there.' Bridport smiled, albeit without much mirth. 'But who am I to question the decisions of government, eh, Wilden? To contest the wisdom of the leaders of the nation? Not I, for sure. I'm a quiet and peaceable fellow, as you know, wouldn't ruffle a feather to save m'life. Besides, I won't give Pitt the excuse to put Sam in command in my place.'

Wilden avoided Bridport's gaze, concentrating instead on the spectacle astern, where the mighty *Queen Charlotte* and a couple of the Ninety-Eights were manoeuvring to fall in line ahead into the flagship's wake. He congratulated himself for not laughing, or even smiling, at Bridport's assessment of himself as a quiet and peaceable man. Difficult personalities evidently ran in the Hood family, for Bridport's brother Samuel, Lord Hood, had recently been relieved of the command of the Mediterranean fleet after a quarrel with the ministry.

'Now, Wilden, you'll want to know my dispositions, eh? That why Pitt's sent you along with me, eh? Want to know why I've not got the fleet standing directly off Brest? Scared that Villaret will seize the chance to bring their fleet out to cause God knows what havoc? Keen to send a critical report back to Downing Street, eh? Eh?'

Wilden gulped again and tried to keep his eyes on the window behind Bridport. *Keep looking at the horizon, Ned. You do not feel ill, Ned. The sea is quite calm, Ned. You will not spew over the admiral, Ned.*

'Admiral, I—'

Bridport waved his hand dismissively.

'All in hand, my dear Wilden, never fear. I've detached Cornwallis with *Royal Sovereign*, four more of the line and a brace of frigates to watch Brest, not that I reckon Villaret will really dare venturing out. He learned his lesson from old Black Dick Howe last year, when Dick dished the Frogs on the Glorious First of June. So I can play nursemaid to Warren and his Frenchmen all the way down to Quiberon, then come north again to cover Brest once more. So that can all be in your report to government, can it not?'

You are not ill. You will not vomit over the admiral. Any other admiral, perhaps. But Bridport, no.

'You do the ministry and the Admiralty a disservice, Lord Bridport. We all have full confidence in your command of this fleet.'

'Ha! Full confidence! *Full* confidence, sir? If Billy Pitt or our esteemed first lord had full confidence in me, they'd make me admiral of the fleet! It's my right as commander of the Channel Fleet, damn it, and Black Dick ain't coming back to sea any time this side of the last trump, that's for certain.'

Wilden nodded but made no attempt at a reply, and not just because he was trying to speak as little as possible. He had played his own part in denying Lord Bridport the title of admiral of the fleet, and the cantankerous admiral was doing no more than demonstrating that Wilden's advice to Earl Spencer, the first lord of the Admiralty, was amply justified.

'Nothing to say to that, eh, Wilden? And you're white, man – I've seen more colour in marsh-mallow. Not the old *mal de mer*, surely? It's damn near a flat calm, man!'

'Some discomfort from the cutter out from Falmouth, my lord. It will surely pass when I've had an opportunity to lie down.'

'Lie down, eh?' sneered Bridport with barely disguised contempt. 'Well, I can lend you my day bed for an hour or two, but beyond that, my lord, I regret that it will be impossible to accommodate you here aboard *Royal George*. The exigencies of a flagship, you understand.'

Wilden understood perfectly. Admiral Lord Bridport's love of his home comforts was almost as much of a byword in the navy as his avaricious pursuit of prize money, and some claimed that if he could somehow hoist sails from his elegant country residence in Somerset, detach it from its foundations and take it to sea as his flagship so he did not have to bestir himself from his drawing room, then the noble admiral would do exactly that. So it was no surprise that he was unwilling to give up even the smallest corner of the admiral's remarkably generous cabin and share it with anyone, let alone a landlubber Admiralty lord who seemed likely to spew all over the immaculately holystoned deck once the ship got properly underway. A landlubber Admiralty lord whom the admiral plainly regarded as nothing more than a spy acting for the prime minister.

'The natural place for you to be would be aboard *Pomone* with Warren, of course, but the last dispatch I had from him said that he's already overburdened with Frenchmen galore. The comte de this and the marquis de that are crawling out of his bilges like damn cockroaches at this very moment, or so he says. So I propose for your own comfort that you go out on one of the other ships in the fleet, a bigger and more comfortable one, then transfer to *Pomone* prior to Warren's squadron entering Quiberon Bay, as close to the time of disembarkation as possible.'

'A most sensible stratagem, if I may say so, my lord,' said Wilden, brazenly flattering the irascible admiral.

'Indeed so, indeed so. In which case, Wilden, I take it you'll have no objection to a billet with the rear-admiral aboard *Sans Pareil*? He volunteered for the honour of hosting you. Seemed most keen to accommodate you, in fact.'

Wilden arranged his face into what he hoped would be taken as a smile of assent, praying that the expression would be taken as a mark of gratitude for what Lord Bridport clearly regarded as an act of considerable generosity.

But a berth on HMS *Sans Pareil* would mean spending several days and nights in the company of Rear-Admiral Lord Hugh Seymour. In Wilden's opinion, it would be infinitely preferable to be gnawed slowly by rats.

CHAPTER NINE

On a Friday morning's tide, *La Verité* cast off from her buoy in the outer harbour of Concarneau, the crew tacking to bring her out into the Baie de la Forêt. It was only her second departure from her home port, the first having been for a brief proving voyage down to Belle-Île. That had gone well, with only a few adjustments necessary to the distribution of ballast. The crew, as Philippe had hoped, seemed to be uniformly competent, lacking the *matelots d'eau douce*, downright lubbers and ships' boys that infested the warships of the Marine Nationale. No doubt squabbles and quarrels would emerge in due course as men learned the measure of each other and the inevitable tensions caused by cooping up nearly two hundred mostly young men in a small wooden hull for weeks on end came to the fore. There was already some discontent in the crew at the presence of the Scot, Drever, but Philippe attributed this to natural suspicion of an enemy countryman. His concern was only with the man's competence, and he judged that the man had not yet shown sufficient qualities to deserve the sort of promotion that Heinrich *fils* continued to request for him. These, though, were insignificant problems when set against the sort of challenges he encountered in his first command in the Marine Nationale, where he had to contend with an openly hostile first lieutenant and an obstreperous, mutinous crew. For now, though, at the outset of the voyage of *La Verité*, with the ship's impressive sailing qualities increasingly apparent and with the prospect of untold prize money at the fore of every mind and uniting even the most disparate elements of the crew, the corsair was a joy to command.

Philippe trained his telescope on Fort du Cabellou on the headland to the south and saw a couple of officers standing on the ramparts with their own telescopes trained on him. Reports of the corsair's departure would be in Brest and Lorient that day, in Paris by the following evening, but it was moot whether anyone would pay much attention. The men in Cabellou soon put down their telescopes and turned away, no doubt feeling that they had seen enough and done their duty. It was not like Philippe's two frigate commands in the Marine Nationale, when his ships' departures from Brest and Toulon attracted plenty of curious sightseers and salutes were exchanged with the forts at the mouths of those harbours. Instead, *La Verité* moved out into the bay unacknowledged, cleared Pointe Beg-Mell and made her course due west for the Pointe de Penmarch, where she would begin her long haul to the north-west.

Philippe stood alongside Augustin Heinrich, white-faced, silent and obviously struggling not to be sick, sailing with the ship as a supernumerary and the plenipotentiary of his father, and Juan Ugarte, who had the watch. The old belief in providence was frowned upon under the Republic, but it was surely providence or something of the kind that had brought Ugarte, a man Philippe liked and trusted, out of captivity in England. He and Ugarte, like all the crew of the frigate *Le Zephyr*, had been taken prisoner when their ship was taken by a superior British man-of-war, but Philippe and a few of the men had managed to escape from a prison hulk in Portsmouth. As a commissioned officer, though, Ugarte had received the same offer that had been made to Philippe, the offer of a very different but rather more comfortable fate.

Philippe had broached the subject when he dined with Ugarte in a venerable tavern in a street just behind the principal wharfage of Concarneau the night after Ugarte's unexpected appearance to offer his services.

'But surely you gave your parole?' demanded Philippe.

The enormous Basque sniffed.

'Gave it, aye, and they sent me to a place called Tenterden, then to a bigger one further inland called Tonbridge. Nice enough, Captain, but so boring, especially in the winters the English have. They'd set up stones all round the town marking the boundary beyond which we couldn't go, and all my comrades, they treated this like it was the frontier of heaven and hell. We're men of honour, they all said, we've given our word, and we can't take even one step beyond the boundary stones. But you know I'm no man of honour, Captain. They might have stuck a uniform on me and called me an *enseigne de vaisseau* in the Marine Nationale, but not even the Republic can make a duck into a racehorse. So one day, I wake up and it's raining again, and I say to myself, "*ergela*, Juan Ugarte. You fool." So I went for a walk and kept walking until I reached the coast. Reckon my word of honour will still be somewhere in Tonbridge, Captain.'

Ugarte's last words to Philippe when the two men parted company aboard the prison hulk in Portsmouth harbour came back to him.

'*Thing is, Citizen Captain, I haven't got a word of honour. I'm just a peasant's brat from the Pyrenees. So I'll spend a few weeks in some nice town somewhere in the country, then just walk out, get myself to a port and find a ship that's got a Basque or two on it.'*

And that, it seemed, was exactly what Juan Ugarte had done. How such a colossal and surely unmissable escapee could possibly have avoided detection on a walk of fifteen hours in unfamiliar country was a question that brought a vague and elusive answer – there was mention of sleeping in a barn by day and walking by night, and an allusion to an accommodating dairymaid – but otherwise, Ugarte's prediction had been borne out in full. His destination, Romney Marsh, was a notorious haunt of smugglers who were perfectly happy even in wartime to transport a man to a remote French beach without asking too many questions, and according to Ugarte one of them had a Basque father who had been shipwrecked on Dungeness years before.

Part of Philippe Kermorvant was outraged. Ugarte's escape from England flouted every principle held by every naval officer – *every gentleman* – in every land. Parole was sacrosanct, a principle as inviolable as a sacred oath, which in a sense it was. If the Marine Nationale wished to make an example, then Ugarte would undoubtedly find himself facing a firing squad or climbing the steps to the guillotine. But there and then, Philippe offered up a silent prayer of thanks to any higher entities that might exist for bringing him the miraculous and fortuitous presence of Juan Ugarte, a man to whom gentlemanly niceties were quite alien.

'Corvette,' said the Basque lieutenant, bringing Philippe back to the present. 'Going round from Brest to Lorient, probably.'

All three men on the quarterdeck of *La Verité* trained their telescopes on a ship a league or so away, coming round onto a course east-south-easterly as she cleared the Pointe de Penmarch. A corvette of twenty-four guns, she flew a *Tricolore* vastly out of proportion to her size that would not have disgraced a Seventy-Four. The corvette closed a little for a closer inspection of the corsair, found nothing to concern her, and bore away. Through his telescope, Philippe could see her captain on the quarterdeck. The fellow was tall but very thin. He wore spectacles and looked to be no more than twelve years of age. That was impossible, Philippe knew, but if boys like this were gaining command of corvettes then the Republic was now granting frigates, or even ships of the line, to almost equally raw and inexperienced captains. *Granting them to men who were not as good as him.*

He dismissed the thought. Envy, jealousy, regret and all their kin were emotions that led ultimately to madness. His father had once written something like that, and Philippe had often known the truth of it. A kind of madness had driven him to seek vengeance against Count Bulgakov for the murders of Tasha and Ivan. He had his revenge on a hillside in Corsica, but the death of his sometime brother-in-law brought him little relief from the grief he still felt for his wife and son. To that, add his bafflement and then growing anger at being dismissed from the Marine Natonale. He knew he could serve France in a better capacity than as the captain of a mere corsair, acting at the behest of an avaricious foreigner. But worst of all was the sight of the garden at Brechelean, *his* garden at *his* chateau, and the sight of Leonore with *that man*, that enemy of the Republic.

As he watched the corvette make her leisurely course toward Lorient, he remembered the day at Concarneau when he received the note written by Olivier, informing him that Leonore was sheltering and nursing a wounded Chouan colonel. He was incredulous. Surely she would not betray him by inviting an enemy within his own walls? He rode at once for the chateau, avoiding the rebel pickets and making his way into the grounds by an old gate unused since his grandfather's day. Looking back dispassionately on his actions, he knew his course was suicidal. He was bound to be killed out of hand or captured, and if the royalist colonel had been shaped by a different mould, Philippe Kermorvant would undoubtedly have died that day. It would not have mattered if he had. His outrage at the traitor Cozanet's invasion of his home paled alongside his fury at Leonore's behaviour. Had she really thought she could keep her betrayal a secret? Not just betrayal – *treason*. What other word could describe the act of sheltering a senior officer in the so-called rebel army? Treason against France, and treason against him. He had intended—

What had he intended? What did he feel for her, and she for him? They had never spoken of it. There had been glances, and sighs, and sometimes shared moments of laughter and contentment. Times when he had been on the point of saying certain words, and he sensed that she would undoubtedly reciprocate in kind. But she was his brother's widow and had as good as sent her husband to the guillotine to save him, Philippe, and that awful choice had erected an invisible barrier between them. When Philippe was honest with himself, which took some weeks after that day at Brechelean, he also knew that if the word 'betrayal' was in play then did it not also describe his liaison in Corsica with the irresistible and passionate force that was Carla Leandri?

The corvette was nearly out of sight. Both Ugarte and Heinrich had gone below, leaving Philippe alone on the quarterdeck of *La Verité*. The voyage was just beginning, but when it ended he knew that he would have to come to a resolution about Leonore. Would he exile her from Brechelean, which he had threatened to do and which was perfectly within his right as the Vicomte de Saint-Victor? Somehow, though, he could not imagine the chateau without Leonore. But neither could he imagine them returning to the way it had been between them, the two of them sitting at opposite ends of the long dining table in the chateau and making polite conversation about the weather. He could only begin to conceive of how dreadful it would be to dine alone at that table. But if neither of those two possible courses, then what?

The words penned by the Chouan colonel, Cozanet, came back to him. *She is a paragon among women, Monsieur le Vicomte, and you are a fortunate man – although whether you realise this is not for me to say.*

From the mouths of babes, from the pens of traitors.

As the captain of *La Verité* agonised, the ship rounded the Pointe de Penmarch and set her course well to the west of Ushant, bound for the west coast of Ireland and the waters of the Atlantic.

CHAPTER TEN

The fleet was underway. The June afternoon was foggy with the air full of drizzle, but conditions were less dense than on the previous day and the sea remained calm enough for Ned Wilden not to feel queasy. The Channel Fleet was on a course that Ned judged to be roughly south-easterly, *Sans Pareil* seconding the flagship, which lay on her larboard beam. On the horizon he could still just make out the forest of sails that betrayed the position of the expeditionary force. He had been on deck a few hours earlier when sails were sighted coming down the Channel, and the youthful midshipman assigned to be his nursemaid reverted briefly to the irrepressible schoolboy he had surely been until very recently. He probably had to be twelve or thirteen, Ned estimated, but he was very small, blond-haired, and looked more like six or seven. Midshipman Jack Kenton had evidently been briefed by his captain to treat their guest as a complete ignoramus, the worst sort of landlubber, so he had clung to Wilden's side like a limpet and explained the parts and workings of the ship to him as if he was a particularly backward younger brother or else a Chinaman or the Man in the Moon, not a lord of the Admiralty. ('This, my lord, is what we seamen call a *belaying pin*', with each syllable of 'belaying' spelled out very, very slowly.) He was effusive about himself: father a vicar in Oxfordshire, dead three years past, mother a saint, older brother an ensign in the Fifty-Second of Foot on campaign in Ceylon, three sisters, and more relatives and neighbours than any child should surely possess. Kenton was inquisitive, too, and keen to learn what great men Wilden had met.

'I certainly have the honour of knowing Mister Pitt,' said Wilden in response to the latest breathless query, 'and he is indeed very tall, rather taller than myself.'

'And the king, my lord?'

'I have had audience of His Majesty on a considerable number of occasions. But I would consider the king to be rather shorter than Mister Pitt.'

Kenton considered this intelligence with the gravity of expression of an ancient philosopher.

'I've seen the king twice. I don't remember the first time, for I was very young, but it was when he visited Saint Giles' Fair in Oxford and my late pa took us all to see him. But the second time was last year when he visited the fleet after the Glorious First of June, my lord.'

'I am aware that a battle was won on that date last year, Mister Kenton.'

Wilden found the absence of deference both amusing and refreshing. He was accustomed in every facet of his life to being treated deferentially, even obsequiously, and the navy was the worst of all for craven fawning. The lieutenants of *Sans Pareil*, of which there were a bewildering seven, had already been falling over themselves to gain the notice of the Admiralty lord embarked with them, undoubtedly hoping he might smooth their paths to post-captain's rank, the golden key that opened the door to wealth, honour, and in the fullness of time and the avoidance of an untimely death, the hoisting of one's own admiral's flag. The infant midshipman, so unaffectedly inquisitive and enthusiastic about everything, was cut from a very different cloth, and Wilden was grateful for it.

Now the boy was pointing to the distant ships of the invasion armada.

'Look, my lord, see the broad pennant flying from the main? That's the commodore's ship, *Pomone*, Forty-Four. Sir John Borlase Warren that is, sir. He's a baronet, sir. Captured three French frigates in one action last year, including *Pomone* herself. A bold man, my lord, a very bold man.'

'I know,' said Wilden patiently. 'I played a part in selecting him for this mission.'

The lad seemed not to have heard.

'Two Seventy-Fours and a Sixty-Four with him, but he still prefers *Pomone* for his broad pennant. His flagship if you prefer, my lord, though a commodore ain't entitled to a proper flag like an admiral. If it was me, my lord, I'd have gone for one of the ones that could give me a bigger cabin. *Thunderer*, most likely, Seventy-Four and merchant built so she's most commodious, they say. Five frigates too, *Anson* being of the same rank as *Pomone*, the others smaller. Maybe sixty transports as well. All in good order by the looks of it.'

'Good enough order, at any rate,' said a loud and familiar voice behind them.

Midshipman Jack Kenton turned and saluted briskly. Wilden merely looked slightly to his side and gave the merest nod of acknowledgement to his host, the captain of HMS *Sans Pareil*.

'I trust Mister Kenton hasn't been wearying you with too many questions, my lord? He has a reputation for loquacity unrivalled in our gunroom. In the entire ship, indeed. Perhaps even the entire fleet. But for all that, he's the makings of a damn fine officer.'

Kenton blushed.

'Not in the slightest, Lord Hugh,' replied Wilden. 'I'm most grateful to you for appointing him as my guide to the hurly-burly of your wooden world.'

Rear-Admiral Lord Hugh Seymour was remarkably tall and strikingly handsome. He was very rich, a consequence of his being a son of the most fabulously wealthy man in Britain, the Marquess of Hertford. His ancestors included kings and queens of England, and one of them had ruled the country as Lord Protector of the kingdom. In truth, the Seymours were probably the closest one could come to royalty among the great families of England without encountering an unfortunate scent of the German. The urbane and brilliant Lord Hugh was one of the closest friends of the Prince of Wales, while the women of the *ton*, without exception and without distinction of age, all secretly loved him. Not so secretly in some cases. Despite his prominence in society he had a reputation as a thinker and an innovator, both vanishingly rare commodities among naval officers, and was responsible for the addition of epaulettes to their uniforms so that their ranks could be more easily distinguished. He had recently been added to the Board of Admiralty, where he sat alongside Wilden, and even more recently promoted to rear-admiral, too recently, in fact, for the customary flag captain usually assigned to a flag officer to be appointed to the ship. In truth it would be no exaggeration to say that Seymour was universally loved, seemingly with only one exception in the entire land.

Ned Wilden hated him.

He found it impossible to say why this was the case, but it was not the first time that the fifth Baron Wilden had found his opinions out of step with the rest of humanity. So, he hated Lord Hugh Seymour in the clubs of Pall Mall. He hated him in church whenever they both attended the same services at Saint George's, Hanover Square. He hated him when they chanced to encounter each other in Hyde Park. He hated him at the Admiralty. And he hated him here most of all, for *here* also meant *now*. Wilden had been rowed over from *Royal George* to *Sans Pareil* on the previous day, his heart sinking further with every swing of the oars. And there his nemesis had been, waiting for him on the deck of his command.

'My dear lord!' cried Seymour, grinning unaffectedly and stepping forward to vigorously shake Wilden's hand once the formalities of the welcoming side party aboard HMS *Sans Pareil* had been concluded. 'Welcome aboard *Sans Pareil*! It is an honour for the ship's company and myself to have such a distinguished passenger embarked! Now, my lord, you'll dine with me in my cabin forthwith? Of course you will. I'm fortunate to have a most splendid cook, the best in the fleet by my humble reckoning. You'll dine much better than you would have done on the flagship, I'll wager!'

Ned Wilden made an expression that might perhaps be construed as a smile of gratitude. He knew what lay ahead, and the hour that followed was purgatory indeed. Seymour talked as if life itself depended on how many spoken words he could utter during it. He talked about the prospects for the expedition (excellent) and their colleagues at the Admiralty (dolts). He held forth upon the condition of France (too strong) and Spain (too weak). He pontificated upon the married state (bliss) and the virtues of his famously beautiful wife (a paragon). Lord Bridport's conversation was wholly self-centred and consisted mainly of bitterness at what he saw as the countless slights against him made by the ministry, but at least the ancient admiral did not attempt to set himself up as an authority on every subject under the sun. Wilden feigned interest and essayed a few forays into conversation. He made a defence of the condition of a single man, but Seymour scoffed at this, assuring Wilden that there was no greater bliss than the married state and that his guest should not deprive himself of it. Wilden had no time for his mother's and sisters' lectures on the same subject, so he would certainly not entertain Hugh Seymour's opinion of the matter.

The whole meal was an ordeal. One of the only two saving graces was the quality of the beef, which amply bore out Seymour's praise of his cook. Wilden had not dined upon such fine meat for a very long time. The other saving grace was that Wilden's senses and stomach no longer made any protest at their enforced excursion to sea. Perhaps he was finally gaining what the mariners called sea legs, Wilden mused, or else perhaps HMS *Sans Pareil* sailed rather more comfortably than the flagship.

'My lord? Lord Wilden?'

Ned looked across the table to his host and realised that his attention must have wandered.

'My apologies, my dear Seymour, I was distracted by the excellence of this meat.'

Seymour smiled.

'Ah, perfectly understandable, my dear fellow. But I was saying, you're fortunate the admiral has given you a berth on this ship. She's French-built, y'know, one of the prizes Lord Howe took last year on the Glorious First. Sleek and fast, unlike the flagship and some of the others.

A better crew, too – more volunteers, fewer pressed men and landsmen, an excellent set of lieutenants and warrant officers. Mids, too. I'm assigning one of them to you for the duration of the voyage. It'll be interesting to see what you make of our Mister Kenton – who is quite a singular young fellow – and he of you.' Seymour smiled. 'No, all things being weighed in the balance, a man couldn't wish for a better command. So God willing, my lord, we'll give you a comfortable and uneventful passage down to Quiberon.'

Unknown to Wilden, Seymour, Bridport, Midshipman Kenton and every man in the Channel Fleet, the prospects for an uneventful passage had just receded dramatically. Just over one hundred and fifty miles to the south-east of where Wilden and Seymour dined, Bridport's vice-admiral, William Cornwallis, with five ships of the line and two frigates, was in search of a French convoy and its escorting squadron known to be in the vicinity of Belle-Île when the sails of another force were spotted on the horizon. The frigate *Phaeton* was detached to investigate, and its initial report suggested that the distant ships were indeed French but of inferior strength to Cornwallis's squadron. Confident of their superiority, Cornwallis and his ships began to close the enemy.

HMS *Triumph* of seventy-four guns was the fourth ship in the British line of battle, sailing in the wakes of *Brunswick*, Cornwallis's flagship *Royal Sovereign* and *Bellerophon*, but ahead of the rearmost ship, *Mars*. The captain of *Triumph*, Sir Erasmus Gower, was a fifty-two-year-old Welshman who had recently returned from an expedition to China. He had been responsible for the delivery and safe return of the first British ambassador to that distant and mysterious empire, tasked with securing an advantageous trade agreement with the Chinese. None ensued, but Gower returned with his reputation unblemished and enhanced, and received as his reward the plum command of *Triumph* in the Channel Fleet.

At eleven in the morning, Gower and his officers trained their telescopes on *Phaeton* as she let fly her topsails, the established signal for the approach of a superior enemy. The captain of *Phaeton* must have utterly misjudged the nature of the force he had sighted, and that misjudgement had been compounded by Cornwallis ordering his squadron to close the distant hulls. Worse, in those waters a superior enemy fleet could mean only one thing. It had to be Admiral Villaret de Joyeuse himself with at least the majority, if not the entirety, of France's Atlantic fleet out of Brest.

'So, gentlemen,' said Gower phlegmatically to the officers nearest him on the quarterdeck, 'not the easy pickings we anticipated after all.'

'Flagship's signalling, sir,' said the signal lieutenant.

'I see it, Mister Chapman. No need to consult the cypher for this one, eh, gentlemen? All ships to tack to starboard and haul away to the south-west. All that the vice-admiral could do in the face of what confronts us. Very well, gentlemen, let's to it!'

The orders were relayed down the chain of command, from Atkins the first lieutenant by way of the warrant and petty officers to the able and ordinary seamen who executed the orders from the quarterdeck. On *Triumph* and her companions, men scurried aloft, others hauled on the ropes that would bring the yards around, and helms were put over. In the distance, their enemies, too, were issuing their orders, but in their case these were to put on more sail and pursue the retreating British squadron. For the force that *Phaeton* had finally counted accurately consisted of twelve ships of the line and eleven frigates, all flying the *Tricolore* of the French Republic. With Bridport's blockading fleet off its station to rendezvous with the expeditionary force for Quiberon, Admiral Villaret de Joyeuse, acting under orders from Paris, had taken advantage and brought out almost the entire Brest fleet.

For Villaret this could be his chance to erase the memory of his bruising defeat at the hands of Lord Howe in the previous year, his chance to destroy an entire English squadron and give the French Republic its first great naval victory of the war. It was a chance the French admiral had to take.

CHAPTER ELEVEN

From the papers of Leonore Kermorvant

Mon cher Philippe.

No. Too intimate.

Monsieur le Vicomte.

No. Too formal.

Brother Philippe.

No, no, no. It makes him sound like a monk.

For at least the tenth time, I crumple my sheet of writing paper and toss it to the floor. I stare out of the window. I get up and walk around the room. No inspiration is to be found in the dusty portrait of Philippe's grandfather (a remarkably ugly man), so I return to my chair, take up another sheet of paper, place it on the desk in front of me and raise my quill once again.

Philippe.

Yes. Better. Neutral, dispassionate. Appropriate.

Philippe. I crave your pardon—

No. Angrily I crumple this sheet too, and it follows its brethren to the floor. Weeks have passed since Philippe's abrupt departure, weeks in which my defiance, my rage at him for his highhanded and unforgiving behaviour, has slowly dissipated. Those emotions have given way to others, some of which I have difficulty acknowledging to myself. This change of heart has been reinforced by the daily, sometimes hourly, reproofs from Martha Penhouet, who insists that I should write to Philippe to crave his pardon. I think the bottom of it all is her less than secret desire to be able to strut about among the shopkeepers of Ploermel and Rennes in the more exalted station of housekeeper to a Vicomte and Vicomtesse de Saint-Victor.

No, despite all dear, infuriating Martha's urging. What have I to crave pardon for? I have done nothing wrong. Nothing passed between me and Colonel Cozanet, and all those employed at the chateau would have sworn the truth of that if Philippe had only taken the trouble to ask them. But no, stubborn, suspicious man as he has revealed himself to be, he adopts the high dignity of the Vicomte de Saint-Victor, then flounces off to his ship without another word. Infuriating man. I should not give him another thought, let alone write him a letter of apology. I should go back to my remaining family in Burgundy. I should certainly not wait here, within the ruinous walls of the chateau of the Kermorvants, merely and meekly to await the return of a man who all too evidently views himself as my lord and master.

No. Put aside the illusions, Leonore. There is nothing for me now in Burgundy, only cousins who to a man are indifferent to my fate. For good or ill my future is tied to this place, and thus it is tied to Philippe Kermorvant.

Philippe. I crave your pardon for inviting into your home — *your home of barely two years, Monsieur le Vicomte who spent most of your life far away from France, whereas it has been my home for ten. Yet the law of France proclaims you to be the owner of my home by right of your birth. Not even a young republic born out of the ideals of* liberté, equalité, fraternité, *has proved willing to challenge such injustices.*

— for inviting into your home an enemy of the Republic. I will not essay to defend my decisions, save to say they were born solely out of human kindness and the urgent necessity of saving a good man's life. But I have had time to reflect on my actions —

– and in hindsight I would undoubtedly do the same again.

But this time I do not crumple the paper. This must be done. Something must be salvaged from the ruins if it can be. The letter must be written. Philippe must hear my justification whether he wishes to or not. He must understand my feelings, which must be expressed candidly. So this letter must be written, even if every word is an agony.

I look back down at the paper and consider how to continue, but before I write another word, I realise there is a foolishly disregarded flaw in my strategy. Philippe is at sea. I am well used to this, for I have always sent him regular reports on matters relating to the estate. But when he commanded ships in the Marine Nationale there was no difficulty in directing letters – to Brest when he commanded a frigate out of that dockyard, Toulon when he had a command in the Mediterranean. The officials in those ports knew exactly where the Republic's ships were meant to be and which outgoing vessels were likely to cross paths with them, enabling mail to be delivered to the intended recipients. Often months late, perhaps, and often in bundles of several at a time, but nowadays the post offices on land can sometimes do little better than that. But he now commands a corsair, and even when we were on speaking terms he never confided in me anything about the mission in which he is presently engaged, nor the identities of ports to which it might be possible to direct mail.

I have a flash of inspiration. The ship's owner will know. Of course he will. But I do not know his name, only that he is a wealthy Swiss merchant of Rennes. I stand and go in search of Olivier.

I find him in the room in the north-west tower that serves as his office. It is one of the only inhabitable rooms in that part of the chateau, and in the days when my late husband, Alexandre, administered the estate himself, it was a veritable quagmire of chaos. Old bills were crammed into pigeonholes alongside the new and pressing ones. Tottering towers of dusty ledgers were scattered at random on shelves and tables. I attempted to tackle the rampant disarray when Alexandre's affections fled from me for successive bottles of brandy, but the task proved beyond me. Now, though, the room is an exemplar of calm and good order. Olivier has arranged everything according to an elaborate system of his own devising. He sits in the centre of the room at a U-shaped desk, letters and papers arranged neatly on either side of him, an account ledger propped up on a reading stand in front of him. He stands as I enter.

'Citizeness Kermorvant,' he says stiffly. 'How may I assist you?'

Relations between us have been cool since I learned it was his letter that had informed Philippe of Colonel Cozanet's presence in the chateau. I barely spoke to him for two or three weeks after Philippe's abrupt departure for Concarneau, but as time passed my attitude changed. Olivier was perfectly right to inform his employer, the owner of the chateau, of something transpiring on his property. No mere 'something', either, but an act that could certainly be construed as treason against the Republic. All of Olivier's loyalty was rightly to the man who had saved him from beggary on the streets of Brest, and it was unfair of me to shun him for merely doing his undoubted duty.

'I need to send a letter to the vicomte,' I say. 'To do that, I need first to write to the armateur of his voyage. You have the man's name and address?'

'I do, Citizeness. But why write to Citizen Heinrich at Rennes when I can supply you with the information you seek?'

'You have it?'

'Of course, Citizeness. The vicomte left directions for mail in case I needed to inform him of any significant matters relating to the estate.'

Matters like his sister-in-law taking in and nursing a rebel, I thought.

'Excellent. Then where may I direct such a letter?'

'The Helder in North Holland, Citizeness.'

'This Helder is—'

'Stralsund, too. And Wismar. Rostock. Danzig. Stettin. Then in Sweden, Gothenburg—'

'Enough! How many ports in all?'

'Seventeen, Citizeness.'

'Seventeen? You write to all of them?'

'Of course, Citizeness.'

'But surely there is one where he is most likely to call? One where mail has the greatest chance of reaching him?'

Olivier shrugged.

'If there is, Citizeness, then the vicomte did not confide that information to me.'

For a normal letter of courtesy, of course, I would write the original and then get someone, most probably the youth standing before me, to write out sixteen copies of it. But the letter I have begun will contain such expressions that it cannot be seen by Olivier, nor any other living being but Philippe. And I cannot face the thought of copying out the words that I must write, the sentiments I must express, a total of seventeen times.

'Very well, Olivier. Then I shall write to this Citizen Heinrich after all in the hope he will be willing to tell me which harbour he has directed the vicomte's ship to use.'

I write to the address in Rennes that Olivier supplies. In normal times a letter can be sent from here to Rennes, and the reply received, within two days. But these are not normal times. The rebellion of the Chouans has disrupted the posts as it has disrupted all else. Besides, Citizen Heinrich may be away from Rennes, attending to business elsewhere.

There is no reply within a week. I brace myself to write seventeen identical letters (completed, now, very heartfelt and very, very long) to all the ports on Olivier's list.

But then a letter arrives, a letter bearing the seal of Citizen Antoine Heinrich.

Its contents are not at all what I expect.

CHAPTER TWELVE

La Verité at sea, fifty-one degrees, thirty minutes of latitude north, twelve degrees, forty-five minutes of longitude west of the Paris Meridian, nine leagues due west of Cape Clear.

As Philippe had hoped at Concarneau, the corsair was proving to be a veritable greyhound of the oceans, taking advantage of the blustery south-westerlies to race past the hostile coast of Ireland at speeds that astonished her captain and brought smiles to the oldest *loups de mer* in the crew. She sailed best with the wind a little off the quarter, but she was easy and nimble in any breeze. They had not yet encountered any heavy weather worthy of the name, but by the time autumn gales prevailed in the Atlantic the corsair would probably be in the more sheltered waters of the Baltic, in the anchorage off The Helder in Holland with a clutch of lucrative prizes, or else back home in Brittany. Philippe had just completed a letter to Antoine Heinrich, the first of a numbered sequence that would be sent home on any French or neutral vessel they encountered that was bound for a French port, or else delivered in due course as part of a batch left with Heinrich's agent in the Batavian Republic for onward dispatch. This letter, at least, was complete. He had started several to Leonore, but the tone was never right and they had all ended as discarded balls of paper.

Philippe put down his pen and walked to his stern window, navigating a course past Augustin Heinrich, who lay on a sea-bed hard against the larboard hull planking in the cabin that Philippe was compelled to share with him. The young man was asleep, a thankful relief from his condition when awake, which alternated between moaning loudly and retching into the bucket positioned alongside the bed.

Under a grey sky and scudding cloud, the horizon astern was clear. Most shipping, certainly all the trades passing through La Manche and the Irish Sea, sailed well to the south, and one of the oddities of the orders from the Swiss *armateur* was Heinrich's insistence that *La Verité* should follow this much longer course northabout around Ireland and the north of Scotland, rather than the more direct passage. French ships, certainly French corsairs out of Dunkirk and Saint-Malo, passed through the Straits of Dover and the southern North Sea all the time, despite the proximity of England's shore. A fatal proximity that had bound the two countries' histories to each other for centuries, making it too easy for each country's rulers to gaze on the opposite shore and imagine taking that small step across such a narrow stretch of water. Philippe himself had followed the course through La Manche earlier in the war, albeit in reverse, aboard the ship that brought him back to France from Russia, the corsair *Quatorze Juliette*. But Antoine Heinrich had displayed what Philippe regarded as uncharacteristic timidity by insisting that his ship took the longer passage and avoided the straits, saying that he considered the risk from the Royal Navy in the Narrow Seas to be too great. Philippe, though, suspected that Heinrich's insistence on the northabout course also had not a little to do with a revelation Heinrich *père* had shared only after Philippe had agreed to take the command. There were secret sealed orders, held in safekeeping by Heinrich *fils*, that were only to be opened when the corsair reached the fifty-fifth degree of latitude. These, both Heinrichs assured him, did not impact to the slightest degree on the ship's broader mission, nor on the ability of all aboard her to obtain the prodigious sums of prize money that had been promised, nor necessitate any significant diversion from her course. Despite his misgivings, Philippe accepted the arrangement. The timely arrival of a letter offering him a command from the minister of Marine would undoubtedly have changed matters, but as it was, he could see no alternative to agreeing to Antoine Heinrich's terms.

His thoughts were interrupted by a furious hammering on the cabin door, followed by the entrance of a breathless young *matelot* whom he recognised as Coiffic, one of the many crew members who hailed from the notorious corsair den of Saint-Malo.

'Captain! Lieutenant Ugarte asks that you come on deck at once!'

There were few situations that Juan Ugarte could not handle himself, so Philippe moved straight away. As he did so, a waking Augustin Heinrich groaned from his sea-bed.

It took only a few strides for Philippe to reach the upper deck of *La Verité*, where he encountered an extraordinary scene. Men were staring and pointing at the main topyard where two of their fellows were engaged in a knife fight, both of them edging to and fro on the foot ropes, one hand grasping the yard while the other stabbed and swung at their opponent. The movement of the ship, the state of the sea and the strength of the wind were not excessive, but the slightest false move would see one or both of them plunging to their death either into the unforgiving ocean or onto the even less lenient deck far below. Several of the ship's petty officers were bellowing at them to stop, but the loudest voice of all, replete with a succession of oaths and curses in Basque, Breton, French and, for good measure, English, came from the giant figure of Juan Ugarte, who was stamping on the quarterdeck with rage. If that did not rouse Augustin Heinrich, thought Philippe, then nothing would.

He recognised one of the two men as the Scot Marcus Drever. The other was a Breton named Marhallac'h who until that moment he had thought a quiet, inoffensive fellow.

'What is this madness?' Philippe demanded of Ugarte. The Basque shook his head.

'God knows, Captain.' God was out of favour in republican France, but Juan Ugarte lived largely by his own laws. 'But whatever the cause, they're both oblivious to commands.'

Philippe heard Ugarte's words, but knew he had to try. The authority of a captain was almost mystical, even aboard a corsair.

'Marhallac'h! Drever! Cease this lunacy! Come down! Come down now!'

But neither man paused, nor seemed even to have heard their captain's order. Drever stabbed again at the Breton, but Marhallac'h swung back and avoided the thrust. A sudden pitch of the hull made both men lose their grip on the yard, but with extraordinary speed they immediately shifted their weight and regained their hold.

Without a word to Ugarte, and without any sort of conscious decision, Philippe went to the starboard main shrouds, swung himself outboard and began to climb.

There were times when madness could only be countered with an even greater measure of madness, and he heard the astonished gasps and chatter as the Vicomte de Saint-Victor hauled himself up the ropes as nimbly as any topman. In truth he had not climbed to a masthead since he was a youngster serving the State of Virginia and then the Continental Congress of the United States, but the return of the old sense of exhilaration at the staggering height, the unrivalled view and the freshness of the air was outweighed by the prospect before him of two men with blades, each seemingly intent on killing the other.

He reached the yard, took hold of it and swung himself onto the footrope. He was nearer to Drever, but the Scot, focused solely on Marhallac'h's knife, did not turn or acknowledge him in any way.

'You, men!' shouted Philippe, trying to ensure he was heard above the moaning and whistling of the wind. 'Marcus Drever! Cease now! Desist! I order it as your captain!'

Marhallac'h, further from the mast, was staring directly at him, realisation finally dawning. But Drever, seemingly oblivious to Philippe's order, stabbed again at his opponent, then turned and waved his knife at his captain. Philippe saw the redness of the Scot's face, saw the unreasoning rage in Drever's eyes, and for a moment he thought the renegade Orcadian was about to lunge at him. He raised his free hand, palm open in the universal gesture of peace.

'Enough,' he yelled to make himself heard above the wind. 'We go down now, all three of us, and resolve the issue between you. We talk as rational men. I do not flog for the mere sake of it, and I will hear you both out before I decide on punishment. You have my word on that.'

Drever's eyes were still furious, but there seemed now to be a slight hesitancy about him. Marhallac'h was already starting to edge his way toward the mast and the shrouds. After another few moments of indecision, Marcus Drever followed him. Philippe breathed heavily, then allowed himself one look at the deck far below and another at the empty ocean all around the corsair before he, too, began his descent.

—

The disciplinary code aboard *La Verité* was based on that of the Marine Nationale, with a few minor variations and a generous dose of that eternally useful catchall, the time-honoured laws and conventions of the sea. No properly constituted naval court would normally include a civilian, but few corsairs could ever have set sail with the son of the principal owner and *armateur* aboard, so Augustin Heinrich sat alongside Philippe and Ugarte as the third judge. Although he was properly clothed and sitting upright on a chair rather than lying sprawled on the sea-bed in a nightshirt, Heinrich's complexion was still ghastly and he held a kerchief very near his mouth as if he expected to vomit at any moment. The door of the cabin was guarded by the corsair's bosun, a surly but capable *Morbihannais* named Madec.

Standing in front of the three judges were the two defendants, Marhallac'h and Drever. Both were silent and sullen, but Drever seemed no longer to be lost in some inner frenzy of rage.

'There is one question only,' said Philippe, opening the inquiry. 'What caused the quarrel between you?'

Neither man said anything immediately, although Marhallac'h took a deep breath and looked around the cabin as though he was seeking the right words. Drever, the more confident and articulate of the two, spoke instead.

'I do my duty,' he mumbled. 'Some have taken agin me, though. Yon Marhallac'h has been the worst.'

'Taken against you?' queried Philippe. 'In what way?'

'They hate me. Call me an enemy of France. A renegade. A spy. Other names.'

Ugarte was incredulous.

'You pull a knife on a man, and on the maintop yard at that, *because he has called you names?*'

'Not just names. Other things too.'

'You've been at sea many years,' continued Ugarte, 'yet you're still offended by what men call you?'

'I didna pull a blade first,' said Drever. 'That was him.'

Philippe glanced at Ugarte, then addressed Marhallac'h.

'Several men who witnessed your confrontation confirm that,' he said. 'So, Marhallac'h, what—'

'Then it is quite clear, Captain,' interrupted Augustin Heinrich, suddenly animated but still as pale as a winding sheet. 'This man, this Marhallac'h, is the sole guilty party here, and Drever was simply acting in self-defence.'

'We must still hear from Marhallac'h, Citizen Heinrich,' said Philippe as patiently as he could. Heinrich took the rebuff with bad grace, gagged as though he was about to vomit, but somehow kept it down.

Philippe turned again to Marhallac'h.

'Well, man? That you attacked Drever is beyond doubt. What do you say in your defence?'

Marhallac'h shuffled on his soles as though the deck of the captain's cabin had suddenly become a bed of hot coals. He was known even to his ship's captain to be a slow and frankly stupid man, the sort of seaman who needed clear orders and simple repetitive tasks. But when Marhallac'h spoke, he did so with unexpected passion. It was as if the words had been bottled up inside him, awaiting their moment.

'It's true no man aboard likes him,' he said of Drever. 'I'm not alone in that, your excellencies. He's a Scot so he's an enemy of France, no matter what he says. But what he says ain't true, Captain. He swears he's a true Jacobin, but he ain't that.'

Marhallac'h seemed about to say more, but then he looked over to Drever and fell silent.

'So what is he?' demanded Ugarte.

'*I* don't believe this, mind, but a lot of the boys, a lot of us Breton boys anyhow…'

'Yes, Marhallac'h?' said Philippe. 'What do they believe?'

'They think he's the Devil, your excellencies.'

Ugarte snorted. Heinrich simply gawped. Only Philippe broke the astonished silence that followed Marhallac'h's incredible statement.

'The *Devil*?'

'Like I say, I don't think that myself, Captain. But some sort of a witch, something of that kind, and as well as that—'

Drever snorted.

'Captain,' said an exasperated Augustin Heinrich, 'this is the very height of absurdity. We live in a time of reason. We are citizens of a republic dedicated to it. Yet a man stands before us accused of being the Devil, or else a necromancer. A patent absurdity, Captain Kermorvant. This Breton declares himself guilty out of his own mouth, sir. I urge that we move to judgement on him at once.'

'In due time, Citizen. But Matelot Marhallac'h, I wish to hear your reasons for thinking this way about Matelot Drever.'

'Captain—' Heinrich protested.

'Remember we form a court of equal judges, Citizen Heinrich. Being the son of our *armateur* entitles you to a place here but it gives your vote no greater weight. So if Lieutenant Ugarte agrees with me, we continue the questioning of Marhallac'h.'

'I so agree,' said Ugarte, who had made his disdain for Augustin Heinrich obvious since the days of fitting out the ship at Concarneau and would oppose anything the young man proposed on principle.

Again with bad grace, Heinrich gave a barely perceptible nod.

'Continue, Matelot Marhallac'h,' said Philippe.

Marhallac'h began to shuffle his feet again and looked at the deck, not at the three judges nor Drever.

'Up there on the yard he laid a curse on me, Captain. I'll swear an oath on that. That's when I pulled my knife on him, your excellencies. But I'm not the only one who's had a fill of him. He'd been full of strange talk since you formed the crew at Concarneau, saying how mermaids and sea-beasts called kelpies were real and that he'd seen them. Once we sailed, he reckoned that the ship was doomed because we'd left Concarneau on a Friday. All his talk unsettled the men, Captain. He would mutter strange oaths and curses—'

Drever smiled, and Ugarte looked up in amazement.

'Oaths and curses? Oaths and curses, Matelot? Damnation, man, if all the sailors in the world who'd ever uttered oaths and curses were put to the blade, none would be left. No ship would ever leave harbour again.'

Marhallac'h looked away.

'Ask any man in the crew. There's not many he hasn't cursed or fallen out with or given the evil eye. Plenty of the men say he's some sort of demon.'

'This is absurd!' Augustin Heinrich protested. 'Captain, surely the case is quite clear! This man attacked Drever with no justification. There is no substance to any of this. Drever is innocent—'

Marhallac'h, increasingly agitated, stepped forward toward Philippe, his hands clasped in supplication.

'Sirs, honoured citizens – hear me out! There's one thing more.'

'Speak it,' said Philippe, 'but if it is of no consequence, I see no reason not to concur with the opinion voiced by Citizen Heinrich.'

'It was like this, Captain,' said Marhallac'h heavily, 'four years ago, just before war was declared, I went on the *pêche à la baleine*, the whaling, out of Saint-Malo. We spent weeks on the coast of Labrador. There were a few other Breton boats, some Basque—' he glanced at Ugarte— 'and some Scots. Some from this Orkney, anyway. The weather was bad, so we spent many nights in the same bays. We drank together as *matelots* do. The Basques and the Scots questioned us about the revolution in France, and there was little talk of anything else. But I remember the Orkney crews telling a story of something that had recently happened in their land. Three children had been killed, they said. Brutally murdered in ways too horrible to relate. But I remember the name of the man they said had done it, who had then fled the country. It was such a simple but unusual name that it stuck in the memory, your honours. The killer's name was Drever.'

Augustin Heinrich rose abruptly from his chair, picked up the chamber pot that he kept to hand at the side of his sea-bed, and retched into it. Ugarte shook his head slowly, as if he had never heard such a preposterous tale. Philippe, though, kept his eyes fixed on Marcus Drever. The Scot, previously so voluble in denying all the accusations levelled at him by Marhallac'h, was silent, his expression venomous, staring hard at the Breton's back. When he spoke, his voice was quieter and more measured than it had been.

'Drever's a common name in my land,' he said. 'But all this is a mere tale, Captain. It's invention, naught else. There's nae proof of any of it. Aye, up there on the yard he accused me of being that other Drever, the child murderer, so I cursed him as any falsely accused innocent would. Then he drew the knife on me, sirs, an' that's honest truth.'

Philippe had heard enough. He held a whispered conference with Ugarte, then with Heinrich when the young man finally returned to his place. When he delivered the verdict, it was categorical.

'There is one fact here,' he said, 'and one alone. A blade was first drawn by Matelot Marhallac'h, and it was he who first attacked Matelot Drever. This one fact was witnessed by many men, including Lieutenant Ugarte, here. All the rest is hearsay and wild rumour. Nothing more than the jealous dislike of an outsider. That being so, we concur that you, Marhallac'h, should receive fifty lashes. Consider yourself fortunate, Matelot, for in the Marine Nationale you would likely have been sentenced to death. Had you killed Drever, that would most certainly have been your fate on this ship too, corsair or no.'

The Breton flinched. Fifty lashes was not an excessive punishment by naval standards, but many men had died from fewer.

'Marcus Drever,' Philippe continued, 'you were the victim of this man's attack. All the rest of Marhallac'h's accusations against you carry no weight.'

The Scot smirked.

'But I stand witness to the fact that you disobeyed your captain's order to desist from your fight with Marhallac'h, and even threatened me with your knife. This, too, was witnessed by Lieutenant Ugarte and several dozen of the crew from the deck. This cannot be disregarded without detriment to the good discipline of the ship. That being so, Matelot Drever, we sentence you to ten lashes.'

CHAPTER THIRTEEN

'*Brunswick*'s still wallowing like a pig, sir,' said Tippett, the second lieutenant of *Triumph*.

Captain Sir Erasmus Gower nodded.

'*Billy Ruffian* ain't much better,' he replied, looking away toward the ship in question. 'Damn me, Cranstoun's desperate! Ditching his poop carronades, by God!'

'And he's readying to follow them with his anchors and boats, like *Brunswick*,' said Tippett, who was studying HMS *Bellerophon* through his telescope.

For several hours Cornwallis's force had retreated slowly before Villaret's superior French numbers, which had formed into two divisions, one to northward with the obvious aim of weathering the British squadron, the other more southerly. But the British ships' progress, sailing beam on to the moderate north-westerly breeze, was hindered by the two most laggardly ships, *Brunswick* and *Bellerophon*, the latter universally nicknamed the *Billy Ruffian*, both usually excellent sailors but now hamstrung by errors in distributing their stores and ballast within their hulls, resulting in the desperate measures ordered by Captain Lord Cranstoun of *Bellerophon*. Consequently, Cornwallis had ordered the brisker *Triumph* and *Mars* to take the rearmost positions in the little fleet, the two ships frequently making or shortening sail to keep their positions in the line. Inevitably, though, this meant the two Seventy-Fours would bear the brunt of the French attack, and Gower watched through his telescope as the enemy ships slowly but steadily closed on his windward quarter.

'Damn me,' he said, 'we'll have to fight 'em with our arse! Master Gunner to the quarterdeck!'

The order was passed to the main gundeck, and within a few minutes the hirsute veteran master gunner of *Triumph* presented himself before Gower. He offered a casual salute.

'Mister Slaughter,' said Gower, 'we'll take two guns off the upper deck for'ard and shift 'em aft, to the wardroom stern ports. Choice of guns at your discretion, Master Gunner, but make it prompt!'

'Aye, aye, Captain!'

'Mister Tippett, all hands to make ready for close action!'

Lieutenant James Tippett saluted, raised his voice trumpet and bawled the order. The Marine drummers took up their positions on the quarterdeck and began to beat out the urgent rhythm that summoned the crew of *Triumph* to their battle stations.

'Mister Lowe!'

Another of the ship's lieutenants, the fourth, presented himself before Gower.

'Sir?'

'The ship needs to be lighter for close action, Mister Lowe. Orders to the carpenter and his crew – stave in the water butts and wine puncheons!'

'All of them, sir?'

'Aye, all of them, Lieutenant!'

'Aye, aye. Captain!'

Gower gave the order to shorten sail once again. Men went about the task grimly but efficiently, somehow avoiding the gun crews who were detaching two of the twenty-four-pounders forward from their carriages and securing them with the ropes that would lower them onto the main deck, where they would be hauled to the stern to strengthen the battery right aft. And all the while the French fleet came on, confident and serene, closing little by little with every minute that passed.

The leading French ship, which had already engaged *Mars*, opened fire on *Triumph*'s starboard quarter and stern.

'Now then, my brave boys, my valiant Triumphs!' cried Gower to the men within earshot. 'Some of you have been with me to China and back on the good old *Lion*, my lads, so let's send the Frogs yonder further still, to hell this time so they can't ever come back! As they bear, Mister Slaughter – *fire!*'

Triumph opened up with the stern chasers and the guns newly installed in the wardroom. *Mars*, sailing abeam, opened fire a few seconds later. For more than two hours, both ships' rearmost guns kept up a ferocious bombardment on the oncoming French ships and received in turn the cannonades of successive assailants. The enemy fire was, as always, slower than that of the better trained and more experienced British gun crews, even though *Triumph*, unlike *Mars*, carried a relatively new crew. Yet as Gower watched and felt the guns on the quarters fire, reload and fire again, he knew at once that something was wrong.

'Mister Slaughter, there!'

'Aye, Captain?'

'We seem to be getting through a prodigious amount of powder, Master Gunner!'

Slaughter grimaced.

'Way it's been for months, sir, in the Channel Fleet at least. Most of the powder's old, from the last war. The Ordnance Board had so much in store, they've been issuing that these past two years. And it's poor stuff in any case, Captain. A mixture of one-third merchants' powder with two-thirds royal to save cost. The French powder's new and a better quality.'

Inwardly Gower, whose long voyage to China had spared him earlier exposure to the shortcomings of the fleet's powder, seethed at the venality of the Ministry and the indifferent complacency of the clerks of the Board of Ordnance. But it did not do for a senior captain to be seen and heard to question higher authority, so a pantomime had to be performed.

'Well, Mister Slaughter,' he declaimed loudly enough for the men nearby to hear, 'we'll have to trust that lesser British powder and the stout hearts of British tars will still be more than ample to dispatch the Frogs! Keep up our fire, Master Gunner, and a song for old England!'

The twenty-four pounder nearest to him fired and recoiled. As the gun crew began their automatic routine of swabbing, loading and hauling, Gower took a few paces forward and began to sing a familiar lyric in his loud and erratic baritone. The men in the nearest gun crews smiled. They were already well used to their captain's propensity for song.

'When Britain first, at Heav'n's command, Arose from out the azure main…'

The hands cheered, and when it came to the chorus, the men of *Triumph* joined in with vigour.

'Rule Britannia! Britannia, rule the waves! Britons never will be slaves!'

The crew went through the favourite repertoire of the lower deck, following all the verses of 'Rule Britannia' with 'Heart of Oak', 'God Save the King' and 'Britons Strike Home', but still the French fleet came on, only the vigorous defence put up by *Triumph* and *Mars* preventing Admiral Villaret's ships from overwhelming the whole of Cornwallis's squadron. Throughout the hours that followed, Gower kept one eye on maintaining *Triumph*'s position in the line, again making or shortening sail as necessary to make allowances for the sluggish *Bellerophon* and *Brunswick*, the other on fighting the ship. *Triumph*'s hull shook as her guns kept up their relentless barrage. But the enemy was scoring frequent hits too, French shot tearing through the rigging and shattering upper timbers. Miraculously there were as yet few casualties, despite the frequent hits on the hull and the large, deadly shards of timber splintering off it, but reports were coming up from below to the effect that the stern was increasingly shattered.

'The two gun crews in the wardroom are quite open to the elements, sir!' reported the breathless, sweating Lieutenant Lowe. 'They've no cover at all. Most of the planking's gone, Captain!'

Gower acknowledged the intelligence, but he knew there was nothing he could do about it. *Triumph* was thirty years old, hardly ancient – the old *Royal William* was well over a hundred – but she had been built at a time when shipwrights constructed hulls with weaker sterns and thinner scantlings than the modern practice preferred.

He glanced over to *Mars*, a new ship, in service for only a few months. Her stern seemed to be in a better state even though she was taking, if anything, an even more brutal pounding from the leading French ships than *Triumph*. The squadron's survival was well and truly in the balance.

'*Phaeton*'s signalling, sir,' said Lieutenant Chapman, his telescope trained northward. 'Strange sail, nor'-nor'-west.'

Gower took up his own telescope and trained it on the distant scout frigate, several miles away from the main body of Cornwallis's squadron.

'Damn me,' he said rhetorically to the nearest officers to him, 'Stopford ain't going to try that old game, is he?'

Robert Stopford, captain of the *Phaeton*, was an intelligent young officer whose abilities Gower rated highly. Somehow, though, he would never have rated Stopford an accomplished actor. But soon afterwards, as Chapman reported *Phaeton*'s signal for four sail, then that the frigate had let fly her topgallant sheets and fired two guns, Gower smiled to himself. Who needed a Kemble strutting the stage at Drury Lane when one had a Stopford? For now, though, the performance was going unappreciated by its intended audience. A colossal broadside from the most immediately adjacent Frenchman smashed into *Triumph*'s stern and quarter, a large, jagged splinter passing no more than inches from Gower's head. Off to leeward, *Mars* continued to take a hammering and was falling away from the line of battle. If *Mars* surrendered or became too shattered to fight, the full force of the French fleet would fall upon *Triumph*, and that contest could have only one outcome. Sir Erasmus Gower was not a man given to introspection or fatalism, but for one fleeting moment he wondered if this would be the day he died.

Gower had been at sea for forty years and knew from experience that time always ceased to have any meaning in battle. It was at once an eternity and the blinking of an eye, a ceaseless pageant of noise – the thunderous roar of the guns, the shouts of officers and men, the screams – and sights – of the wounded, the actions of the crew, the movements of the enemy, the blood and shattered bodies – all cloaked in drifting clouds of acrid smoke. There were a hundred and one emotions in the blinking of an eye, courage, foolishness, fear, exhilaration, joy, grief, excitement, alarm, relief, elation, despair, many others, all at once or in succession. A captain had a hundred and one things to weigh in every moment, and it was impossible to get any sense of the wider engagement. There was an instant when the flagship *Royal Sovereign* hove into view, her bow emerging from the smoke like some vast, ancient sea monster, Cornwallis bringing her into play by wearing round to support the increasingly shattered *Mars*, her rigging in tatters, and *Triumph*, in turn, altered course to second the admiral. The colossal roar of *Sovereign*'s battery awed every man who saw and heard it, even the jaded, cynical Gower, and the flagship's bold intervention caused four French ships to fall off, giving *Mars* the breathing space to manoeuvre once again back into the line of battle.

Even so, the situation of Cornwallis's squadron was still desperate. The French still had a huge numerical advantage, and were sure to overwhelm the British ships before they could fall into the safe haven of Bridport's main fleet, still far over the horizon to the north-west. But as afternoon turned to evening, a miracle occurred.

'Sir!' cried Henderson, the youngest but keenest of *Triumph*'s midshipmen. 'Look, sir! The French are starting to haul their wind, sir! They're breaking off the action!'

'Great God, sir,' said Lieutenant Atkins to Gower, 'the lad's right! They're shortening sail! That must be the meaning of the signal flying from their flagship. Villaret's giving up, Sir Erasmus!'

Gower made no reply. He could scarcely believe it. The French still held all the cards, the day should still be theirs, by morning Sir Erasmus Gower should be either a prisoner breakfasting on snails or a corpse feeding the fishes of the Atlantic, while his command would be rechristened *Le Triomphe* and would fly the hated republican Tricolour. Yet there was no mistake. The French were breaking off the action. They had total victory in their grasp, but they were abandoning the fight.

'The Frenchies must reckon the Old Lady's close, sir!' laughed Midshipman Henderson, uttering the derogatory but wildly popular nickname for Lord Bridport.

Atkins clipped the boy's ear as if he was an errant schoolboy.

'A deal more respect for the Admiral, if you please, Mister Henderson!'

Gower ignored the exchange. All of his attention was fixed on the extraordinary sight of the French falling away, the distance between the two wildly mismatched fleets increasing with every minute that passed. For all his irreverence, though, the young midshipman was surely correct. Gower could think of no other reason why the enemy would abandon such an advantage and what would surely have been a rare, inevitable and crushing victory over their eternal adversary. They had evidently convinced themselves that Lord Bridport and the entire

Channel Fleet were just over the horizon, or at least much nearer than they actually were, and that false deduction could only be due to the ingenuity of Captain Robert Stopford of *Phaeton*. His earlier signal, letting fly his topgallant sheets and firing two guns, was the time-hallowed signal for the sighting of a fleet. Some time later, although it was difficult to make out signals so far away amid the smoke and confusion of battle, Lieutenant Chapman reported *Phaeton*'s supplementary signal that the newly sighted fleet was friendly and consisted of ships of the line. It was one of the oldest tricks of the mariner's trade, known to all seamen the world over, but it seemed that astonishingly, blessedly, the French had fallen for it.

Sir Erasmus Gower did not count himself an especially religious man, but he offered up a silent prayer of thanks to God for the deliverance of *Triumph* and the rest of Cornwallis's squadron, for the quick thinking of Captain Robert Stopford, and for the gullibility of Admiral Villaret de Joyeuse. Then he turned to the mundane business of ordering Carpenter Martin and his crew to temporarily seal the gaping holes in the stern by stretching hammocks over them, after which HMS *Triumph* and the rest of Cornwallis's squadron would set their course for old England.

CHAPTER FOURTEEN

La Verité at sea, fifty-three and seven tenths degrees of latitude north, thirteen and three tenths of longitude west of the Paris Meridian.

It would be an easy prize.

A substantial and heavily laden brig, its course suggesting it was making for Glasgow, Galway or one of the other ports in the north-west of Ireland or west of Scotland. Most likely Glasgow, Philippe thought, given the prosperity of that port. The target knew what *La Verité* was and was making an effort to run for it, although her master and crew must have known it was a forlorn hope. Perhaps he hoped for a fortunate encounter with a British frigate or privateer out of Plymouth, Lough Swilly or the Clyde that would save him from the murderous horde of Frenchies in the oncoming corsair. Only such a miracle would save him, for the weather certainly would not. Both ships were upon a brisk, gusting strong, south-westerly wind, but *La Verité* was by far the faster and more manoeuvrable of the two. The captain of the brig would undoubtedly know this, so all he could do was play out a charade of resistance and pray for that elusive miracle.

Surprisingly, one supernumerary member of the ship's company of the privateer seemed unhappy with the pursuit Philippe had ordered.

'We shouldn't delay, Captain,' said the young man at his side with unexpected urgency. 'Even a few hours – it was never my father's intention that we should take prizes in these waters. Not until we reach the cruising grounds that were agreed.'

'A delay of a few hours will make no difference, Citizen Heinrich, to the prospects in the North Sea and the Baltic. None at all. Not even a few days, probably not even a few weeks. The war will not end in so short a time, believe me. And are you saying, Citizen, that your father would want us to pass up an easy opportunity to add a fat purse to his coffers?'

'It was not in the agreement,' said Augustin Heinrich with some petulance. 'It is not in your orders.'

'Nor was there any sort of prohibition against taking any prize that might present itself this side of the British Isles. Perhaps it's in those mysterious sealed orders from your father that are not to be opened until we reach the fifty-fifth degree of latitude. But we've not yet crossed the fifty-fourth, so until then, Citizen, I have full authority to employ the ship as I see fit.'

Heinrich shaped to protest but thought better of it. He strode forward, making his way to the fo'c'sle where he could watch the capture of the prize without resuming his disagreement with Philippe.

'Never known anyone turn down the chance to take such an easy prize as this, *mon Captaine*,' said Ugarte, looking puzzled. 'But then, there's plenty will say the Swiss are a very odd breed. Too many mountains, too little sea. Put a Switzer on the ocean and it's like putting a fish in a tavern.'

Philippe smiled. He would not go down the road of criticising his employer, but he could not really disagree with his lieutenant. Heinrich was a lubber through and through who was only now overcoming the incessant and violent seasickness that had afflicted him ever since they left Concarneau. He would never make a seaman, but as Ugarte would undoubtedly say, what Switzer ever had? Since the floggings of Drever and Marhallac'h, though, the *armateur*'s son had been withdrawn, speaking as little as possible to Philippe at meals. He had dissented from the sentence decreed by Philippe and Ugarte, but nevertheless witnessed the floggings being carried out. He winced as the first lash struck Drever's back, drawing blood at once, but although Bosun Medan laid on vigorously, the Scot's ten strokes were over quickly and he walked away from the hurdle to which he had been tied. No man stepped forward to assist him with his wounds. At the end of Marhallac'h's fifty, though, by which time the Breton's back was lacerated into an ugly patchwork of blood and welts, a score or more of his shipmates rushed forward to help him.

La Verité was closing rapidly on the merchantman's starboard quarter. Philippe summoned the gunner, Vuillermoz, who knuckled his forehead in naval fashion as he came before his captain.

'Master Gunner, prepare a warning shot into his rigging once we come within range.'

'*Commande*, Citizen Captain!' he cried in naval fashion.

Vuillermoz went forward and ordered the crew of the foremost larboard gun to man and load their weapon. The wadding and shot were rammed home. Vuillermoz adjusted the aim, but before he could fire, the chase fired a speculative round from the two guns on its quarter. Neither shot hit *La Verité* nor even came close, her balls throwing up water well short of the corsair's starboard bow. Even if the gunners aboard the chase found their range, Philippe and every man in his crew now knew they were very unlikely to hurt *La Verité*. Some merchantmen had well-trained and regularly drilled gun crews working immaculately maintained ordnance, but it was already abundantly clear that this was not one of those ships.

'Ha! Pop guns,' said Ugarte. 'Who's he going to scare with those? My old mother?'

'Ready a boarding party, Lieutenant Ugarte, in case this fellow keeps up this show of fight, no matter how feeble his ordnance. Twenty men should be more than enough, the usual arms.'

'*Commande!*' Ugarte replied.

A few minutes later, the potential boarders mustered on deck. Pistols and cutlasses were distributed, and the men massed on the fo'c'sle and along the ship's rail to intimidate the merchant crew. The two ships were very close now, the men aloft on *La Verité* taking in sail to prepare for close action. Up for'ard, Vuillermoz judged his moment, waited for the signal from Philippe, then gave the order to fire. The corsair's twelve-pounder made a mightier noise than the small guns on the chase, and the shot tore through the mizzen sail and several of the shrouds.

The men on *La Verité* watched as what appeared to be a shouting match developed on the quarterdeck of the merchantman. Several men were yelling at a lone figure who was presumably her captain. Philippe had witnessed such a scene at first hand and knew exactly what he was witnessing across the water. Representatives of the crew, the oldest hands, probably a few of the mates too, would be berating their captain and urging him to surrender, their only concern being the preservation of their own lives. The captain would be making a show of resistance so that if and when word of the precise circumstances of his ship's capture got back to the owners, he could put his hand on his heart or upon a Bible and swear that he had done everything in his power to resist, but had been forced to give in to the overwhelming force of the enemy pursuing him and the craven cowardice of his worthless crew. Such scenes had probably been played out on the world's oceans for two thousand years or more.

Two thousand years with the usual outcome. To the obvious disappointment of the men assigned to the boarding party, the merchantman's English colours came down, the ship took in all sail and hove to, and Philippe sent *Verité*'s boat under Vuillermoz to take possession. Then he turned to Ugarte.

'Choose a prize crew, Lieutenant. Six men should be sufficient, at least two capable of taking the helm. Orders to proceed with all expedition to Concarneau, Douarnenez or Morlaix as wind and tide permit, upon arrival to present themselves and the ship to the authorities there. I will write a letter to be forwarded to Citizen Heinrich once the prize makes port.'

'*Commande!*'

Ugarte strode down into the waist of the corsair to select the prize crew, and Philippe turned his attention back to the prize. It was a promising start to their voyage, especially if the ship's cargo proved to be lucrative...

There were raised voices further for'ard, and the antagonists were Juan Ugarte and Augustin Heinrich.

Philippe made his way from the quarterdeck and found the young Swiss red-faced and weeping angry tears as he harangued Ugarte.

'You cannot order this!' Heinrich bawled. 'He cannot go – ah, Captain, you must put a stop to this!'

'A stop to what, Citizen Heinrich?'

'I named six men to the prize crew,' said Ugarte, 'and this – this *gentleman* objects to the choice of one of them.'

'Which?' demanded Philippe.

'Him,' said Ugarte, pointing at the nearby figure of the Scot, Drever.

Philippe had said nothing to his lieutenant, but it did not surprise him that Ugarte would seek to take the first opportunity of removing the Scot from the crew of the corsair. Since the floggings, Drever had been shunned even more overtly by the men. The popular Marhallac'h was still unfit for duty and had to lie face down in his hammock. Ugarte reckoned that only the prospect of the riches offered by the Heinrichs prevented the men of *La Verité* from simply sending Marcus Drever over the side in the middle of the night, the fate that had befallen countless Jonahs at sea since time immemorial.

Philippe turned to Augustin Heinrich.

'Your reasons, Citizen Heinrich?'

Philippe recalled the enlisting of the crew at Concarneau, where Heinrich had sought to favour Marcus Drever with immediate promotion, and the court where they had judged Drever and Marhallac'h, with Heinrich arguing for entire leniency for the Scot. Too many years at sea, at war, and seeing every side of man's nature made Philippe think at once of sodomy, but how could the cultivated and wealthy merchant's son possibly know a mere mariner from a remote part of the enemy's territory, let alone make him his catamite? And what if there was at least some grain of truth in Marhallac'h's wild accusations of sorcery and child murder?

Heinrich looked baffled by the question.

'I need give no reason, Captain. I am the son of this ship's owner and his representative on board. I know I would have my father's entire support in saying this.'

The young man's pomposity irritated Philippe, but there was something more to the young man's stubbornness, something that Philippe Kermorvant could not quite identify. Still, the discipline of the ship and the immutable hierarchy of the sea had to be maintained.

'I only have your word for that, Citizen, and when this ship is at sea I and I alone make all decisions about her day-to-day activities. Nominating and dispatching a prize crew undoubtedly falls within my responsibilities, not yours.'

Heinrich was slowly returning to a more even temper, his eyes seemingly fixed on some invisible point on the deck and entirely unaware of the incredulous stares of the men within earshot. Then he looked up and fixed a fierce expression on Philippe.

'You have more than my word on the subject, Captain Kermorvant,' he said. 'You have the intentions and orders of my father, stated unequivocally and in writing. All will be made clear when we reach the fifty-fifth degree of latitude and you open your sealed orders. Meanwhile, take my word for it. The man Drever remains with this ship and is not to be sent in any prize crew.'

Philippe's immediate instinct was to argue the case, but he managed to keep silent. It would be disastrous for him to argue with Augustin Heinrich within the view and earshot of many of the crew. Corsair men, unlike naval crews, were not driven by loyalty to a country and a flag, no matter how reluctantly many of those in the Marine Nationale or any other navy on earth trod the decks of their ships. Corsair men served for money, served in the belief that at the end of the voyage, the success of their cruise and the resources of the owner or owners of their ship would ensure that they were rewarded handsomely and in timely fashion. Even in the American war, when many of the men with whom Philippe had served were driven principally by love of their homeland and hatred of the English, there had also been a powerful mercenary instinct at play. If the crew of *La Verité* suspected there was disunity between their captain and their owner, as represented by the owner's son, then the entire discipline of the ship's company was likely to collapse.

Besides, there were many other men who could fill a place in a prize crew equally well.

'Very well,' said Philippe. 'Matelot Drever remains with the ship. Lieutenant Ugarte, choose another for the prize crew.'

'Commande!'

CHAPTER FIFTEEN

Philippe put down his sextant. He glanced across to Ugarte, who was still taking his own noonday fix of their position. If both men agreed, then the moment would have come.

At last the Basque lowered his instrument and growled, 'By observation, fifty-five degrees north.'

'Concur,' said Philippe, 'and thus to be recorded in the ship's journal.'

The horizon was clear. *La Verité* was sailing large on a fair breeze, out of sight of land to the west of County Donegal and the northernmost extent of Ireland. Since the capture of their prize, the *Earl of Galloway* of Glasgow, there had been no further alarms beyond sightings of a few distant fishing craft that Philippe deemed not worthy of pursuit.

'Well, *mon Capitaine*,' said Ugarte, 'this is the moment, then. Finally, we learn what's in these precious secret orders.'

Philippe nodded. The question of what Antoine Heinrich might or might not have ordered from his comfortable residence in Rennes had intrigued and at times worried Philippe throughout their voyage, especially so since the strange incidents with the Scot, Drever. Perhaps *La Verité* would be ordered to rendezvous secretly with some other ship, or to intercept a certain vessel sailing from a certain port on a certain day, the purpose of such orders never to be known. Perhaps they were ordered to a hostile shore to embark a spy – or even to disembark one, although he could hardly credit Heinrich *fils* as a credible agent of any kind. The nervous, self-important, easily irritated Switzer would be an even less likely assassin. But then, did the secret orders somehow pertain to the man Drever, whose cause Augustin Heinrich had pleaded a little too passionately? Might Drever be, say, the leader-in-exile of a Scottish rebellion aimed at severing the union with England and setting up a republic on French lines? No, Philippe decided, this was all far too fanciful. Despite all the wild stories about him that Marhallac'h had aired, Marcus Drever was nothing but a common seaman – sly, wholly illiterate, given to drink and no leader of men. He could see no circumstances in which he would even consider him for a position as a master's mate, as Augustin Heinrich had originally proposed.

In any event, it was time to have the questions answered.

Philippe made a final scan of the horizon, contented himself that there were no sails in sight and no clouds threatening a storm, then went below. He found Augustin Heinrich in the commodious cabin at the stern that they still shared, and to his surprise the young man was on his feet. He had spent the entire morning lying once again upon his sea-bed where he had sometimes spent entire days of their voyage, his landlubber's constitution seemingly unable to adjust to even the ordinary movement of the ship. Now, though, Heinrich was standing. He already had the canvas-bound package in his hand and held it out for Philippe to take.

'Do not judge my father too harshly,' Heinrich said.

The enigmatic remark disconcerted Philippe, but he took the package, untied the string that held the canvas in place, then drew out the letter within and broke Antoine Heinrich's seal. He sat down on one of the two chairs afforded by the cabin and began to read.

> Captain Kermorvant. Whichever you please.
> I do not know if you will be able to forgive me for the deception my son and I have exercised upon you.
> No, deception is too strong a word. Not entirely a deception, then. The principal part of the mission that we agreed at Rennes and Concarneau remains unchanged. Your public orders setting out your targets in the North Sea and Baltic trades of France's enemies remain entirely valid. I look forward in due course to all of us, yourself included, prospering mightily from the prizes I confidently expect you to garner.
> All this remains as we discussed and has not varied a single jot. However, there is one additional element to the mission that I did not reveal before you sailed. I did not do so because I feared that if you knew of it then you would refuse to undertake the voyage, and I have made the stipulation about not opening these orders until you reached the fifty-fifth degree northward of latitude in the belief that you would then be too committed to the expedition. Perhaps I am wrong in this. After all, I am Swiss and not greatly knowledgeable in the seaman's mysteries. Then

again, you may be so outraged but what you may wish to regard as my deceit, and by the additional task I propose you undertake on my behalf that you will wish to have nothing more to do with me, my son or your mission as, in good faith, you formerly believed it to be. Perhaps after reading these words of mine you will give order for our ship to turn back and return to France. Perhaps you will throw my son overboard for his part in this deceit, although I must warn you, Monsieur le Vicomte, that if you do such a thing I will destroy everything and everyone you hold dear and pursue you to the very ends of the earth. Believe me in this, for I am not a forgiving man.

But I do not believe you will.

Why do I have such confidence that you will not reject what I have to tell you? I know you are a man who has known and lost a great love. I have contacts and correspondents in every country of Europe, so I know of the wife and son you had in Russia. I know how they were butchered by your brother-in-law, and I know how you duelled with that blood-soaked murderer in Corsica and killed him. So I trust that you understand passion and are a man who knows how it feels to lose the love of your heart.

The truth, then. I have a wife, the stepmother to my son. She is many years younger than me but she has been the joy and consolation of my years in France, through all the tumults of the revolution and the shadow of the guillotine, which is no respecter of neutrality or national borders. In the year Ninety-Three, though, she was taken from me most cruelly. We were in Valenciennes, where I had business, and found ourselves trapped in that town when it was placed under siege by the English and the Austrians. You will know, of course, that the town ultimately surrendered. All the conventions of warfare were observed to the letter. Civilians were unmolested and the French troops were allowed to march out with full honours. But my wife was abducted from me, sir, snatched away by the evil designs of a deranged lecher wearing a red uniform. This man carried her away, back to the place whence he came, and will certainly have inflicted the most unspeakable horrors upon her during these last two years.

The place where she is held prisoner by this heartless brute, this monster of iniquity, is on one of the islands that are called Orkney. My son will show you the exact place upon a map. So I appeal to you, Captain, Monsieur le Vicomte, as a man who has known the anguish of forced parting from the one he loves. In the name of God, or Reason, or your wife and son, as you prefer, I beg you to restore my dear wife to her loving husband. This, sir, is why I commanded our ship to make its way to the Baltic by the northern route around the north of Scotland, even though you argued for the faster passage through La Manche. You will find my wife by means of my son and the man Drever, present in your crew, who is of those islands and will act as your pilot and guide. His services have been bought at a high price, but his assistance will, I trust, achieve my purpose. With their aid I wish you to find my wife, free her from her unimaginable captivity, and convey her and my son to The Helder in what we must call the Batavian Republic. My son will escort her home from that place and you will be wholly free to revert to your original orders and pursue your original mission. If The Helder proves unreachable for whatever reason, then you have my authority to disembark them at any port in Norway that may suit the purpose.

The one remaining piece of information you require is the name of my enemy, now, I trust, your adversary too. His name alone hints at something pagan. At something evil. The name of this depraved fiend is Major Thorfinn Rendall.

Craving your forgiveness, your sympathy and your agreement to this purpose,

I remain, Monsieur le Vicomte, your admiring and respectful friend,

Antoine Heinrich

'There is no syndicate,' said Augustin Heinrich.

He and Philippe Kermorvant were sitting in the captain's cabin of *La Verité* shortly after Philippe had read the astonishing additional orders from Heinrich's father. Outside the stern windows, the waves rose and fell gently enough for Heinrich *fils* to experience little discomfort. The wake of the corsair cleaved its path gently through a calm ocean.

'All those worthy citizens of the Republic and all those distinguished names my father said were the joint owners – they were all chimeras, Captain, mere fictions devised to impress you. I have a share, you have a share, but all the other shares are owned by him. This ship was built at his expense alone. Almost all the profits would have been his, too, but for once my father is not driven by profit. This ship exists, and you and the crew were engaged to sail it, for only one reason, and that is to bring my stepmother back to him.'

Philippe's anger did not manifest itself in a raging display of temper. He was furious with Antoine Heinrich and his son, but the sheer scale of the deception practised on him was so breathtaking that it carried him some way beyond mere rage.

'I do not like being duped, Citizen Heinrich. I resent being lied to.'

'No. Of course not. What man does? And my father has apologised for our deception. I add my own apologies, for what they are worth. But I beg you, sir, I beg you with all my heart, agree to this one modest request of ours. My father did not lie when he told you he had considerable influence with members of the Committee of Public Safety and the National Convention. Do this one thing, this one little thing, and it can be your way back into the Marine Nationale. Even more than that, we will pay you and every man in the crew double what was agreed at Rennes, along with even larger shares of the proceeds from the prizes you take during the rest of the voyage.'

Philippe was controlling his fury only with great difficulty. So much had suddenly become clear – the curious insistence on a longer route to reach their intended cruising area, Augustin Heinrich's inexplicable favour for the renegade Marcus Drever, Heinrich *père*'s unwillingness to stint on any element of the corsair's voyage. But it was still outrageous, and to Philippe's mind it all displayed an utter contempt for the sensibilities of the captain the Heinrichs had gone to such lengths to recruit. He could blame none but himself. At Rennes, he should have followed the instinct, the still small voice, that told him not to trust Antoine Heinrich. He had been seduced by the prospect of riches that Heinrich held out, and then, at Concarneau when he could still have withdrawn with his honour intact, he had been blinded by anger at Leonore's actions in bringing a Chouan rebel into his home. All such regrets were too late now.

'You and your father might have bribed the man Drever to betray his country, Citizen,' said Philippe indignantly, 'but I am cut from quite a different cloth. Besides, this mission to rescue your stepmother demands that I take this ship into enemy waters, land on enemy soil, snatch a prisoner from the custody of a British Army officer, then get away unscathed. It is not a modest request at all, Citizen Heinrich.'

'But you must do it, sir! *You must!*'

'This isn't a man-of-war, Citizen, it's a corsair. The captain can't merely give an order and expect it to be obeyed without question or demur. The crew has to be persuaded, cajoled—'

'Bribed?'

'Convinced. If the carrying away of your stepmother miscarries in any way, men could be killed. The ship could easily be captured and every man aboard left to rot in an English prison for the rest of the war. *Liberté, égalité, fraternité*, Citizen Heinrich – if you're going to ask men to risk their lives to rescue your stepmother, you've got to let them vote on it.'

Augustin Heinrich, a man brought up to believe that anything and anybody could be bought and commanded, seemed to think hard about this, but at last he nodded. Philippe, sick of the man's presence and of having been taken for a fool by the Heinrichs, made his way back to the quarterdeck, where Ugarte barely concealed his impatience as his captain inspected the compass, the set of the sails and the horizon.

'Well, sir?' he said at last, unable to contain his curiosity about the contents of the secret orders any longer.

'Not now, Lieutenant. Not now.'

'*Oui, mon Captaine!*'

—

The vote took place the next day. The ship was under an easy sail in a gentle breeze, well to the west and out of sight of the islands called the Hebrides. The men were crammed into the waist and fo'c'sle. Philippe did not speak. That left the field clear for Augustin Heinrich to speak with a fervour and conviction concealed until that moment. He appealed to all those who had known love. He asked them rhetorically how they would feel if those loves were torn from their arms. He likened Major Thorfinn Rendall to a modern-day Caligula, and although hardly any of his listeners knew who Caligula was, Heinrich's vivid descriptions delivered a clear enough message. The fellow had previously unknown skills as an orator, Ugarte whispered, and might have made an excellent candidate for the National Convention if only he were French. But Philippe could see from the men's eyes, from their impatient shuffling and murmuring, that they remained unconvinced. Heinrich tried another tack, trying to persuade them that the isles of Orkney were undefended, inhabited only by a few peasants who were bound to fly before French valour and republican zeal. There would be no risk from British forces, none at all. Still the men mumbled and exchanged wary glances with each other. Marcus Drever, descended from those same 'peasants', stood a little apart, his face creased with displeasure. Finally, though, Heinrich came to his peroration, and here the mood changed. The promise of double pay and more prize money animated the men, and to his shame, Philippe knew he shared their sentiments. The captain's share of the riches promised by the Heinrichs would be not inconsiderable, and the chateau and estate of Brechelean were in need of substantial restoration after the years of neglect under his half-brother, Alexandre, and the subsequent ravages caused by the revolution and civil war in Brittany. For all his doubts about the Heinrichs, their motives and their methods, he knew that in the final reckoning he was driven by avarice just as much as the lowest *matelot* in the crew.

Philippe Kermorvant had never felt less proud of himself.

When it came to the vote the result was overwhelming. A few men abstained, to the jeers and cat-calling of their shipmates, but the overwhelming majority voted to find and rescue the missing Madame Heinrich.

'Congratulations, Citizen, your oratory has won the day,' said Philippe, with little grace, as Heinrich *fils* came aft.

The young man was grinning and flushed with excitement.

'Destiny, Monsieur le Vicomte. We will regain that which was taken from us. Lay your course for the isles of Orkney, Captain!'

CHAPTER SIXTEEN

From the papers of Leonore Kermorvant

'I am honoured to make your acquaintance, Citizeness Kermorvant,' says Antoine Heinrich, 'or perhaps you prefer to be known as Madame la Vicomtesse?'

He stares at me inquisitively and for rather too long. I give him what I trust is my best expression of surprise and condescension.

'I regret that you are mistaken, Citizen. I am not the wife of the Vicomte de Saint-Victor.'

His remarkably ugly face registers utter confusion. Roman, standing just inside the door to act as my chaperone and guard, smirks.

'Forgive me, madame, but I thought – that is to say, I assume – then you are the vicomte's sister?'

'I am not, and he has no sister. We share the same surname because his brother was my husband.'

He frowns, seemingly struggling to digest this information. I am being harsh on him, there in his gaudily furnished apartment in Rennes overlooking the vast remnants of the cathedral, but he is not the first to assume that because Philippe and I share the same name and live under the same roof, we must surely be husband and wife. I do not feel inclined to make light of the matter, as I invariably do with all the others who make the same mistake. But by sending an invitation in his reply to my letter to him, this Antoine Heinrich has insisted that I come to Rennes in person, *a return journey of an entire day demanding an intolerably early start, simply to give me an address that he could easily have provided in one line of a letter.*

I do not like this Citizen Heinrich and wonder why Philippe has any truck with the man. Unwigged and quite bald, with a broad, flat nose and large ears that stick out most laughably, he is one of the ugliest men I have ever seen. His head is bald and glistening, it being a warm day. His face resembles that of one of the least elegant dogs kennelled at the Chateau de Brechelean, the ratter Adonis, the choice of name being one of my late husband's best jests in the final years of his life. Despite an evidently lavish use of perfume, the Swiss merchant stinks of sweat and something else that I do not wish to consider.

'His brother was your husband, Citizeness? The gentleman in question is deceased?'

It is none of his business, but Alexandre's death is a matter of public record so there is little point in denying it.

'My husband went to the guillotine two years ago, Citizen.'

'Ah. The time of the Terror, then. You have my sympathies, madame. Yet you have continued to live in your brother-in-law's residence?'

'With respect, Citizen, your inquisitiveness about the condition of affairs between myself and Philippe – that is, the vicomte – may be regarded as bordering on impertinence, sir.'

'Forgive me, madame,' he says smoothly, 'I intended no such affront. I am Swiss, and we are a questioning people. A blunt people. Our manners may seem a little uncouth in comparison with the much greater refinement of the French. I am not of bourgeois birth and have only attained my current position by dint of ceaseless struggle and hard work. I regret I have had little time or indeed inclination to learn the finer points of etiquette.'

'I accept your apology, sir, but I ask you once again to supply me with the information I seek, the only reason for my being

here. Once you have done so I will take my leave and trouble you no longer.'

'So soon, Citizeness? But my cook has been preparing a light repast for us.'

'No repast will be necessary, Citizen Heinrich. We need to set out as soon as possible to ensure we return to the chateau before nightfall.'

I nod to Roman, who is impatient to be on the road. Quite apart from the very real risks posed by Chouans and robbers on Breton roads at night, I suspect he has an assignation tonight with one of the maids.

'As you wish, madame. The likeliest port of call for the ship is The Helder, where I have an agent. But I would advise you against using the regular posts. There is a constant risk of ambush and interception here in the west, then the notorious incompetence of the postmasters along the entire route. Those in the Batavian Republic are corrupt to a man. No, Madame Kermorvant, letters to the vicomte are best directed to me at this address, and I will ensure they are forwarded in the packets containing my own correspondence. I employ a network of private couriers who are entirely dependable.'

The idea of entrusting my letters to this man appals me. My expression and my hesitancy before I reply must surely betray my feelings.

'My thanks, Citizen Heinrich,' I finally manage to say, 'but that will not be necessary. Merely supply me with the name of your agent at The Helder and I will trust to the posts.'

'But I insist on it, dear lady.' I shudder. Any man who calls me 'dear lady' deserves a knife in the ribs. 'I have a packet ready to be sent to The Helder within the hour. You have a letter to the vicomte with you? It will be on its way much sooner if you allow me to send it with mine.'

I am torn. The letter sits within my purse, for I had already intended to post it from Rennes, a city of that size being certain to be better served by the mails than an obscure chateau in the midst of a war-torn region contested between the Chouans and the Blues. But the letter is so intimate and contains such frank expressions and declarations that the prospect of Heinrich opening and reading it makes me shiver. Nonetheless, it is surely believable that a merchant of his rank, with all his wealth and his contacts in many countries, would have means of getting mail to its destinations more rapidly and securely than any available to the common public. Besides, I reassure myself, men of business like Citizen Heinrich depend utterly on confidentiality in their affairs. I must distinguish the appearance, manners and, yes, the smell of the man before me from the way he makes his living, and that gives me cause to think he will treat my letter as sacrosanct. And my urgent desire to have the letter find Philippe as soon as possible makes me dismiss any lingering doubts.

I reach down to my purse and take out the letter. Antoine Heinrich smiles, a truly ghastly spectacle of uneven brown teeth.

'Belocien, take Madame Kermorvant's letter and add it to the packet bound for Holland.'

The man called Belocien, who had been introduced as a clerk and factotum but who has more of the taciturn look of a battle-weary soldier, comes forward and takes the envelope from me with a stiff bow of his head.

'My thanks, Citizen Heinrich,' I say. 'But I do not understand why you could not simply write to me to tell me to forward mail to Captain Kermorvant through you without insisting that I must come here to Rennes.'

Heinrich smiled.

'Forgive me for inconveniencing you in any way, my dear Madame Kermorvant, but it was merely the curiosity of an old and, as you have rightly said, an impertinent man. But the

vicomte talked of you often and extolled your many virtues, so I was keen to meet the woman he clearly esteems so highly.'

This is a blatant lie. I cannot imagine that Philippe has mentioned me at all, certainly not since our falling out over Cozanet, for if he had, Antoine Heinrich would surely not have assumed that I must be Philippe's wife. No, the only possible source of that error must be my own hand, signing a letter to this merchant of Rennes as Leonore Kermorvant. But even allowing for a false deduction being drawn from that simple signature, why would Antoine Henrich be so determined to invite me here to meet me in person?

I am increasingly uneasy. There is something about this man I do not trust, despite having just entrusted him with perhaps the most important letter I have ever written. It is too late to retrieve it, but I sense I might just have made a terrible error in handing it to Antoine Heinrich's unlikely clerk. I recall a homily given by our village priest just before the revolution, when he opined that an ugly body signified an ugly soul. Alexandre, far gone in drink and bearing the awful scars of the goring that had rendered him impotent, stood up, strode to the pulpit, pulled the priest from it and pummelled him, all the while screaming drunkenly that no one, not even a man of God, should denounce another living being merely for their appearance. It was one of the rare occasions in those last years when I inwardly cheered my husband, and an incident so memorable that it has remained fixed in my memory. But it occurs to me that if there is any proof at all of the priest's contention that an ugly body signifies an ugly soul, then Antoine Heinrich provides that proof.

I am thinking of ways to reclaim my letter and extricate myself from the room without being intolerably rude when I hear the beating of a drum and the sound of a marching band coming ever closer. Heinrich stands, goes to the windows, summons his attendant to open them, then beckons me to join him. I do so *reluctantly, but Roman, perhaps sensing my discomfort, comes across and stands a few paces behind me.*

From the window I have a clear view down into the square before the west front of the cathedral. A crowd has formed on either side of the road, and they are cheering the band as it passes. Behind it comes an infantry regiment, its ranks cheered to the skies by the onlookers, some of whom wave hats bearing red, white and blue cockades or, in a few cases, the red berets of the sans-culottes. Shouts and chants begin – vive la France! vive la République! *After the first regiment and before the second, which is just entering the square, ride several senior officers, one of whom is a little ahead of the others, mounted on a large and impressive black stallion. This officer wears a general's uniform but seems remarkably young for such a rank, being surely no older than his mid-twenties. His dark hair is thick, bushy and wild, making him look more like the sort of artist who scratches out a living from a pitiful garret. The cheers are especially loud for this man.*

'General Hoche,' says Antoine Heinrich. 'Shifting his headquarters from here to Vannes, it seems.'

My own curiosity gets the better of me.

'Why so?'

'Nearer the coast, Citizeness. Better placed to repel the invasion when it comes.'

'What invasion?'

Heinrich preens himself. He is a truly repulsive man.

'I have it on the most excellent authority,' he says pompously, 'that the royalist emigré army has sailed from England under the escort of Admiral Bridport, intending to land somewhere on the coast of the Morbihan. Hoche is the man ordered to defend against it. He is little older than my son, madame, and was not even a lieutenant three years ago. Yet now he is the man entrusted with saving the Republic.'

For one brief moment I forget my revulsion at Antoine Heinrich's lies and his unwelcome presence far too close to my left shoulder. Instead I gaze down at the young General Hoche, so stately upon his horse, and realise he is the man ordered to slaughter dear Georges Cozanet, his fellow Chouans, and the army of exiles coming to their aid. I am as loyal to the Republic as any woman in France, but somewhere deep within me, a quiet voice whispers its hope that this General Hoche fails in his mission.

Hoche passes out of sight, the cheers of the spectators echoing after him, and I realise the timely appearance of the general and his regiments has given me the perfect opportunity to take my leave of Citizen Heinrich. I try to do so without looking him in the eye, for therein, I am now convinced, lurks a very ugly soul indeed.

CHAPTER SEVENTEEN

'Your first sea battle, my lord!' cried Hugh Seymour loudly and heartily. 'I wish you joy of it!'

Joy was not the principal emotion Ned Wilden was feeling as he stood on the quarterdeck of *Sans Pareil* surrounded by Seymour, several of his seven lieutenants, midshipmen, warrant officers and others. One of the scouting frigates had sighted the French fleet early on the previous morning, the enemy ships coming away from Belle-Île, some forty miles distant, with their course seemingly set for Brest. Bridport had signalled for *Sans Pareil* and five other ships known for their particularly good sailing qualities to move ahead of the flagship and lead the pursuit of the enemy fleet, then some twelve miles away. Seymour was all business, giving his orders briskly and without any of the tedious prolixity that Ned Wilden had often witnessed at the Admiralty table or in the clubrooms of Pall Mall. The officers and men of *Sans Pareil*, including the boy warrior Jack Kenton, plainly worshipped this Hugh Seymour, a version of the man that Wilden had never encountered before. But as the prospect of battle grew ever more imminent, so the bloodline of the knightly and warlike Saint Maurs of Wolf Hall shone through ever more clearly in their descendant.

All the while as *Sans Pareil* and her consorts closed the French fleet, Wilden's constant attendant, the impossibly young Midshipman Kenton, was jabbering delightedly but incomprehensibly about the likes of luffing up, fore topgallants and other such nautical gibberish. Wilden needed to divert him, or at least to get him speaking words and sentences that bore some resemblance to the King's English.

'Will it be the first battle for you too, Mister Kenton?'

'Oh no, my lord! I was on *Barfleur* last year at the Glorious First. Captain Collingwood commended me most generously to Lord Howe, most generously indeed, and Black Dick – sorry, sir, Lord Howe that is – he was most kindly to me. Before that I was on *Crescent* with Captain Saumarez when we beat the *Réunion*, afterwards on *Artois* with Captain Nagle when we took the *Révolutionnaire*. The lads in the gunroom call me Lucky Jack Kenton, I've seen that much action. More than most post-captains, Lord Hugh reckons, and there's only been two years of war.'

'Then I pray that your luck holds, Mister Kenton, and that some of it rubs off on me.'

The boy grinned.

'Don't fret, my lord. We'll look after you, Lord Hugh and I.'

All through the day of the twenty-second of June the British ships pursued the enemy, but the winds were light and sometimes entirely lacking, making it a day of frustration for every man in the fleet. Now, though, on the morning of the twenty-third the sun was coming up over the far distant French mainland, and Wilden, a great lover of his bed, realised to his surprise that he had gone the entire night without sleep.

For there, *there*, was the enemy. There was the French, the loathsome Tricolour of their murderous republic in plain sight. Some five miles away, the distance between the two fleets having more than halved during the night despite the negligible breezes that both Seymour and Kenton bemoaned. Wilden felt an unfamiliar emotion, perhaps one-third anticipation, one-third raw hatred, one-third even rawer fear. Since the war began, the French had always been remote, a distant foe as invisible and inhuman as Satan or the ghost in *The Castle of Otranto*. There had been Frenchmen galore in London, royalist exiles torn from their homes and native country, and Wilden had come to know many of them well, especially during the recent preparations for the Quiberon expedition. But the French republicans, the fanatics, the Jacobins, the so-called *sans-culottes*, were a different matter. It had been relatively easy to imagine stratagems to defeat these faceless foes, the blood-crazed atheists who had guillotined their king and queen, but Wilden had never really imagined what it would be like to look a French republican in the eye or even just to see their flag flying from the hulls of their men-of-war.

Yet now, there they were.

The drummers beat to quarters and the men of *Sans Pareil* took up their positions at their battle stations. Many of them were smiling, their faces bright with anticipation of the action to come.

'Trust the Frenchies to run, my lord!' exclaimed the grinning Kenton with a blend of disdain and childish enthusiasm. 'Cravens, every man of 'em!'

'Cravens with a purpose, Mister Kenton,' said Lord Hugh Seymour, lowering his telescope. 'Villaret's trying to draw us onto the lee shore, force us to turn away and give him a clear run into Lorient. Many a fine hull's perished on Brittany's cliffs. But that won't concern Lord Bridport, mark my words!'

As *Sans Pareil* and her consorts slowly drew ever closer to the retreating French fleet, it became evident that one of the enemy ships was falling well behind the others.

'That's the old *Alexander*, my lord,' said Kenton. 'She was one of ours until the Frenchies took her last year. Always a shocking sailor, the old *Alex*, so she can't have been any better for the Frogs. That's *Orion* and *Irresistible* making to leeward to engage her.'

Wilden looked at his young mentor in astonishment.

'You can tell them apart? You can tell one ship from another at this distance?'

'Aye, of course! Begging your pardon, my lord.'

Kenton's expression conveyed a mixture of pity and contempt in equal measures. The midshipman's unspoken reply, *you mean you can't?*, hung in the air. The notion that a man entrusted with the office of a lord of the Admiralty could not tell individual ships apart was obviously anathema to the tiny midshipman, and Wilden felt a pang of shame. This mere child, this stripling who had been a babe in arms only a very few years before, knew far more of seamanship and warfare than the fifth Baron Wilden ever would. He was already a veteran of three engagements and was surely on course for a glorious career to rival and perhaps exceed Seymour's. Men five times his senior knuckled their foreheads to salute Jack Kenton whenever he passed them by or gave them a command. In return, Kenton knew all of their names and had a word for each and every man, words delivered with that elusive combination of good humour, unquestionable command and detached dignity that Wilden had come to recognise in Hugh Seymour and most of the lieutenants of

Sans Pareil. Ned Pardew had been the fifth Baron Wilden since the day of his birth, but he was never as at ease with his social inferiors as Jack Kenton was until he was perhaps twice the age the boy was now. In truth, Wilden suspected that the young midshipman might very well already possess more assurance, innate air of command and respect from his inferiors than his noble and vastly senior charge.

Yet Wilden was about to step into Kenton's world, Seymour's world, Bridport's world. The world of Mars, the world of battle. A world for which he was manifestly unsuited. Seymour had suggested that Wilden might wish to spend the duration of the coming engagement down on the orlop deck with the surgeon, but he had indignantly rejected the suggestion. Part of him wanted nothing more than to be in the lowest, safest part of the ship, for Ned Wilden was not a man in whose breast the flame of martial ardour had ever burned brightly. But a peer of England, and a lord of the Admiralty to boot, had to set an example of courage to the lower orders. Besides, he would not allow Hugh Seymour the satisfaction of seeing him scuttle below decks at the first sniff of action, giving Seymour an anecdote at Wilden's expense that would delight many a bibulous gathering in the clubs of Mayfair. Besides, the prospect of spending several hours in the makeshift surgery on the orlop appalled a man who had always been revolted by the sight of blood. So Ned Wilden had smiled condescendingly and told Seymour that he was proud to stand, and if necessary die, beside the gallant tars of Old England. But he knew all too well that this bravado would mean one thing.

He was about to experience his first battle.

The mighty *Queen Charlotte* of one hundred guns was leading the British line, closely seconded by *Orion*, Seventy-Four. *Sans Pareil* and the other fast ships were close behind, Bridport's flagship and the rest of the fleet some distance astern. The British fleet, like the French retreating ahead of them, had all sail set to try and catch the light winds, incessantly making adjustments to respond to each slight change in the negligible breeze, but even so the movements of the ships of both fleets were painfully slow. The French were trying to run for the Île de Groix, an island of only a few square miles with cliffs fringing its northern half, now little more than a mile or two away from the French vanguard. Kenton kept up a running commentary, but even the garrulous child was silent for long periods when nothing at all happened. At last, though, the ship the French called the *Alexandre* came within range of Bridport's van. She put up a show of resistance from her stern guns, but the frigate that had been sent to tow her to safety swiftly abandoned the attempt when the leading British ships opened fire. Wilden watched, astonished, as *Queen Charlotte*'s broadsides, then those of *Orion*, finally poured into the stricken enemy ship, the cacophony of the guns giving Ned Wilden his baptism in a fight at sea.

Sans Pareil was coming up as rapidly as the feeble breezes allowed, but Seymour showed little inclination to engage the shattered *Alexandre* in his turn.

'Isn't she an easy prize, Admiral?' asked Wilden, assuming the deference to which he knew Seymour was entitled on his own quarterdeck.

'Aye, easy enough, but so easy she'll keep. Our duty is to second *Queen Charlotte*, and that means we have two targets, one after the other. See that big three-decker with the Tricolour at her main, my lord? That's their flagship, *Le Peuple*, one hundred and twenty gubs. That's Villaret himself. So he's our man, and he's what Douglas in *Queen Charlotte* will have in his sights. But first, my lord, we need to grapple this fellow ahead, the one the brave old *Charlotte*'s now engaging. And that means Mister Kenton, here, needs to return to his station.'

Kenton saluted his admiral, nodded and smiled to Wilden, and said, 'I wish you all good fortune, my lord, and will look forward to toasting our triumph with you.'

The boy's cheeriness infected even the unemotional Wilden, who grinned in return.

'I am obliged to you, Mister Kenton, and will most certainly hold you to that promise.'

Then Lucky Jack Kenton saluted Ned Wilden and went forward.

It was difficult to hear Seymour's and Kenton's words, or even his own, for the guns of *Queen Charlotte* and her French opponent – the name at the stern, now visible, revealed her to be *Le Formidable* – were now thundering. Wilden was accustomed to the storms that frequently rolled over into Shropshire from the Welsh hills, but he had never seen or heard anything to resemble the apocalyptic spectacle unfolding before him. The scene assailed all of his senses, for now, although the south-easterly wind carried away most of the fog of battle, he could smell the bitter tang of gunpowder. Surely battle at sea could not get more hellish?

But despite taking heavy damage in its masts and sails from the Frenchman's guns, *Queen Charlotte* was already pulling ahead, her captain, a valiant Scot named Andrew Snape Douglas, intent only on duelling Villaret himself in the flagship *Peuple*. Seymour was fully engaged in giving his orders, all of his quarterdeck officers were absorbed in their duties, and Kenton was nowhere to be seen. Seamen scurrying hither and thither bumped into Wilden, knuckled their foreheads, gave him a perfunctory 'sorry, m'lud' and returned to their stations. Suddenly Wilden felt desperately alone, all too obviously a civilian thrust into a strange, perilous world for which he was not equipped and where he was not welcome. He was not even wearing a sword, a weapon he detested. He had his pistols, but they were intended to ward off London's footpads and not France's wooden leviathans nor the hundreds of atheist fanatics they carried. He was an encumbrance to every man on *Sans Pareil*, a useless passenger, an obstacle pointlessly occupying a space on the deck where a fighting man could be. He was of even less use than a widow's man, those fictitious entities entered in ships' books so their wages could be allotted for the relief of widows of those who fell in battle.

Sans Pareil was coming up level with *Le Formidable*, and even a lubber like Wilden could plainly see the terrible toll the French had already paid in their duel with *Queen Charlotte*. Shot holes peppered the enemy ship's hull, her upperworks and rigging were desperately torn, bloodied bodies and parts of bodies were being thrown over the side, and a small fire had broken out on the poop deck. Astern and minute by minute, Bridport's *Royal George* and the other, slower ships of the fleet were coming up to join the fray. Wilden watched, fascinated, as the starboard gun crews of *Sans Pareil* ran out their weapons and awaited the order they knew was coming. He saw Seymour staring intently at the enemy, judging distance, speed, wind, pitch and roll. Then the command –

'*Fire!*'

More hellish by far. Wilden felt the entire hull of *Sans Pareil* shudder as the cannon recoiled. The flames spewing from the gun barrels were truly a vision of the infernal underworld. He thought for several moments that the broadside had surely rendered him deaf, and thanked God as he began to hear the cheers of the gun crews and the orders of their officers. The men were already reloading the guns, intent on reducing *Le Formidable* to matchwood. The fire on the French ship's poop deck was now raging unchecked, and Wilden glimpsed blazing bodies immolated in the flames. But the French still resisted. The answering broadside was far feebler than that fired by *Sans Pareil*, but Wilden felt the impact as several shots struck the stout English oak of her starboard side. A shot severed a shroud no more than a few feet from him. A man fell to the deck, screaming with pain and clutching his stomach. None went to his aid, so Wilden ran to him, lifted him, and nearly spewed at the sight of the fellow's guts, exposed through an ugly wound.

'Oh Jesu,' cried the wounded sailor, 'oh Jesu, oh Jesu – that my Abigail be made a widow...'

Wilden looked about desperately.

'You men!' he shouted to two of the nearest gun crew. 'Get this man to the surgeon!'

''E's already gone, m'lud!'

'We can't leave our posts, m'lud!'

Wilden looked back down at the wounded man. But his eyes were frozen open, staring not at Wilden or his shipmates but into eternity. The men of the gun crew had already turned away, intent only on readying their weapon for the next broadside. Reluctantly, Wilden laid the corpse on the deck, stood, and looked around him. The deck of *San Pareil* was full of men attending remorselessly to their duties, their efforts punctuated by orders from those in authority. The air was thick with gunsmoke and the thicker black clouds rolling over them from the fire aboard *Le Formidable*. There were occasional shots from muskets and swivel guns, but for the moment the main batteries of the two combatants were silent. *Sans Pareil* was slowly moving away from her shattered opponent.

'My lord! My lord, are you hit? Are you wounded, sir?'

It was Lord Mark Kerr, the sixth lieutenant, his cutlass held firmly in his hand. Of all *Sans Pareil*'s lieutenants, he was the only one who had shown no interest in overtly soliciting the lord of the Admiralty for advancement. But as a younger son of the Marquess of Lothian, who owned vast tracts of the Scottish border country, Lord Mark's success in life was undoubtedly assured regardless of any intervention from elsewhere, so he had no need to fawn on anyone.

'Wounded? No...'

Wilden looked at his hands and arms, then down to his chest, and saw that he was thoroughly smeared with the blood of the man who had died in his arms.

'The blood of another,' he said. 'I am unhurt, Lord Mark.'

'Thank God! But sir, Lord Hugh urgently requests that you go below at once!'

Wilden glanced across to the burning poop deck of *Le Formidable*. Despite the precariousness and sheer terror of his situation, he found it impossible to suppress a smile. As captain of *Sans Pareil*, Seymour was perfectly entitled to order Wilden to go below. Come to that, he was perfectly entitled to order his fellow Admiralty lord placed in irons. It was even possible that by couching it as a request rather than an order, Seymour, a man whom he had damned without reservation until so very recently, was genuinely driven by concern for Wilden's safety. But Seymour, the consummate courtier, would not dare take the risk of treating a known confidante of the prime minister so rudely as to order him or incarcerate him.

'My compliments to Lord Hugh, Lieutenant,' said Wilden, 'but I am perfectly comfortable where I am.'

'As you say, my lord. But I reckon the battle is going to get a good deal hotter.'

CHAPTER EIGHTEEN

La Verité *at sea, fifty-eight degrees, fifty minutes of latitude north, five degrees, twenty minutes of longitude west of the Paris Meridian, a league west of the island called Hoy*

Philippe studied the towering sea cliffs of the islands now troublingly close to the east. Rain was stinging his eyes, but he could see the waves, high and angry, breaking onto the sea-stacks and the cliffs, implacable red-grey walls of rock. Philippe cursed the Heinrichs for their duplicity in bringing him and the ship to this bleak and infernal destination. They should not be here at all, pursuing a personal obsession of Antoine Heinrich when they should be in open water, sweeping up prizes for their own profit and the benefit of France. As the corsair drew ever nearer to the shore, Philippe knew for sure that he should have returned a different answer to Antoine Heinrich when the question was posed that day at Rennes. This was not a hospitable shore, and the strong rain-bearing westerly driving *La Verité* could easily become a ship-killing wind forcing them onto the unforgiving rocks and to their deaths. In that event, no amount of money would have been worth the consequence. The sails of the corsair were reefed, the one exception being the fore topsail, but for the moment *La Verité* had ample sea-room. But even if they were spared the rocks, it remained inescapable that this, the cliffs and islands before them, formed an integral part of Britain. This was the enemy's shore, and they were about to sail into the very heart of an enemy harbour.

For the hundredth time since the revelation at the fifty-fifth degree of latitude, Philippe silently cursed himself for saying *oui* to Antoine Heinrich that day at Rennes.

Ugarte was off watch and asleep below, Augustin Heinrich once again confined to his sea-bed with an unsurprising recurrence of serious *mal de mer*, and Philippe shared the sodden quarterdeck with the universally detested native of these islands, Marcus Drever, now finally fulfilling his role as pilot to guide the ship on the evening flood tide into the broad, placid harbour that both the charts and the Scot's assurances insisted lay somewhere behind the formidable cliffs and away from the violent waves breaking on the rocks of Orkney.

'Hoy,' said Drever, gesturing toward the brooding cliff-girt island on the starboard quarter, 'and the peedie isle in the Flow's mouth is called Graemsay. We'll make our course sooth o' that, Captain, by way of Burra Sound. Reckon we should anchor just off Graemsay Kirk, just opposite Moaness where there's a break in the foul ground, an' wait for when it's darkest. No exciseman'll come oot Stromness the night, an' tomorrow's the Sabbath, so no folk aboot then. We won't get any attention 'til Monday, an' by then we'll be lang gan oot the Flow.'

Philippe followed perhaps one word in three of Drever's discourse, but the meaning was clear enough. He had noted the small town of Stromness on the chart, lying on the north side of the western channel that led into the broad expanse of Scapa Flow. It was said to be a place frequented by the ships of the company that traded to the north of Canada, sometimes a harbour of refuge for ships seeking respite from Atlantic storms, but never a harbour that saw the warships of King George's navy, whose concerns were all far to the south where all of England's enemies were located. Philippe could only hope that this intelligence, and the confidence of the renegade Drever, did not prove false.

'You're certain there's no battery on either shore?' Philippe asked.

Since the incidents of the prize crew and the knife fight with Marhallac'h, Philippe found it wholly impossible to trust Marcus Drever. The suspicion aired by the Breton, that Drever might be not just a traitor to his country but a child murderer, was now common knowledge throughout the crew. It clung to the man and could not be shaken, with only the knowledge that he was directly employed by the Heinrichs saving the Scot from the multitude of ways in which a crew could quietly dispose of a hated shipmate. Drever had never been popular among the rest of the crew, but for the last few days he had been brutally ostracised by his shipmates. While ordinary *matelots* would always clutch at even thinner pretexts to christen a man a Jonah, a curse on the ship, its crew and its voyage, even Philippe felt uncomfortable dealing with the rogue Orcadian. Now, though, in his native waters Drever had come into his own as the de facto pilot of the corsair, yet Philippe could not rid himself his doubts about the man and the nature of his relationship with Augustin Heinrich.

'Battery?' scoffed Drever. 'Why'd any man think to have batteries on the Flow? An' our colours'll no concern any braw laddie on Hoy or Mainland. Always been Yanks coming in for refuge or to take on water, before an' since yon rebellion they had.'

The privateer was flying her false colours, the Stars and Stripes of the infant United States of America, the land of Philippe's birth and upbringing. A newborn land for which he had served in his first ships and fought his first battles. So he found the deceit in which he was now engaged uncomfortable, and he knew his old childhood friend Sam Arbon, now a member of the American House of Representatives, and his other old comrades-in-arms would have chided him vehemently for such disrespect to the flag under which they had fought. But although both Drever and Augustin Heinrich assured him that these remote northern isles had no defences to speak of, *La Verité* could hardly sail into what the charts showed to be a vast natural harbour in British waters under her own colours, the republican *Tricolore*.

At Drever's suggestion *La Verité*'s course was a little north of north-north-east, keeping her well away from the implacable shore of the substantial and forbidding island that the Scot named as Hoy. When Drever signalled for a change of course, Philippe gave the orders to come due easterly, then, shortly afterwards, east-south-east and finally south-south-east to come into the mouth of the channel shown on the charts and named by Drever as Burra Sound. The leadsman's call revealed ample water below the corsair's keel at every stage of their passage, the safe channel having a sandy bottom but even the shelving rock on either side giving more than enough clearance. As Drever had indicated, there were no signs of any defensive batteries or of any other vessels.

Between the two substantial islands to the north and south, the ones named by Drever as Mainland and Hoy, lay a far more modest, flatter island upon which stood a few hovels, a nondescript church and a large herd of long-haired cows grazing on grass that seemed remarkably green and lush for such a northerly latitude. Like all the land in sight on the larger islands, no trees were visible anywhere, their absence due, said Drever, to the prevalence of strong winds that made it impossible for anything higher than a bush to flourish.

At Drever's behest, Philippe ordered another course change to come more easterly, keeping close to the shore of the low island that Drever named as Graemsay.

'*Sept toises… six toises… cinq toises… quatre toises…*'

The leadsman's regular calls provided reassurance that ample water still lay beneath the corsair's keel. The seabed now was of rock, the ground firm, and *La Verité* came to an anchor within easy hailing distance of an austere rectangular building of dull grey stone that Drever proclaimed to be Graemsay kirk, this being, it seemed, the Scottish word for a church. The stark, unadorned rectangular structure suggested a faith far more austere than the Catholicism in which Philippe had been raised by his devout mother and which the revolution in France had decisively overthrown.

It was now well into the evening, although there was yet little sign of impending darkness. The sky remained as grey and ugly as it had all day, threatening a storm but never managing to deliver it other than in brief, intermittent squalls of rain. Philippe studied the island of Graemsay, alert to any sign of hostile intent. He could make out a few figures on the shore and further inland – there an old man staring curiously at the incoming ship, there a mother and child throwing pebbles into the water who gave the corsair barely a second glance – but no sign of any who might be taken for sentries or lookouts of some sort. No sign of a military presence of any kind. The war seemed so remote as to be utterly unknown to these ancient, windswept islands and the inhabitants who made up the sparse population.

Tonight, that would change.

Ugarte came on deck, inspected the scene around him, then sniffed loudly.

'Not much of a place,' he said. 'Not much of a prison for this Señora Heinrich.'

'Not our concern, Lieutenant, although if it proves to be so then so much the better.'

Rescue the damned woman, get out of enemy waters as quickly as possible, rid themselves of Marcus Drever once and for all, land Augustin Heinrich and his stepmother at The Helder, satisfy Heinrich père by doing so, resume their real business of cruising the sea and taking prizes, garner the profits…

Philippe had mapped it out in his mind. It should all be so very simple.

The corsair swung at single anchor for several hours. As Drever had predicted, no functionary came out from the town of Stromness, which lay out of sight behind the island in the mouth of the capacious anchorage called the Flow. The few inhabitants of the island of Graemsay seemingly accepted that the ship was there but that its presence was of no concern to them, the American colours attracting no curiosity but seemingly sufficient to reassure the inhabitants that the strange ship presented no threat. Men who could speak English tolerably well were stationed as lookouts, able to respond to any questions from curious inhabitants without arousing suspicion. One of the carpenter's crew, a bright youth called Gorrec, had spent several years working in a shipyard in Boston and was able to assume a passable accent to field the one shouted query from a young fisherman, informing him that the ship at anchor off his island was the *Secretary Hamilton* out of Providence, Rhode Island. The fisherman went away, seemingly satisfied with the response. Meanwhile Philippe and Ugarte went for'ard and aft, down to the cramped messes and along the upper deck, selecting and arming the men who would be needed for the landing party. The German, Teschow, would be one, Drever another, for he alone knew the precise geography and nature of the islands. He assured Philippe that a force of no more than twenty should be ample for the mission. Their destination, on an island even smaller than this Graemsay, would be unsuspecting and undefended apart from a handful of servants and farmhands, Drever said.

On their return to the quarterdeck Philippe found that Augustin Heinrich had finally risen from his bed and come on deck. He was very pale but dressed, upright, and not retching.

'Your condition is improved, Citizen?' asked Philippe.

Heinrich attempted a complacent smile of reassurance.

'This anchorage is kinder to my health, Captain. And the goal is so close now. How can I languish below when winning back Anne-Catherine, freeing her from the intolerable slavery she has endured, is within my grasp?'

There was something about Heinrich's response that perplexed Philippe.

'You are close to your stepmother, Citizen?'

Heinrich *fils* seemed to consider the question an impertinence. He flushed and mumbled a response.

'I have the greatest respect for her, Captain. She and I – she is only a little older than me – my father made a good choice of a second wife.'

'Your father's love for her must be powerful.'

Heinrich looked at Philippe sharply.

'Your meaning, Captain?' he snapped.

The vehemence of the young man's response startled Philippe.

'It is no small thing, Citizen, to fit out a ship and engage a crew. No small expense. No small risk to send that ship into the very heart of an enemy harbour. The prize must be very precious.'

The tension and hostility faded from Heinrich's features.

'No small thing at all, sir, although, of course, this is merely a brief diversion from your greater mission. From your greater profit, Captain. But as for risk, look about you. There are no ships in this place. No soldiers to oppose us. Hardly any people at all. Drever told us all of this when we employed him, and he was right.'

Heinrich, clearly impatient to be under way again, remained on deck for the next few hours. The hours of midnight, one and two passed. Although still grey and threatening, the sky remained stubbornly light, a phenomenon of northern summers that Philippe remembered from his time in Russia. At three, with Drever back on the quarterdeck to act as pilot, Philippe gave the order to weigh anchor and loose the topsails. With the wind still south-westerly and strengthening, *La Verité* made headway once more, Drever ordering occasional slight course changes as the ship moved slowly south-east toward the low-lying black masses of several more islands, barely distinguishable in the gloomy half-light of the summer night. Philippe knew from his chart that the nearest of them, the smallest, was named Cava, and the largest, furthest away, Flotta. Neither of them concerned him unless they sheltered a British warship or contained a garrison, and there was no sign of either. All of Philippe's concern, as well as that of Augustin Heinrich, was on the middle island, the one named on the chart as Fara. That was where Thorfinn Rendall, the abductor of Madame Anne-Catherine Heinrich, had his lairdly seat. That was where Augustin Heinrich's stepmother would be found.

CHAPTER NINETEEN

HMS *Sans Pareil* was clear of the burning *Le Formidable*. Seymour was intent on coming up with the French flagship, *Le Peuple*, which had already been engaged by Captain Douglas in the mighty *Queen Charlotte*. But Wilden, still resolutely standing on the quarterdeck in the midst of the smoke and fury despite Seymour's constant imprecations for him to go below, could see the mighty one-hundred-gun *Charlotte* falling away from the French, her sails and rigging in tatters after a ferocious exchange of fire. Through the pervasive smoke, hanging thickly over the fleets in the inconveniently light winds, Wilden could see the ghostly shapes of other British ships ahead and abeam of *Sans Pareil*. He wished he still had in attendance his ebullient walking encyclopaedia, Midshipman Jack Kenton, who would have been able definitively to identify the ships for him, but from memory and the sight of the large command flags flying from the foremasts he assumed that he could see *Queen*, the flagship of Vice-Admiral Sir Alan Gardner, and *London*, Vice-Admiral John Colpoys. There were a couple of Seventy-Fours too, and Kenton could undoubtedly have identified them in the blink of an eye, but with the lad at his station well for'ard the two ships could have been Noah's Ark and the Ship of Fools for all Wilden knew. Astern he caught occasional glimpses of *Royal George*, Lord Bridport's flagship, and her fellow sluggards still struggling to come up to join the battle, while dead ahead the French continued to retreat slowly eastwards toward the Île de Groix. The island was so close now that its shore batteries were opening up on the British fleet with a few speculative shots at the very limit of their guns' range. Bridport would be fuming, probably even stamping in rage on his quarterdeck, because he knew he had to complete his victory before Villaret's fleet could get into the waters between Groix and the dockyard of Lorient, where they would be safe. Bridport would want as many prizes as possible, thereby accruing for himself a fortune in prize money, but every minute brought the French closer to safety and threatened to thwart the Old Lady's ambition.

'Damn this fellow!' cried Seymour, pointing at a large French ship which was slowly interposing itself between *Sans Pareil* and the enemy flagship.

'She's *Tigre*, Seventy-Four, sir!' said Quinton, the fourth lieutenant. 'The last list we had out of France showed her captain as one Bedout, a Canadian.'

'No matter where he sprang from, he wants to stop me getting at Villaret, by God!' exclaimed Seymour. 'Very well, gentlemen. Let's make this Captain Bedout regret it!'

Wilden had never witnessed a land battle, but from what he had read in accounts of the likes of Cromwell and the great Duke of Marlborough, the action was meant to be incessant from the moment the two armies began to engage. Not so at sea. Minutes that dragged into infinities might pass before a ship came within range of its next assailant, a strange period where no guns might fire but a score or more of slight adjustments of the helm or the sail pattern might be ordered. The distances were much greater too, with several miles still separating the rearmost British ships from the foremost French. The battle in which Wilden found himself reluctantly engaged was particularly frustrating, or so Seymour and the lieutenants present on the quarterdeck said, because of the still barely noticeable breezes that made the painfully slow movements of the ships resemble some kind of dumb show upon a stage. It took perhaps twenty minutes for *Sans Pareil* and *Tigre* to be in position and within close enough range for them to exchange broadsides. But at that moment, as Wilden had already come to realise, everything changed. Inaction gave way in a mere moment to action of the most frenzied, most desperate, most brutal kind.

'*Fire!*' ordered Seymour, and the thirty-six-, twenty-four- and twelve-pounder guns of *Sans Pareil* spat flame and smoke, their recoils sending a shiver through the hull. The gun crews immediately began the reloading sequence, each gun captain urging his men to ever greater efforts to outdo their neighbours and above all to outshoot the damned Frenchies yonder.

A few seconds later *Tigre* replied, and Wilden felt the impact as three or four shot struck the planking of *Sans Pareil*.

'Barely even a fleabite, my lord!' yelled the exultant Seymour. 'This is no tiger we fight, by God – hardly the equal of a dowager's tabby, I'll wager!'

For the next half hour, Wilden felt himself in the very epitome of hell. *Sans Pareil* fired broadside after broadside, every one wreaking more havoc on their French opponent. *Le Tigre* was shattered in her hull and her rigging, her broadsides increasingly erratic, slow and intermittent. Still the French ship resisted, though, to the obvious astonishment and frustration of Seymour and his officers. The casual dismissal of *Le Tigre*'s fighting qualities had been swiftly forgotten. The two ships were now so close that Wilden could see individual faces on the enemy's deck and saw what must have been dozens of men hit, bleeding and dying. Bodies were slung unceremoniously over the side or through the gunports. Increasingly difficult to manoeuvre and with her sails too torn to keep up with the rest of her fleet, but still putting up a remarkably defiant resistance, *Tigre* slowly fell out of the makeshift French formation. By doing so, she lay directly in the path of the oncoming vice-admirals' flagships, *Queen* and *London*, which joined their fire to *Sans Pareil*'s.

'They are brave fellows, facing these odds,' said Wilden to Seymour of the men of *Le Tigre*.

'Foolish fellows to hold out for so long. This Captain Bedout should have struck an age ago. Perhaps he hopes Villaret will come round and save them, but the ships around him seem intent only on flight.'

Wilden spotted young Kenton, shoving his way through the gun crews in the waist of the upper deck and looking purposeful, perhaps coming to make a report from his battle station. He smiled when he saw Wilden, and Ned reciprocated. But in that moment the guns of *Le Tigre* fired one last ragged, forlorn broadside at *Sans Pareil*. Part of the rail shattered, the smaller oak splinters wounding a couple of men in the nearest guncrew, who staggered away from their positions. The sight distracted Wilden momentarily, but when he looked again at Kenton, he saw a jagged shard of wood protruding from the lad's cheek. At that angle the splinter must have driven up into his brain, killing the boy instantly. Kenton fell to the deck. He did not even have the time to utter a sound of any sort.

Wilden gasped, then sprinted from his position on the quarterdeck, took the companionway in two strides, and ran to the fallen midshipman, lifting his inert body from the deck. Kenton was entirely still, his face calm and serene but disfigured by the horrific death-wound and the shard that had inflicted it. Wilden knelt down and closed Kenton's eyes. The lad was still warm. He could not be dead. He was so young, so full of joy for life. He could not be dead. It was wrong. It was unfair. It mocked the very existence of God. Why had the fatal splinter not struck him, Wilden, instead of this lively, good-natured child? Why had God ordained that Kenton, poor Kenton, who might one day have made a great captain or even a great admiral, should die this day?

Shock gave way almost immediately as a tide of rage overwhelmed him. He carefully laid the impossibly tiny body of poor Kenton back down on the deck, covering it with torn canvas that must have been ripped out of one of the sails by a French shot. Then Ned Wilden stood, drew one of his pistols, and fired it at *Le Tigre*. He knew it was futile – the French ship was well out of pistol range – but Wilden could feel tears soaking his cheeks and knew for the first time in his life what bloodlust felt like.

'My lord! You must go below, sir, for pity's sake!'

Wilden turned. William Stevens, the chaplain of *Sans Pareil*, a youth whom he had thought insipid and otherworldly whenever they shared a table in the wardroom, was kneeling by Kenton's body, ignoring the continuing French fire and interrupting his intonation of the prayers for the dead to address him.

Instead of complying with the chaplain's injunction, Ned Wilden knelt down beside the body of Lucky Jack Kenton, whose good fortune had deserted him all too soon. How would his poor mother take the news of her son's death? Did she have sufficient means of support? He would make it his business to find out.

As he mumbled the words, taking his lead from the chaplain, he knew that the boy's death was affecting him more powerfully than that of any since the loss of one of his servants, the man who had been like a father to him since his earliest days, in a riot during the previous year.

'Wash it, we pray thee, in the blood of that immaculate lamb, that was slain to take away the sins of the world...'

Lord Wilden was weeping uncontrollably and barely able to form the words. This for a boy he had barely known, yet who had made a greater impact on him than a hundred grown men. An unseemly spectacle, demeaning for a peer of the realm and a lord of the Admiralty in the presence of hundreds of men from the lower orders.

But no man was looking at him. No man cared for his grief, not even the chaplain, who was intent only on praying for the soul of the dead midshipman. The men of *Sans Pareil* were intent only on the mechanical actions of prime, fire, reload, time and time again, as they bombarded *Le Tigre* incessantly. Wilden's grief was so profound that he did not at first notice the firing had stopped, nor did he register the loud cheers and hollering from the men of *Sans Pareil*. A glance behind him revealed that the Tricolour flying from the ensign staff of *Le Tigre* had come down. The French had finally surrendered. How poor Kenton would have cheered.

Edward, Lord Wilden, had never married and had no intention of doing so. He had no son, nor ever would have. But as he looked down through tearful eyes on the shattered but peaceful features of Midshipman Kenton, he wondered whether any son of his might have looked and behaved a little like this valiant lad.

CHAPTER TWENTY

The eastern sky was already becoming lighter as the landing party from *La Verité*, embarked in the ship's longboat, made landfall on the low-lying, insubstantial island of Fara, set in the southern part of the vast harbour close to the much larger, towering bulk of Hoy. The ship lay at anchor off the north-easternmost point of the island in *huit toises*, eight fathoms. The last hour or so had seen less rain but the wind was still blowing hard, perhaps even strengthening a little. Ugarte had the acting command with orders to run for the sea if there was any sign of an enemy man-of-war, but both he and Philippe knew that the order was almost certainly superfluous. The great anchorage, ringed by hills and islands like some colossal giant's amphitheatre, was empty of anything that might challenge the corsair. Away to the north, close to the shore of the island called Mainland, were a few small craft that Drever called yawls; small, low hulls with straight stems and raking sternposts. Inshore fishermen, undoubtedly, and with none of them showing any sign of sailing out to approach Fara, no threat to the corsair. What might await them ashore was quite another case, and as Philippe leapt from the longboat and ordered the craft to be hauled up onto the island's rocky shore, he felt an unwelcome sense of disquiet. Something about this landing, about their entire expedition, felt somehow wrong, especially since the revelation of the secret orders. But apart from his resentment of the duplicity of the Heinrichs, he could not identify any cause or justification for the feeling. So far, everything had gone exactly as the Heinrichs and their agent, Drever, had said it would and was as they wished it to go. Yet the feeling remained.

He strode up the slight slope that divided the shore from the farmland of Fara, gesturing for the men of the landing party to fan out on either side of him and Heinrich, who was as eager as a puppy. Ahead lay the low, dark shapes of a dozen or so hovels, scattered across the level area of the island and the slopes of the low hillock at its centre. There was no sign of life in any of the cottages, the only other waking creatures on the island seemingly being a small herd of cattle, grazing on the eastern side of the island. The hillock was crowned by the only building of substance, the only house with two storeys and two gables. In France, even in the poorest regions of Brittany, this would barely have counted as a worthy farmhouse for a tenant, but Drever insisted that this was their target. This was Fara House, he said, and within its walls the devilish Major Thorfinn Rendall, the laird of Fara, held prisoner the wife of Antoine Heinrich.

The landing party advanced cautiously toward the house, men peering into the gloom all around them, alert for any threat. The ground was firm and level, so it was easy for the men to keep their footing. There was still no light from any of the cottages, but as they got nearer, Philippe could see a dim light through one of the ground floor windows of the larger building. It was not yet five in the morning, but in Fara House someone was already awake and about, perhaps even the reviled Major Rendall himself…

The thought that had been nagging at Philippe for days, just out of reach beyond the limit of his conscious thoughts, came into focus. It was a thought that had been forming since the opening of the additional orders from Heinrich *père* at fifty-five degrees north. It was a thought that, if he had been able properly to consider and articulate it in time, might have tipped the balance of the crew's vote in a different direction. And if he had thought of it that fateful day at Rennes, the voyage itself may never have begun.

He put out his arm to halt Augustin Heinrich who was nearly breaking into a run, so eager was he to reach the house.

'What, damn it?' snapped the young man. 'We are nearly there, Captain – look, man, there are no guards or defences, nothing to stand in our way—'

'Thorfinn Rendall,' said Philippe, looking sharply at Heinrich, 'the man who you and your father say abducted your stepmother.'

'Him? The devil who holds her within those walls? What of him? We're moments away from killing him and freeing her! Mere moments, Captain!'

'A major in the British Army, yes? Major of a line regiment, if he was in the Valenciennes campaign?'

'What of it?' hissed Heinrich, whose expression, clearly visible in the dim light of early morning, was fast turning from irritation to fury.

'Then why is he here? How could you and your father be certain he would be here? If he's an officer on active service, surely he would still be with his regiment, not in his home. A major in the British Army would be the equivalent of, what, a *chef de bataillon* in the Army of the

Republic, and men of that rank do not generally retire in the middle of a war, Citizen Heinrich.'

Heinrich gaped at Philippe as though he had no comprehension of his words.

'She's just there, man! Within those walls! We must free her, free her *now*! Why does it matter about Rendall, or what rank he holds in the damned British Army? Why should we care about that villain?'

Drever, who was within earshot, interjected.

'Captain, I'd left Orkney before Major Rendall came back from the war, but the tale I heard—'

'Enough, Drever!' snapped Heinrich. 'No more hesitation! We advance on the house and take it. I demand it! Now, Captain Kermorvant!

Heinrich was agitated beyond any reasonable measure. Philippe looked around, over the pathetic cottages of the islanders toward the towering black mass of Hoy to the south and the lower lands of the larger island to the north, which Drever named Mainland. The sky was lighter now, and he could make out individual features of the landscape more distinctly. *La Verité* was still the only substantial vessel in the broad anchorage, the unmistakeable form of Juan Ugarte at her quarterdeck rail. Nobody had emerged from any of the cottages, where a handful of candles had now been lit. There was no sign of any troops, or indeed of any living being other than the incurious cows. There was no threat. Unless the abductor Rendall had concealed a brigade of Highlanders within the rough, heavily weathered walls of Fara House, there was nothing to prevent the men of the corsair commandeering the entire island and doing exactly what Augustin Heinrich wished. Despite his misgivings, Philippe signalled for the men to advance the last few paces to the house.

He reached the wall by the window where the single visible light shone and pressed himself against the austere stonework, Heinrich by his side. Still no sound came from within the house. No sign of life. No screams of an imprisoned and brutalised woman.

The window was unshuttered. In the relative stillness of the morning, with the breeze momentarily negligible, Philippe could hear a faint voice from within the house. A woman's voice. A calm, gentle woman's voice, not raised in any way, not screaming for help or crying out in agony. A woman's voice reading in French-accented English.

"'I may believe as much or as little as I please of this,' said Manfred; 'but I will hear thy own story before I examine into the truth of it. Tell me, what reason did the princess give thee for making her escape? Thy life depends on thy answer.'

"'She told me,' replied Theodore, 'that she was on the brink of destruction, and that if she could not escape from the castle, she was in danger in a few moments of being made miserable for ever.'

"'And on this slight foundation, on a silly girl's report,' said Manfred, 'thou didst hazard my displeasure?'

"'I fear no man's displeasure,' said Theodore, 'when a woman in distress puts herself under my protection.'"

Philippe recognised the words as being from *The Castle of Otranto*, a book he had read years before in America. It was not right. Nothing was right. But he was committed, all of them were committed, and there was no going back. Cocking his pistol and gesturing for Augustin Heinrich to stay back, Philippe swung around and peered through the window.

The scene before him held no Gothic horrors. A young woman, presumably Anne-Catherine Heinrich, dressed in a woollen shawl over a nightgown, was sitting on a tall chair backed with wicker or straw to one side of a fireplace, the book held in her hand. She was reading by the light of several lanterns and naked candles to a man lying on a chaise longue, an item of furniture that seemed utterly out of place in the sparsely furnished, low-ceilinged room and the bare, wild islands that lay all around it. The man seemed at ease, listening intently to every word. The look between him and his companion, and that between her and him, was familiar to Philippe. It was the look Tasha had bestowed on him so often in the blissful time in their little house in Kronstadt before the dark shadow of her brother Bulgakov had separated them forever. It was the look of two people entirely content in each other's company. It was the look of two people deeply in love. Here, though, that look had even more potency. For the man on the chaise longue was horribly damaged, his left leg and half his left arm missing, the left side of his face a mass of scar tissue.

Augustin Heinrich could contain himself no longer. He sprang out from Philippe's side so that he was directly outside the window, gasped at the spectacle before him, and before Philippe could restrain him, screamed, '*Anne-Catherine!*' and began to hammer on the window frame. The woman and the injured man looked up in alarm and saw the two faces in the glass. The man's response was unhurried, with no hint of fear or even concern. He raised himself slowly with his one good arm, swinging himself off the chaise longue and standing with the aid of a crutch. There was a sword on the wall above the fireplace, two pistols on a small table to the man's left, but he reached for none of these weapons. Instead, he stared at the faces in the window. It was difficult to tell because of the hideous disfigurement of his face, but Philippe could have sworn the man was smiling. The woman's reaction was quite different, and at once told Philippe a story as Gothic as the book she had been reading from. She screamed and screamed again, but the screams and the twisted, enraged expression on her face were not caused by the unwelcome intrusion. They were caused by the sight of Augustin Heinrich and the sound of him calling her name.

CHAPTER TWENTY-ONE

The men of *La Verité* had no need to break down the door of Fava Hall. It was opened for them by a strapping young woman of no more than twenty, dishevelled, dressed in rough plaid and evidently just risen from her bed, who announced herself as the housekeeper and who seemed singularly unabashed by the unexpected arrival on her doorstep of a party of armed Frenchmen. Augustin Heinrich brushed past her impatiently, both Philippe and Marcus Drever following in his wake, and nearly ran into the room they had just been spying on. He made directly for his stepmother, arms wide to embrace her, but she took a step sideways and slapped him with remarkable force.

'You *bastard!*' she screamed, her expression twisted and red with hatred. 'You villain! You filth! You *pervert!*'

'Anne-Catherine,' Heinrich said urgently, seemingly oblivious to her tirade against him, 'my love. I came for you – I came all this distance to bring you away from this man—'

'*My love?*' yelled Anne-Catherine Heinrich. 'Your love? You understand the word almost as little as your father.'

'The younger Heinrich,' said the crippled man, Major Thorfinn Rendall, in fair French delivered in a rough, rasping voice. 'By God, that you had the gumption to come all this way. I wouldn't have believed you capable of such a thing. And I see you've brought a little army, Marcus Drever among them. Well, then, Marcus Drever, the child-killer, the traitor, the poorest spawn of these islands, returns home after all this time. The only homecoming awaiting you takes the form of a gallows in front of Saint Magnus's, Marcus Drever.'

The Orcadian sneered, but Philippe paid little attention to the exchange between him and Rendall. Anne-Catherine Heinrich, a tall blond woman with striking, refined features, had her hands on her hips, glaring viciously at Augustin Heinrich as if weighing where she would deliver her next blow. The young Switzer, still visibly reeling from the ferocity of her slap, was now seemingly on the verge of tears.

'We can be happy together, Anne-Catherine,' he begged, his voice nearly breaking. 'We can be far away from my father – you'll never need to see him again, I swear it. I promise I'll keep you safe from him. We can go far away from him and from here, from this man, this *cripple*…'

He gestured toward Rendall, who seemed greatly amused despite the presence in his house of several heavily armed Frenchmen intent on abducting his companion.

'Well, my dear,' he said light-heartedly, 'it seems that the younger Herr Heinrich, here, has dreams of taking you away from me. And why would you not go with him, eh? Why stay on this feeble windy island in the remotest part of Britain, many miles from any respectable society, wasting your life on a broken half-man? Go with him, Anne-Catherine. Augustin is quite a presentable fellow, and an ingenious one too, I'll wager, so I'm sure he'll be able to do what he says and find you a place on this wide earth where his father won't be able to find you. This gallant captain will carry you there, I'm certain – my apologies, sir, I have not done you the courtesy of asking for your name.'

Philippe's unease was running rampant, the absence of any signs of confinement giving a lie to the story spun by the Heinrichs. It had all been a lie. He had been complicit in the desperate schemes of two desperate men, father and son. His chest and stomach felt as though they were in the grip of a vice. But as Major Thorfinn Rendall addressed him directly for the first time, he steadied himself and replied as confidently as he could manage.

'Kermorvant, Major. Captain of the corsair *La Verité* in the service of the French Republic, one and indivisible.'

Thorfinn Rendall's eyes narrowed.

'Kermorvant of the *Verité*? Now those are two names I've seen in the same sentence before.'

Rendall took firmer hold of the crutch and took a step forward. Four or five pistols, including those of Philippe and Augustin Heinrich, swung to aim at the shattered frame of the erstwhile soldier, but Rendall ignored them, similarly ignored his own weapons that were still easily within his reach, and swung himself the three paces to the nearest bookcase.

'Finn!' cried Anne-Catherine, who made to go to him. But Drever reached her first, grabbed her arm, spun her round and held his pistol to her head.

Rendall, seemingly unperturbed, took a book from one of the higher shelves and, one-handed, flipped it open to the title page.

'*Verité*. Well, that's it indeed. As this edition tells us, that was the pen name of the illustrious philosopher Edouard Kermorvant, Vicomte de Saint-Victor. An interesting writer, although many of his ideas are quite deluded, of course. Your father, perhaps, Captain?'

'I cannot deny it.'

'You are his eldest son, and thus the current vicomte?' Philippe nodded, and Thorfinn Rendall bowed his head in mock deference. 'Forgive me, my lord, but I'd rate you a distinctly unlikely captain for a mere privateer. An even unlikelier kidnapper, at that.'

He looked at Anne-Catherine Heinrich, who still had her arms pinioned to her back, and her stepson.

'This is no kidnap,' said Augustin Heinrich with feeling. 'My stepmother was abducted from her husband and family, from *me*, by this man!' He pointed at Rendall. 'He is the villain here! Anne-Catherine, my dearest, you will come with us now – come with *me*. We will make a new life together!'

'With you, Augustin?' she said as she struggled vainly against Drever's grip. '*With you?* After all your father did to me? After all your collusion in his perversions? Go with you? A new life *with you?* Finn saved me from you and your father! He loves me, and I love him!'

Heinrich laughed, but it was not the laugh Philippe had heard in Rennes, Concarneau or the captain's cabin of the corsair on the rare occasions when Augustin Heinrich was well enough to dine with him. Now there was a terrible mania about the younger Heinrich, a derangement of the senses. Perhaps the mania was born of his unrequited love for his stepmother, but it may have owed an equal portion to simply having Antoine Heinrich for a father.

'Love *that?*' protested Heinrich *fils*, the words strangled. 'Look at him! His body is torn! It is shattered! He is a cripple! What woman would possibly want to waste her life on a creature like that? But you know I love you,

Anne-Catherine. I have always loved you since the day you married my father. No, before that – the day I first saw you! So heed the man who loves you, Anne-Catherine. Captain Kermorvant will carry us to freedom! We'll be together at last, never to be parted again. I have my own money and I have a body that's whole! I can give you all that this cripple can't!'

'Finn is more of a man than you and your father together,' said Anne-Catherine acidly, almost spitting the words at her stepson.

The barb struck Augustin Heinrich like a sword thrust. He momentarily lost his balance and swayed like a drunkard. The movement distracted Drever and Anne-Catherine broke free of the Orcadian's grip, ignoring the possibility that the renegade would pull his trigger, and ran to Thorfinn Rendall, throwing herself against him and gripping him tightly. His free arm dropped the volume of *Verité*'s writings and enfolded her. Rendall kissed the top of her head.

'We *will* be together!' shouted Augustin Heinrich. 'We will! Drever, take her and this time don't let go of her!'

The Orcadian stepped forward, his pistol levelled at the head of Thorfinn Rendall, and Philippe saw how the business truly stood. Augustin Heinrich had never possessed any intention of taking Anne-Catherine back to his father and the life of slavery she had lived with him. Augustin Heinrich wanted her for himself, and expected Philippe and the crew of *La Verité* to become complicit in his plan. But it was obvious from the scene he had just witnessed that the lady herself wanted no part of either Heinrich, *père* or *fils*. She wanted the desperately broken husk of a man to whom she clung.

Philippe kept his pistol level but turned his aim away from Rendall.

'Stand down, Drever,' he ordered in English.

Drever turned and saw Philippe's pistol pointing directly at him. He looked back questioningly at Augustin Heinrich, whose expression was confused and desperate.

'I pay you,' he snarled at Philippe. 'I *own* you.'

'Your father pays me and every man in the crew, this one included. Your father, not you. You own none of us, Heinrich, and neither does your father. Lower your weapon, Drever.'

The Scot looked desperately from man to man, back to Thorfinn Rendall and Anne-Catherine Heinrich, then back to Philippe.

'*Lower your weapon!*' repeated Philippe.

Drever's eyes were wild and desperate. He began to comply but then swung round to fire at Philippe. His finger never pulled the trigger. There was only one spark, one sound, one shot. Philippe's pistol ball ripped a bloody hole in the Orcadian's forehead, and Marcus Drever fell dead to the floor.

Anne-Catherine Heinrich screamed, and some of the men of *La Verité* gasped. Three or four lowered their weapons, but the others wavered, not knowing who now led them nor at whom they should aim. Some still had their guns trained on Rendall, a couple were pointing them at Augustin Heinrich, but three had their guns levelled uncertainly at their captain. Heinrich, seeing the confusion, pointed furiously at Philippe.

'Shoot him! Kill him! He's a traitor to France! I pay you! I'll reward you! Take me and the woman, there, to the nearest friendly port. You'll be rich, my friends, richer than you could ever imagine!'

One of the Bretons, a relatively young master's mate called Tibeuf, was more forward than the rest and recovered more quickly from the shock of what had just played out before the landing party. He still had his gun on Thorfinn Rendall, but he was staring at Augustin Heinrich.

'So who's going to steer us to the port where you'll pay us, eh, Citizen? You? You're a Switzer and a lubber who's spent all the voyage puking. Can you make sense of a chart and lay a course? Can you read the winds and the tides? Can you even tell bow from stern, eh?'

'The lieutenant! Ugarte!' yelled the increasingly wretched and forlorn Augustin Heinrich. 'I'll buy him – he'll command the ship!'

'Ugarte?' said Tibeuf incredulously. 'You know he served with the captain before? All the old navy men stick together.' A few members of the landing party nodded in agreement. 'Ugarte won't take your gold, Citizen – that's assuming you've got any gold to give. Ain't it all your old pappy's?'

A few of the other men growled at that.

'You must give us passage!' pleaded Heinrich. '*You must!* Anne-Catherine, tell them – tell them it's what you want!'

Anne-Catherine Heinrich had still been staring at the body of Marcus Drever, but now she looked up as though seeing the scene before her for the first time.

'All I want is here,' she said, gripping Thorfinn Rendall's arm more tightly.

Augustin Heinrich half-turned, as if looking for a means of escape. But Tibeuf's pistol was fixed on him now. A couple of the other crewmen from *La Verité* had similarly changed their aim, and one of them, the burly Rostocker Teschow, filled the only doorway in and out of the room. Even if he somehow escaped from the house, Heinrich was on a tiny island in the midst of an archipelago far from France or his native Switzerland, with no vessel anywhere in sight that could carry him away from it. He was on British soil, and there was ample evidence that he had served republican France, the avowed enemy of Great Britain. He had no hope of escape.

Augustin Heinrich fell to his knees. His eyes swam with tears but stayed fixed on his stepmother, who looked on him with undisguised contempt. He seemed about to form more words, but they never came.

Then he raised his pistol to his forehead and blew out his brains.

CHAPTER TWENTY-TWO

The bodies of Augustin Heinrich and Marcus Drever had been removed to an outbuilding of Fava House. The room where they died had been restored to a condition of mundane domesticity by Rendall's housemaid, who scrubbed the blood and brains from the floor with no comment beyond a slight shake of her head. Philippe sat opposite Anne-Catherine Heinrich and Thorfinn Rendall, drinking a glass of Scotland's fearsome 'water of life'. The best remedy for all ills at any time of day, Rendall claimed. Philippe had encountered it before, on merchant voyages to Scottish harbours after the end of the revolutionary war, and wondered how such a ferocious liquid, even more potent than the vodka beloved of his Russian friends, could possibly remedy anything.

Philippe had ordered the men to wait for him outside, where the sun was now fully up and a few curious villagers were emerging from their cottages to tend to the cattle or their beached boats. *La Verité*, where Ugarte would know nothing of the extraordinary events that had unfolded ashore, was plainly visible through one of the windows, still gently swinging at single anchor. The only other sign of life was a curious seal who seemed to be intently studying the proceedings on Fava.

Philippe knew he needed to return to his ship. No matter how peaceful the scene in Fava House might now be, *La Verité* lay in a vast natural harbour, surrounded on all sides by islands that formed part of King George's dominions. The enemies of France and of Philippe Kermorvant were literally on every side. The corsair crew needed to get under way immediately and hope they could get out of the colossal snare in which they were trapped before its teeth could close and trap them.

Thorfinn Rendall, sitting once again on the chaise longue, seemed to divine Philippe's discomfort.

'You have done us a great service, Captain,' said Rendall, his hand firmly in that of the woman he loved. 'You have undoubtedly saved my life, and prevented Anne-Catherine and I from being parted forever. Prevented her from being returned to the hell of captivity and the unspeakable perversions of the elder Heinrich to which she was subjected' – Philippe saw Anne-Catherine's lower lip tremble at that – 'or else placed instead in the son's cage. A cage built out of an obsession as deranged as his father's'.

'Augustin's passion for me grew out of pity,' said Anne-Catherine quietly and slowly, seemingly taking great care to choose exactly the right words. She was not looking at Philippe nor even Thorfinn Rendall, but staring at the now barely visible stain on the floor that marked the spot where Augustin Heinrich died. 'I think at first he was ashamed and disgusted by the humiliation and degradation to which his father submitted me. Worse than the treatment of the lowest slave in a harem, he once said. Antoine was an avid devotee of the writings of the Marquis de Sade – you have read his works, Captain?'

'No, madame,' said Philippe, 'but I have heard of them. I am aware of their nature.'

Anne-Catherine Heinrich nodded.

'But over time, I sensed that Augustin's pity also turned into lust of his own. Like father, like son.'

'Thank God they were all trapped in Valenciennes when the allies besieged it,' said Rendall.

'Antoine's greed kept us there too long,' interjected Anne-Catherine. 'He was meant to be meeting some German merchants to sign several very large contracts, but they were delayed by the campaigns along the Rhine.'

'And Heinrich kept waiting for them,' said Rendall. 'My regiment was part of the Duke of York's army that took the town. And that was how we met, Captain, my Anne-Catherine and I.'

She gazed affectionately at Thorfinn Rendall and said, 'We had a short time together before…'

'Before I sustained these wounds, Captain, and was compelled to retire from active service.'

Compelled to retire. The man's very survival, the fact that he still lived and breathed, was evidently a minor miracle of modern medicine, but the bitterness underpinning the word 'compelled' suggested that if he could, Thorfinn Rendall would still be on a campaign and seeking the next battlefield.

Both Rendall and Anne-Catherine fell silent, seemingly lost in their memories. His surviving thumb gently caressed her fingers, which in turn gently brushed his own.

There was a gruesome untold tale here, Philippe realised. The hideous abuse and humiliations inflicted by Heinrich *père*, the growing and unspoken obsession of Heinrich *fils*, the exact means of Anne-Catherine Heinrich's escape from Valenciennes and the clutches of her husband and his son, Thorfinn Rendall's part in that escape, her all-consuming love for a man who must have nearly died of his hideous wounds – wounds received, perhaps, in the very act of bringing this beautiful woman out of hellish captivity.

Some men would seek to pry, to carry out a prurient interrogation of the couple. Philippe, as the man who had saved both their lives and who possessed all the armed force in that place and at that moment, was in a perfect position to be such a man. But all he felt in the presence of the couple before him was humility. They had overcome the horrors of war, the Heinrichs and Thorfinn Rendall's appalling injuries. They surely contended with the judgement and incomprehension of the ignorant every day of their lives. Through it all and against it all, their love swept each and every obstacle aside.

He had once known such a love and trusted that he would know it again. He had an unbidden thought of Leonore, but it was interrupted.

'You have done us the greatest service,' said Thorfinn Rendall. 'So allow me to do you a service in return, Captain Kermorvant.'

Anne-Catherine Heinrich looked at her lover adoringly and gave him a slight nod. Rendall took a sip of his whisky, then addressed Philippe again.

'The Volunteer regiment of these islands is aware of your presence. Your arrival in the Flow was reported from Graemsay to Stromness, thence to Kirkwall. Flying American colours was the flimsiest of disguises, Captain, and folk saw through it in an instant. Many of the people hereabouts make their livings from the sea in one way or another. They know American ships and American crews when they see them, and they know a ship that looks French-built and a crew that looks to be full of Frenchmen, no matter how ingeniously the

English speakers in your crew are brought to the fore. So your course was reported to the Volunteers soon enough. There will be telescopes fixed on your ship as I speak, no doubt of it. So as soon as enough of the men can be mustered and can requisition sufficient boats, they'll be across here. And even in such a poor and thinly inhabited place as these islands, Captain, we can field more than enough Volunteers to outnumber your crew several times over and set up ample field artillery to sink your ship. Volunteers who, to a man, are descendants of the fierce Northmen of old. They knew how to fight and annihilate their enemies, Captain, and so do we, their blood kin. Therefore, I would strongly urge you to leave the Flow as soon as you can.'

Philippe silently cursed himself for relying too much on the confident assertions of the renegade murderer Drever and the blasé, arrogant complacency of Augustin Heinrich. He had fallen too easily into the trap of underestimating the islanders, of assuming they were simple, primitive folk who scratched out a living at the edge of the world. It was the same fatal error that the British themselves had committed when attempting to put down the great rebellion in their American colonies, and had come up instead against those formidable, determined men with whom Philippe and his young friends had fought.

Philippe Kermorvant would not repeat the same mistake. He and the men of *La Verité* would not linger to try the mettle of the Orkney Volunteer Regiment.

'My thanks, Major Rendall, I shall heed your advice.'

The crippled soldier held up his hand.

'There is more, Captain. There is a Russian frigate in Kirkwall Bay on the north side of Mainland. She became detached from the main squadron sailing to join Admiral

Duncan's fleet in the North Sea, was damaged in a storm, and went into Kirkwall to repair. The last report I had from my factor there, received only yesterday, indicates that the works on her are complete and that she is ready for sea. Her captain will doubtless be acquainted by now with your presence.'

'The Republic I serve is not at war with Russia, sir.'

'Technically not, perhaps – not yet. But I have met Captain Komarov, and he seems to be a man in a desperate hurry to fight Frenchmen. The sort of man who will gladly sink you first and resolve any difficult questions from his empress and her ministers afterwards.'

Komarov. *Pavel Nikolaiovich Komarov*. It could be none other. The Russian navy under the Empress Catherine had been relatively small, and all the officers, certainly all the captains in the Baltic fleet, knew each other and socialised with each other. Philippe recalled the splendid reception in Princess Tereshkova's salon in Saint Petersburg in October 1792, not long before Tasha and Ivan were murdered and, blinded by grief, Philippe Kermorvant had left Russia for good, intent on offering his services to France. News had just been received that King Louis XVI had been deposed and a republic proclaimed. While the news privately delighted Philippe and amused his friend Kharabadze, it outraged Komarov of the *Drakon*. Komarov was already very drunk and spent the rest of the evening berating the French and proclaiming that the empress should immediately declare war on the treacherous republicans. If Philippe's recollection served him right, the fate Pavel Nikolaiovich Komarov had in mind for Citizen Robespierre was so gruesome that two or three ladies of the court nearly fainted.

Thorfinn Rendall was right. Pavel Nikolaiovich Komarov was not a man who would worry overmuch about the legal or diplomatic niceties of whether there was or was not a formal state of war between the Russian Empire and the French Republic.

Philippe downed the last of his whisky, set his glass upon the side table and stood, intending to take an immediate leave of Rendall and Anne-Catherine Heinrich. The crippled soldier, too, stood, unaided.

'Anne-Catherine,' he said, 'the chart, if you please. Well, Captain Kermorvant, as I see it your problem is that you killed your pilot for these islands.'

The thought had already occurred to Philippe. Marcus Drever might have been a vile child murderer and a traitor to his country, as well as a strange and difficult man, but his knowledge of the islands and their navigation had been invaluable. Philippe and Ugarte were both experienced navigators and could undoubtedly lay a course for one of the countless channels that lay between the islands surrounding the mighty harbour called the Flow. But whether their charts showed all the hidden rocks or other unmarked obstacles would be a lottery without the advice of Marcus Drever or some other man knowledgeable of the local waters.

Anne-Catherine Heinrich went to the large chest of drawers in one corner of the room, opened a middle drawer, took out a large sea-chart and laid it on the dining table. With his crutch, Rendall reached the table in two strides.

'When I was a boy,' said Thorfinn Rendall, 'and before I was recalled to the colours when the war began – when I was a whole man, in other words – I often sailed around the Flow and out into the waters beyond. I crossed to

Scotland itself many times, and once conned my own yawl to Shetland. So I'm not wholly ignorant of your craft, Captain.'

Rendall handed his crutch to Anne-Catherine, steadied himself on the table with one hand and pointed at the chart with the other.

'We are here, on Fara. You are anchored *there*, with Cava there, Flotta there and, of course, Hoy to our south and west. The wind is south-westerly and gusting, so you'd be ill advised to beat back for Graemsay Sound or Clestrain Sound, past Stromness – I take it you entered the Flow that way? Quite apart from having most probably to tack your way out, the local volunteers thereabouts will be quick to get into position and those channels are easy to cover. So you're left with easterly or south-easterly as your likeliest exits from the Flow. Now, you have all *these* channels between the southern islands and each other and, *here*, Holm Sound between Burray and Mainland, with Lamb Holm, here, in the midst of that channel. So you could simply take the most direct course upon the wind and either set your course that way or round the Calf of Flotta and Roan Head, *here*, and leave the Flow southerly, by way of Hoxa Sound. But the Volunteers will be expecting that too, Captain. I'll wager they'll already be setting up what artillery they possess on Hoxa Head, here, or thereabouts. And there's the other element – the Russian ship. If Captain Komarov feels inclined to chase you down, he'll sail from Kirkwall Bay by way of the String, here, through Shapinsay Sound, then come south-west between Deerness and Copinsay and strive to enter the Flow by way of Holm Sound or Water Sound. Much would depend on how quickly he can set sail from

Kirkwall, and that will probably depend on how willingly the Volunteers share their intelligence of your presence.'

Oh, Komarov would be inclined toward the pursuit, Philippe had no doubt of it, and doubly so if he somehow came to know the identity of his quarry. They had never been friends, and Komarov had always been inclined to utter disparaging remarks about the foreigners who came to offer their services to the Empress Catherine – Philippe, Admiral John Paul Jones, Admiral Samuel Grieg, all the others. No love was lost between Pavel Nikolaiovich Komarov and Philippe Kermorvant, Vicomte de Saint-Victor.

'So what do you advise, Major?'

'This course, here. By Gutter Sound and Weddel Sound, past Lyness and Hackness out into Cantick Sound. Once beyond Cantick Head you're out into the Pentland Firth. The open sea, Captain.'

Philippe studied the chart and the course that Rendall was proposing. It was all too confined, and although the course seemed to be clear of skerries and other obstacles, much of it was too close to land for his liking. If the Orkney Volunteers could set up field artillery in time on the coasts of Hoy or Flotta, or on the island called Switha that lay directly in the middle of the channel being proposed... And what if Thorfinn Rendall was not the amiable, honourable, grateful fellow he appeared to be? What if he was deliberately directing into a trap a ship, her captain and her crew, of a country that had inflicted upon him such shattering wounds?

There was no alternative. Any delay would increase the risk that the local volunteers would mobilise in full strength and attack the ship, or that Komarov would bring his ship around, block their escape and give him the glory of sinking the first enemy ship in the imminent war between Russia and France.

Philippe Kermorvant vowed that come what may, he would not hand Pavel Nikolaiovich Komarov that satisfaction.

CHAPTER TWENTY-THREE

Wilden was rowed across from *Sans Pareil*, anchored in the lee of the Île de Houat, and stepped onto the deck of HMS *Pomone* to the usual greeting from the side party. He had parted from Lord Hugh Seymour and his officers with a degree of regret. The Seymour he had encountered at sea, in his own command and in battle, had been an entirely different beast to the Seymour who sat on the Board of Admiralty and haunted the clubs of Saint James's. Lord Hugh, his lieutenants, and indeed all the men of *Sans Pareil*, had been brave men, fearless and loyal, truly the valiant tars of Old England lionised in popular songs. After their victories over *Le Formidable* and *Le Tigre*, he had witnessed them unhesitatingly pursue the monstrous French flagship, *Le Peuple*, and exchange broadsides with her. In truth, though, Wilden remembered little of the latter stages of the Battle of Groix, as Lord Bridport had apparently christened it. He dimly recalled the towering sides of *Le Peuple*, and the astonishment among Seymour's lieutenants when Bridport wore around and broke off the battle without securing the entire destruction of the French fleet, a reward that seemed to be well within his grasp having already taken three prizes before disengaging. Wilden only had thoughts for his fallen young friend, Midshipman Jack Kenton, whose body was committed to the sea somewhere north-west of Belle-Île. In due course he would raise Bridport's unaccountable behaviour with both the prime minister and the first lord of the Admiralty, and he would make an effort to obtain an address for Kenton's mother so he could write to her with an account of her son's kindness to him and his heroic death in his country's service. No, better still he would make it his business to find where she lived and call to pay his respects to her in person, giving her what account he could of the death of her son. For now, though, he had to turn his thoughts to other concerns and above all to the mission entrusted to him by William Pitt.

Wilden's new if very temporary berth was a smart forty-four-gun frigate, like Hugh Seymour's command, a prize taken from the French in the previous year, and her crew were drawn up in immaculate order to receive him. But he was immediately aware of a less expected sound than the bosun's whistle piping the still: that of voices raised below deck. Not just raised, in all truth. Two men were screaming at each other with occasional and unsuccessful interventions from others who were trying to mollify them. All of the voices spoke very loud, very agitated and very furious French.

Commodore Sir John Borlase Warren, the captain of *Pomone*, saluted Wilden, simultaneously raising his eyebrows in an expression that conveyed many centuries of English exasperation with their Gallic neighbours.

Wilden acknowledged both Warren's salute and his unspoken warning. He hoped that his own expression conveyed a sense of reassurance to the stalwart commodore.

For Edward, Lord Wilden, knew exactly why the most senior commanders of the French royalist expeditionary force were bellowing at each other like fishermen in an alehouse. This was the precise reason why the prime minister had sent him to Quiberon.

Warren led Wilden below to the great cabin of *Pomone*, the source of the fracas. There was no cessation of the argument, nor any diminution of the fury, as the commodore and the Admiralty lord stepped into the cabin. A few of the French royalist *emigrés* within turned to glance at the new arrivals, but otherwise the attention of every man present was fixed on the scene playing out before them.

A very tall, narrow-faced, bare-headed, notably tanned man of fifty or thereabouts stood in the middle of the cabin, screaming into the face of a shorter, slimmer, bewigged, sharper-featured but equally animated fellow who was perhaps ten years younger. Despite the educated but angry French they were speaking, or rather yelling, both wore the red uniforms of generals in the British Army. With only two exceptions, the newly arrived civilian Wilden and the blue-uniformed Warren, the other men in the cabin, to the number of a dozen or so, wore similar garb denoting various senior ranks.

'*I* am the commanding general of this entire expedition!' yelled the taller man, the Comte de Puisaye. 'Appointed by the regent himself! This whole project was my idea, my plan, my very—'

He became aware of Wilden's presence in the cabin, and the short, bewigged man on the receiving end of the tirade, the Comte d'Hervilly, took advantage of the interruption to smile a greeting.

'My Lord Wilden,' he said in English before reverting to his native tongue. 'Tell him if you please.'

Wilden took a deep breath. He had known this moment was likely to come since that hour in William

Pitt's company in a snow-blanketed Downing Street. They both knew that the plan they had devised, and had refined in the intervening months, would inevitably lead to such a scene as this, and for that reason they had taken every possible measure to ensure it remained a secret until the last possible moment.

Wilden tried to imagine that Billy Pitt was standing in his place and guessing at what the prime minister would say and do. *Calmness, Ned*, Pitt had said. *Cool the tempers. Defuse the situation.*

'*Messieurs*,' said Wilden in his accentless French, 'I suggest that we discuss this matter without an audience.'

The Frenchmen in the cabin, be they generals, colonels or the usual gaggle of staff officers, looked outraged and some were clearly ready to protest loudly and vehemently, but the bewigged man nodded reluctantly and the others began to shuffle out, murmuring angrily. French they might be, within touching distance of French soil they might be, but they were aboard a British warship, wearing British uniforms, and in the presence of a lord of the British Admiralty acting as emissary for the British prime minister, and that trumped everything.

When he was alone with Puisaye and Hervilly, Wilden strode to the chair at the head of Warren's table, sat down, and beckoned the two red-coated generals to sit in turn, one on either side of him.

'Now, *messieurs*, I take it the matter that agitates you is the question of the command?'

The tall man, the Comte de Puisaye, bridled at that.

'There is no question of the command,' he said haughtily. 'I command. This entire expedition has been undertaken at my instigation. It is my brainchild. That is recognised and understood by all. I, and I alone, have the confidence of the Chouans. I have the commission of the regent, the Comte de Provence, to be commander-in-chief of the Royal and Catholic Army of France. I have the approval of your own prime minister, Lord Wilden!'

'Up to a point,' said Wilden calmly, 'but so does the Comte d'Hervilly here. And he holds a British commission, not one from the Regent of France. A commission signed by both the said prime minister and His Majesty King George the Third.'

Puisaye went very pale. Hervilly sniffed, a trace of a smirk on his lips.

'A dual command?' blustered Puisaye, recovering from the argument-crushing deployment of King George's name. 'No, sir! Such a thing offends every law of war!'

'And what do you know of the laws of war, eh?' scoffed Hervilly, speaking up at last. 'Who is the soldier here, in this cabin? Lord Wilden knows. William Pitt knows. *You* know, Puisaye, even if you're too damn proud to admit it. Every man in this expedition knows. I fought in America, I commanded the cavalry of the late king's guard. I'm a soldier to my bones. But you, Puisaye? A politician through and through! It's not long since you were proud to serve in the National Convention of the so-called Republic and to call yourself a Girondin and a revolutionary, and all the world knows it!'

There was the crux of the matter. As Pitt and Wilden had discussed many times, the truth was that there was relatively little to choose between Puisaye and Hervilly in terms of military experience. But while Puisaye undoubtedly had the stronger contacts and greater credibility among the Chouan rebels, the fact was that his political career until rather too recently had been exactly as Hervilly described. The *emigrés* were composed overwhelmingly of men who had narrowly escaped revolutionary France with their lives, who had lost their estates and whose brothers, fathers or sons had perished on the guillotine. To such men, the Comte de Puisaye was anathema. There would have been no issue if the originally designated commander-in-chief had sailed with the expedition, for the credentials of the Comte d'Artois were unchallengeable. A prince of the Bourbon blood royal, Artois was brother to the guillotined Louis the Sixteenth, uncle to the imprisoned and nominal Louis the Seventeenth, brother to the titular Regent of France, the Comte de Provence. Artois would undoubtedly be regarded with awe and reverence by the Chouans and the *emigrés* alike, though what the rest of France would make of a man with a reputation for unremitting fanaticism and bigotry was a moot point. But pressing, if unspecified, matters had detained Artois elsewhere, and that left Ned Wilden struggling to keep the peace between the two men commanding in his stead.

'You don't know Brittany,' Puisaye retaliated, almost spitting the words at Hervilly. 'I've been with the Chouans, I've fought with them, I know their leaders intimately—'

'*Messieurs, messieurs!*' said Wilden impatiently, raising his hand to quieten them. 'No one doubts the estimable qualities that both of you possess. I do not, and the prime minister certainly does not. But Monsieur le Comte d'Hervilly is correct in one respect. He is a soldier, so our feeling, the prime minister and I, is that he should bear responsibility for what I may call the soldierly elements of the expedition. The command of the *emigré* troops, the disembarkation itself, the dispositions against enemy positions, decisions on the deployment of individual units, all such matters will fall to the Comte d'Hervilly. The direction of the greater strategy of the campaign – objectives, supplies, above all the alliance with the Chouans – rests with Monsieur le Comte de Puisaye. Nothing could be clearer, *messieurs*.'

Puisaye grimaced and shook his head.

'Nothing clearer to an Englishman, perhaps,' he said angrily.

But Puisaye was defeated. He might boast of the two – no – three hundred thousand Chouans he claimed to have at his beck and call, but he knew they would be nothing without the binding force of the *emigré* army and the resources of the British state, notably the funds that had launched the expedition and the raw power of the Royal Navy epitomised by *Pomone* herself.

When all was weighed, Puisaye knew all that. He and Hervilly continued to glower at each other and at Wilden, the representative of Britain and above all of her prime minister, but at least the shouting had stopped. Wilden doubted whether the matter had been settled. Indeed, there was every prospect that his intervention would make matters worse, as he had warned Pitt it would. But that could not be helped now.

CHAPTER TWENTY-FOUR

Wilden stood alongside Sir John Warren on the quarterdeck of *Pomone* as the invasion force, guided only by the leads and compasses of the leading ships, moved slowly north, further into Quiberon Bay. It was gone midnight, conditions still quite light just a few days after the summer solstice, and the fog that had plagued their approach to the bay was finally lifting. Lights were visible away to port in the small villages along the peninsula of Quiberon and the compact fortress that stood on isthmus connecting the peninsula to the mainland. The fort, renamed Sans-Culotte by the revolutionaries, was visible from *Pomone* as an ominous low mass, dominating access to and from Quiberon itself. The fort was too far away to impede the landing so for now the expeditionary force would avoid it, although it would obviously have to be secured early in the campaign.

Pomone and the first of the transports already had their boats alongside, and French officers were issuing orders to their men to begin embarking into these landing craft. The noise with which sailors and soldiers alike undertook their duties surprised Wilden. Surely the enemy ashore, or at least those in the fort, would be alerted? But he swiftly realised that it did not matter one jot how much noise the invading army made. A fleet of nearly seventy ships could hardly approach the French coast unobserved, and the troops' natural excitement at setting foot once again in their native land was entirely understandable. So at about one in the morning, amid a cacophony of chatter and cheering, the first of the boats set off for the coast of France, Hervilly himself in the headmost of them. There were mutterings among some of the other French officers that Hervilly had delayed the landing for twenty-four hours while the bay was properly reconnoitred, but Wilden ignored them. Hervilly's caution was merely proof of his being a sensible and meticulous general, while the *emigré* officers were still in shock at the turn of events which had seen an English lord of the Admiralty suddenly appear among them and abruptly overturn what they had come to regard as their chain of command. Of the Comte de Puisaye, still smarting at the perceived affront to his authority, there was no sign.

The first landing boats grounded in two coves just to the west of the village of Carnac. From *Pomone*, Wilden and Warren heard some scattered, piecemeal musket fire, but it was too sporadic to suggest a vast defending force willing to fight to the death. The royalist fire that replied to it was more intense and came from both sides of the republican position. By the time the first slight glow of the sun was visible through the clearing mist, the royalist bridgehead ashore seemed to be firmly established. Through his telescope, Wilden could see only the white standard of the Bourbons flying at the landing places and from the sand dunes fringing them.

'So now we see if the promises were true, my lord,' said Warren. 'Now we see if the Chouans come in.'

'Then it's time for me to go ashore, Sir John. The Chouans will have their own commanders. I fear some days of arguing over protocols and precedence might lie ahead.'

'Concerns I am deeply relieved to leave with you, my lord,' said the smiling Warren. 'But, of course, the prime minister and your colleagues at the Admiralty would rightly condemn me if I did not see to your safety. I've detailed two Marines to attend you ashore.'

'Surely there's no need for that, Sir John? Our allied Frenchmen are so numerous!'

'Numerous and allied they might be, my lord, but with respect, they're still French. So I pray you, sir, indulge me in this.'

Wilden inclined his head.

'As you will, Sir John.'

By the time the sun was fully up, the system for landing the expeditionary force was well established. Boats went in an unremitting procession from the ships to the landing places, then went back immediately to collect another contingent of soldiers, stores or ammunition. The Frenchmen, overjoyed to be returning at last to their native land, sang as the boats crossed the calm waters of Quiberon Bay. But each boat, each *emigré* regiment, had its own song, and the invasion of France swiftly turned into a discordant cacophony of competing scurrilous ditties.

Wilden disembarked from *Pomone* at a little after eight in the company of his two Marine guards, a burly, garrulous Scot named Jardine and a sullen Irishman called Lynch. They were to go ashore with a boatful of *emigré* troops from Hervilly's own regiment who barely acknowledged their presence, so intent were they on the goal that was now so tantalisingly close. Many men were weeping as the shore of France drew nearer, and when the first of them leapt ashore as the boat grounded, they fell to their knees and kissed the sand. Others sang the royal anthem, the 'Marche Henri Quatre'. It was an emotional scene, and even Ned Wilden found himself moved.

There was noise from the east, the sounds of a large number of people on the move toward the landing beach. The Frenchmen must have heard it, but they showed no sign of reacting or forming themselves into any sort of military formation. Wilden exchanged a glance with Jardine, the older and more experienced of his two escorts, but the Scot looked equally as puzzled. Were they about to die at the hands of a Republican counter-attack, slaughtered on the sand before they could even set foot on proper ground?

But the republicans would not be shouting '*Vive le roi!*' in happy and excited voices. The republicans would not be sending out women and children to fight their battles. The first of the newcomers emerged from behind a bend in the road that ran from the forest down to the beach. A half-dozen young women were the first to appear, screaming with delight when they saw the first line of royalist pickets and throwing themselves into the arms of the nearest troops. A gaggle of matrons, all weeping, then a human flood of peasants of all ages, although women and the old predominated. But there were younger men too, and many of these ran into the water, some even going in chest high, to help pull the army's boats ashore. Despite the imprecations of their officers, many of the troops forming on the beach ran forward to embrace the huge, ecstatic welcoming party of native Bretons.

Wilden saw Hervilly at the other end of the beach, surrounded by a gaggle of his staff officers and a line of sentries struggling to keep the Breton women from mobbing the would-be liberator. Wilden walked over to him.

'A splendid reception, Monsieur le Comte!' said Wilden cheerfully.

Hervilly shrugged. 'No more than their duty, my lord. They are mere peasants, after all. But Brittany, more than anywhere else in France, has always been loyal to the Bourbon kings. Once the Chouans come in… Puisaye says they're bringing seventy thousand men to join us and that there are another two hundred thousand of them ready to rise all over Brittany and the Vendée once we give them the lead. Imagine that, my lord! We shall sweep all before us. On to Lorient, then Vannes, then Paris! Death to the Republic, the Most Christian King seated back in Versailles! Truly, you are part of a crusade, Lord Wilden.'

Hervilly gestured across the beach. *Emigré* troops were embracing and being embraced by peasant women as though they were long-parted lovers. A few were dancing for joy, and there were repeated shouts of *'Vive le roi!'* But there were unsettling sights too. A tall, proud-looking staff officer pushed away a young, dirty-faced woman who tried to embrace him. A couple of privates from the *emigré* army exchanged angry words and then punches with three of the local men. But the rare notes of discord were lost amid the overwhelming air of jubilation. Notes of reverence, too, especially when the ancient Bishop of Dol came ashore accompanied by two dozen priests, a ceremonial cross borne before them by a young *emigré* officer. The priests sang lustily a hymn that Wilden recognised as a '*Te Deum*'. Exiles and Breton natives alike made the sign of the cross or prostrated themselves. The return of a bishop and a crucifix symbolised like nothing else the return of the old religion to France, and it triggered another wave of sobbing and wailing.

Beyond, out in the bay and seemingly oblivious to the scenes of rejoicing ashore, a couple of Warren's smaller vessels were manoeuvring closer to the shore to unleash their batteries against Fort Sans-Culotte, while the expedition's flotilla of boats continued to ferry ashore the men of the Catholic and Royal Army of France. But of the commander-in-chief of the expedition, the Comte de Puisaye, there was still no sign.

Hervilly was standing on the beach, issuing orders to his subordinates, when Wilden heard a new sound in the distance. Jardine, the old soldier, heard it at the same time and nudged his younger comrade, Marine Lynch. But Wilden knew the sound well enough. He heard it every day from his office at the Admiralty building in Whitehall when troops were practising drill on Horse Guards or parading down Whitehall proper. The sound of drums giving a martial beat.

A new shout went up among the huge crowd of people thronging the beach.

'Les Chouans!'

The Chouans were coming to join forces with their brethren. They poured down the roads, so many of them that they spilled out into the forests fringing the beach and emerged suddenly from the trees. Wilden and his escorts watched in open-mouthed astonishment as more and more of the armed Breton rebels crowded onto the beaches of Carnac to welcome their exiled comrades back to France.

'So, this is an army, then?' said Jardine, gazing critically at the astonishing combinations of clothing and arms borne by the Chouans. Then he remembered himself and added a mumbled, 'My lord'.

As a fighting force, the Chouans were certainly unimpressive. Puisaye had led Wilden to expect a vast legion, a properly constituted army, yet the men before him were raw peasants wearing clothes that were little better than rags and carrying a bewildering variety of weapons that ranged from modern muskets to scythes brought straight from the fields and halberds that looked so ancient that they might have seen service in the Hundred Years War. Many carried no weapons at all, the only marks that identified them as soldiers being the white cockades in their hats or the Sacred Hearts on their chests. These, it seemed, were the men who were going to liberate France from the atheist fanatics and restore both a Bourbon King and the True Church.

Some of the Chouans were on horseback, and one rider detached himself from what appeared to be his regiment to ride toward Wilden. He was quite a young man, certainly younger than Wilden himself, and unlike almost all the men he seemingly commanded and those of the *emigré* army, he wore what had clearly once been part of the white uniform of a captain in the old royal army.

'You, *monsieur*!' he cried. 'Can you direct me to Monsieur le General the Comte de Puisaye?'

'I cannot, sir. The comte is still aboard HMS *Pomone*, I believe. General the Comte d'Hervilly, however, is just over yonder.'

'I don't know any Hervilly,' said the mounted Chouan contemptuously. 'I'll only deal with Puisaye. But you, sir – you're English?'

'I am. I am Wilden.'

'Wilden who? Wilden what?'

'Lord Wilden, sir.'

'*Lord* Wilden? I'm honoured, my lord.' The Breton grinned, then looked thoughtful. 'Y'know, I saw your name in a book quite recently. You're some sort of cousin to the Vicomte de Saint-Victor, no? Your family has an entire chapter devoted to it in a book of genealogies in the library of the Chateau de Brechelean.'

Ned Wilden was curious to know how this Chouan commander had been in the home of his French cousin, Philippe Kermorvant, whom Wilden had tried unsuccessfully to recruit for the royalist cause and therefore for that of Great Britain. Perhaps he had even met Philippe there, for as far as Wilden knew his cousin had obtained no new command since he had lost that of a frigate in the Mediterranean. But social proprieties had to be observed first.

'You have the advantage of me, sir.'

The Chouan swung himself out of the saddle, grimaced as he landed on the sand, suggesting the presence of a recent wound, and presented himself before Wilden, bowing his head and then holding out his hand in the English fashion.

'Then allow me to enlighten you, my lord. My name is Georges Cozanet. I have the honour to hold a commission as a colonel in the Catholic and Royal Army from His Royal Highness the Regent.'

On hearing Cozanet's rank, Jardine and Lynch came to attention. Wilden took the proffered hand. A colonel of the Chouans, no less, and one who had been at cousin Philippe's home very recently. How strangely the world sometimes turned.

CHAPTER TWENTY-FIVE

The royalist army was striking its first blow. Several days of establishing a perimeter, digging in, landing the remaining troops and supplies from Warren's fleet in the bay and, in Wilden's case, fruitless shuttling between the French commanders and trying to smooth injured sensibilities, gave way to a sudden burst of decisive action. Fort Sans-Culotte, on the west side of the isthmus, lay in its rear, preventing land access to the rest of the Quiberon peninsula, and had to be taken. At five in the morning, two of Warren's frigates moved across the bay to attack a republican battery as a diversion while the commodore, with two of the other frigates and a number of the transports, landed Puisaye and several thousand Chouans and regular royalist troops on the beach to the south of the fort. Meanwhile, Hervilly, with several thousand more men, advanced onto the isthmus from the north, encircling the republican garrison. Wilden rode with them, alongside Cozanet at the head of his regiment. He had held several conferences with Hervilly and Puisaye, both separately and together, trying to reconcile them to each other and to the notion of a divided command, but to no avail. Perhaps a victory, in the form of the capture of the fort, would prove more successful in reconciling the mutually antagonistic royalist generals, although Wilden suspected this would be wishful thinking. Riding astride an excellent Breton horse, breathing the fresh breezes coming off the sea as all around him the royalist forces manoeuvred into position, was a welcome diversion from the disillusioning reality of acting as the prime minister's personal envoy.

Unlike many of the French officers – indeed, very much unlike Puisaye and Hervilly – Cozanet proved a welcoming and amiable fellow who was perfectly willing to tolerate what must have been the irritating presence of an Englishman of indeterminate but clearly eminent status and authority. He was also happy to describe his encounter with Wilden's cousin Philippe and his sister-in-law, Leonore, and even provided Wilden with an item of intelligence that might prove useful. It was no surprise, thought Ned Wilden, that a man of Philippe's experience and merit had been offered a privateer, and no surprise that the ship in question was set for a cruise in the North Sea and Baltic. But the name of the mission's instigator, a Swiss merchant domiciled in France named Heinrich, intrigued Wilden. He had heard that name before in an entirely different context, he was sure of it. He had a vague recollection of a night at Brooks's a couple of years earlier and a tale told by Windham, the war secretary, of something that occurred when the Duke of York's army occupied Valenciennes. But the claret had flowed too well that evening, and he could not now remember the detail.

The recollection was still eluding him as he and Cozanet reined in before the fort, beyond the range of whatever artillery it contained. Hervilly's force was forming up, occupying the whole breadth of the isthmus. The *emigré* regiments were to the fore, the disorganised masses of the Chouans positioned behind them. Hervilly had made it very clear that he did not wish for any intermingling of the different elements of the royalist army, at least not until he was confident in the qualities of his Breton allies.

'They can't have more than a few hundred men in there,' said Cozanet, pointing toward the low grey ramparts of Fort Sans-Culotte. 'There's only one outcome today, Lord Wilden. It just depends how long it takes the garrison commander to accept it.'

The royalist troops, now formed in their ranks, made ready for an assault, a few pieces of field artillery being brought into position as a makeshift battery while one of Warren's ships, the *Anson*, lay menacingly off the coast immediately to the west of the fort. Wilden had never witnessed a siege, nor even seen land artillery fired in anger, and felt both excitement and dread at the prospect. This was nearer and more intimate than the fight he had witnessed aboard HMS *Sans Pareil*, where most of the men involved on both sides had been hidden from view, concealed within the hulls of their ships. Here, though, the long lines of royalist troops were all around him, thousands of men with a common purpose, and it was possible with the naked eye to see the men lining the ramparts of the fort. Cozanet's only emotion seemed to be impatience, an eagerness to be among the republican defenders to commit as much slaughter as possible on them. But for nearly an hour, nothing happened. The royalists continued to make their dispositions. The republicans looked down from their ramparts, the Tricolour flying limply above their heads. Then the fort's gate opened and a single officer rode out under a flag of truce, making for the royalist lines.

'So the horse trading begins already,' said Cozanet as the horseman approached. 'Disappointing. But they must have recognised their position is hopeless. They'll want terms, Hervilly'll demand unconditional surrender, no quarter given without it, the Blues will prevaricate and hold out for better. The usual chess game of a capitulation.'

They were too far from Hervilly to hear the exchange, but it must have proceeded very much as Cozanet forecast. The enemy officer was before Hervilly for only a few minutes before he turned his horse and rode back toward the fort, far too short an interval for any meaningful parley to take place.

'*Et voila*,' said Cozanet a little while later as the Tricolour came down and a large white flag was hoisted in its stead. 'Let us pray, my lord, that all of our victories prove so painless.'

They rode into the surrendered fort with Hervilly and the vanguard of his army, and stood close to him as he took the surrender of the garrison commander. The Blue troops laid down their weapons, and the royalists cheered loudly as the white banner with fleur-de-lis ran up the flagpole of the former Fort Sans-Culotte, which immediately reverted to its original name of Fort Penthièvre.

The royalists were barely beginning to savour their victory when there was a commotion at the gates of the fort, and the Comte de Puisaye, tall and erect upon a large black stallion, rode in at the head of his own vanguard.

'Wilden!' he bawled as he dismounted. 'Lord Wilden! Why did you not prevent this travesty?'

'Your army has just won its first victory, sir,' said Wilden, marshalling all his dignity despite the insult offered to it. 'How, pray, can that be a travesty?'

'Why, *I* should have accepted the surrender, of course! As the commander-in-chief of this expedition! As the representative of the King of France! Not *him*!'

He nodded grudgingly toward Hervilly, whom he otherwise failed to acknowledge in any way.

Wilden, exasperated and amused in equal measure, struggled to maintain an equable disposition.

'Surely, *monsieur*, all that matters is that the fort has surrendered? That it is yours?'

'*Ours*, Lord Wilden,' said Puisaye, barely concealing his rage and impatience. 'It has surrendered to both kings. It is a victory for the alliance I negotiated with Monsieur Pitt. We must hoist your flag, sir! We must break out the English colours alongside those of King Louis'!'

Hervilly was within earshot but he made no move to oppose Puisaye's order. As it was, Puisaye beckoned to Wilden's two Marine guards, the only British troops present in the fort, and one of the comte's aides presented them with a folded Union flag. At a somewhat bewildered nod from Wilden, Jardine and Lynch went up to the ramparts, and after a few minutes the familiar red, white and blue broke out alongside the Bourbon colours. A makeshift band, formed from some of the *emigrés* and Chouans with a priest incongruously playing the trumpet, delivered an utterly appalling, almost unrecognisable rendition of 'God Save the King'. Despite the awkwardness of the situation, Wilden felt a thrill of pride as he watched the flag unfurl. Billy Pitt would be delighted if he could witness it. The king would undoubtedly be in ecstasies, and certainly would be when he eventually heard of it. Instead, that day in the west of Brittany, Ned Wilden was a surrogate for them both.

The victorious generals and their British guest took a late but triumphant breakfast in the large room that had served until that morning as the republican officers' mess. A tricorn hat that still sported a red, white and blue cockade was ceremonially burned, but the laughter that accompanied the incident was the only jollity of the occasion. As was now both custom and a diplomatic necessity, Wilden sat between Hervilly and Puisaye, who were still barely able to look at each other. He made conversation with each in turn, although both men tended to be of the school that elevated themselves as the sole topic for discussion. Cozanet, an altogether more interesting and collegiate companion, was at the far end of a table peopled exclusively by roughly dressed Chouan officers, a marked contrast to the immaculate and brand new red uniforms of the *emigrés* who clustered around the men of authority.

There was a moment when Puisaye was talking to the Bishop of Dol, on his left, Hervilly to the Chouan leader Charette, when a movement at Cozanet's side caught Wilden's eye. A Breton, presumably one of Cozanet's own men, was presenting him with a note. There was a mumbled conversation, then Cozanet used his knife to break the seal of the message. He read it and stared at it for several seconds, his expression darkening. Then he stood and walked over to stand in front of the table where Wilden sat, presenting the note to Puisaye with a deep bow of reverence. The nominal commander of the expeditionary force read it, blinked, and nodded to Cozanet, who returned to his place.

Puisaye stood, tapping a spoon on the table for order. The royalist officers, even Hervilly, fell silent.

'Word has been received,' said Puisaye, holding up the note, 'from our friends in Paris, corroborated by a number of unimpeachable authorities. Alas, my friends, our worst fears have come true. The rumours are confirmed beyond all doubt. The king is dead.'

The royalist and Chouan generals lowered their eyes and crossed themselves. The aged Bishop of Dol began to murmur a Latin prayer. Wilden had never felt more of a foreigner. Some of the French officers were in tears, even though the king they mourned had never reigned over France as Louis the Seventeenth and had died in a filthy, disease-ridden prison cell in Paris at the age of just ten. But there was ever a permanence, a relentlessness, to royalty, and at length Puisaye loudly and solemnly articulated the words that had to be spoken.

'*Le roi et mort,*' he announced gravely and deliberately. '*Vive le roi!*'

Hervilly, the Bishop, Cozanet and all the other officers stood and repeated the words. Wilden mumbled them, but whether the newly proclaimed Louis the Eighteenth, the next youngest brother of the dead boy-king's guillotined father, would ever reign over France, and whether it would be this very expedition, this very army, that restored him to his throne, were distinctly moot points. But it was not a time to air such doubts.

'*Vive le roi!*' said Wilden, albeit very nearly inaudibly.

CHAPTER TWENTY-SIX

La Verité weighed and began to move from her anchorage off the north-westerly point of the island of Fara. It was still the middle of the afternoon, and the ship had been in the Flow for less than twenty-four hours. In that short time, though, every single assumption and every single element underpinning the voyage had been overturned. The entire mission was a sham, an insane odyssey conceived by one vain, arrogant, perverted and obsessive man to take back a woman he regarded as his private property. He had been defeated in his purpose by the duplicity of his own son, who wanted the same woman for himself. Philippe and every man in the crew had been pawns of the Heinrichs, but now the younger Heinrich, along with the pawn he had employed, lay dead in an outbuilding on an obscure Scottish island.

As the sails unfurled and the ship slowly began to gain momentum, Philippe tried to devise a course of action. The cruise into the North Sea and Baltic, taking prizes galore, seemed a chimera, a vanishing illusion that had never truly been real. Would the men now obey orders to sail on such a voyage? What guarantee did they have that Antoine Heinrich would pay them any of the proceeds if they did succeed in taking prizes? Enough of the men had been present to witness what happened in Fara House, and they would undoubtedly have reported it graphically to their messmates. They had witnessed the suicide of Heinrich's son, and there was every chance that Heinrich *père* would blame them – would blame Philippe especially – for the death. They had failed to bring back his wife, the object of his all-consuming lust, and they had taken the part of an enemy of both Antoine Heinrich and the French Republic, the part of a British officer, Major Thorfinn Rendall. Heinrich *père* might have been lying about his impressive connections in the National Convention and the Committee of Public Safety, just as he had lied about the actual purpose of the cruise of *La Verité*, but Philippe suspected that in this particular instance, the Swiss *armateur* had been speaking no more than the simple and deeply uncomfortable truth.

None of it, of course, would matter one jot if they did not escape the labyrinth formed by the Orkney isles, the potential opposition from the local volunteer troops, and above all the prospect of Pavel Nikolaiovich Komarov and his ship, somewhere out there beyond the land masses to the east.

'Too deep for the lead,' said Ugarte as the leadsman delivered his report. 'A good channel, Captain.'

Philippe, drawn back from his swirling thoughts, looked at the dark and massive hills of the island of Hoy, their presence filling the entire landscape to the west.

'*Droit comme ça, timmonier!*' he cried. Steady as she goes, helm.

He allowed himself a last glance over the port quarter, to Fara House, where Anne-Catherine Heinrich and Thorfinn Rendall were free to resume their strange yet undoubtedly deep and sincere romance. Another thought of Leonore came into his mind, but he could not imagine how the increasingly frequent thoughts he had of her could possibly have anything to do with what he had witnessed that day. Perhaps, though, the unburied corpses of Augustin Heinrich and Marcus Drever testified to the power of the love of Finn Rendall and his Anne-Catherine, just as the execution of his own half-brother Alexandre—

'Sail ho!'

'Where away?'

Ugarte was pointing through the broad channel to port, between the islands of Fara and Flotta. Philippe raised his telescope and saw at once what the lookout had identified. There, off to the north-east, over toward the shore of the island called Mainland and emerging from the channel Thorfinn Rendall had identified on his chart as Holm Sound, was a large warship, completing a tack into the teeth of the strong south-westerly.

It was a ship and a flag that Philippe recognised. *Drakon*, heavy frigate of forty-four guns, thirty of them eighteen-pounders. Over three hundred men. Flying from her ensign staff, a diagonal blue cross upon a white ground. The flag under which Philippe himself had sailed. The flag under which he had commanded. The flag of Russia.

It was Komarov.

Moments later, sight of the *Drakon* was lost behind the low isle of Flotta. A few curious folk who would have been counted as peasants in France watched *La Verité* from that shore, but ships, unlike the cattle grazing all around them, were of little concern in the scheme of their lives.

Philippe tried to keep *Drakon* clear of his mind. He went to the chart table, checked his course again against the compass, and ordered a slight course change more to south by east to ensure that *La Verité* cleared the island of Switha. He dared not order all sail yet, not until they were clearer, but Komarov would have more open water and might be able to make more sail than the corsair. It would be a close race, he feared. Every moment he expected and dreaded to see the bows of the Russian frigate emerge from behind the southernmost point of Flotta, the promontory the charts named as Stanger Head.

'Courses yet, captain?' asked Ugarte, who had to be feeling the same emotions.

'A little longer under topsails alone, Lieutenant. If we still had Drever – but we do not, and for now the rocks of the shoreline are a bigger threat than the frigate.'

'*Commande, mon Capitaine.*'

The men of *La Verité* were at the guns. There was very nearly universal silence as the ship moved through the Sound, making for the channel to the west and south of the small island called Switha. Every man of the corsair knew that if the Russian ship got ahead of them, the battle would be brief, murderous, and many of them would not survive it.

The corsair's bosun, Medan, presented himself before Philippe.

'Which flag should we hoist, Captain? That American one again?'

'No, Citizen. If we're to fight, let it be under our own colours.'

'*Commande, mon Capitaine!*'

A few moments, the *Tricolore* was hoisted from the mizzen shrouds. The strong south-westerly caught it immediately, and the familiar red, white and blue of the Republic spilled out to cheers from the men on deck.

'Helm four points more to starboard!' Philippe commanded.

The bows of the corsair came more southerly. The open sea was now plainly visible dead ahead, and there was still no sign of Komarov. Switha, the island ahead of them, the last island in the archipelago, was relatively low. Surely if *Drakon* was still behind it, her topmasts would be visible above the rough pasture and low, turf-roofed cottages that occupied the majority of the island?

The lookout's urgent cry—

Philippe, Ugarte and the other men on deck saw the frigate over to the north-east, sailing in the midst of the channel between Flotta and the promontory Thorfinn Rendall had identified as Hoxa Head. Komarov was taking no chances, not risking a course that took him closer to the islands. Perhaps he had no local pilot, or no source of advice like the magnanimous Thorfinn Rendall. But there was movement on the frigate, and Philippe trained his telescope on her. Komarov's crew were setting more sail and manning their guns ready for action. Philippe saw the eyes of his men turning to him, pleading for an immediate response. But *La Verité* was in a narrower channel, there were headlands to port and starboard, there might still be uncharted rocks...

Ugarte gestured toward the island called Switha. Men in red uniforms were hauling three – no four – field guns into position on the south-western shore. Somehow the Volunteer regiment of the islands had got some artillery across to the island and were setting up a makeshift battery.

Caution to the winds.

'Toutes voiles dehors!' Philippe bellowed, to be seconded by Ugarte and the other officers. All sail.

Men went to their designated ropes and very nearly the full spread of the corsair's canvas unfurled. *La Verité* was sailing south-south-east, the wind favourable between west by south and west-south-west, and the ship picked up speed rapidly.

'Master gunner!' cried Philippe.

Vuillermoz presented himself and saluted.

'Oui, mon Capitaine!'

'Larboard battery, Citizen. Get those fellows over there on the island to keep their damned heads down. Fire at your discretion!'

'Commande!'

Before Vuillermoz could give the commands to his gun crews, one of the guns on Switha fired a single shot. The ball went high, punching a hole in the main topsail, and before the enemy gunners could fire another the larboard battery of *La Verité* opened up, very nearly in unison.

'Very good, Master Gunner!' shouted Philippe.

Heirs to the ferocious Northmen of old they may have been, as Thorfinn Rendall had claimed, but the Volunteers on Switha, at least, evidently had no stomach for a fight against such a manifestly more powerful battery as that carried by *La Verité*. Having tasted the power of the corsair's broadside, they were already abandoning their positions and running for cover. But they would be no more than farmers and tradesmen given the most rudimentary military training while all the regiments of the regular army, and even the county militias, were committed to the campaigns against France.

Komarov's gun crews on *Drakon* would be an entirely different proposition, but only if *Drakon* caught *La Verité*. Philippe turned his attention back to the Russian frigate. Komarov had his studdingsails aloft, trying to seize the advantage of every breath of the brisk wind coming from his starboard beam. *Drakon* was a fearsome sight, and he could see several of the men of the corsair staring at her silently. But in one sense, they were equal. These waters would be just as unfamiliar to Komarov as they were to Philippe, Ugarte and their men. Perhaps Komarov had aboard a local pilot who could cancel the advantage Philippe had obtained from Thorfinn Rendall's generous imparting of local knowledge, but it was by no means certain.

There was yet another element to the equation. Philippe had served in Russian warships. He had commanded a frigate in the Empress Catherine's service, albeit a much smaller one than *Drakon*. The Russian ship was much older than both his *Strela* and his current command, and Philippe knew from his own experience that the Russian navy, made complacent by the relatively benign waters of the Baltic and the Black Sea, devoted less attention to the maintenance of its ships than the British or even the French. All things being equal, *Drakon*'s hull would be more foul than the newly built *La Verité*. The frigate was, or ought to be, much slower than the sleek new corsair. But if they were not equal, or if Thorfinn Rendall's instructions proved false and *La Verité* grounded, and the corsair felt the weight of the Russian frigate's vastly heavier broadside...

'He's coming to starboard,' said Ugarte. 'Reckons he can catch us.'

'Then we shall disabuse him of the notion, Lieutenant Ugarte. *Bonnettes!* Studdingsails!'

It was still a gamble. They were still relatively close to the shore of the island of Hoy. But it was time for *La Verité*'s paces to stand comparison with those of *Drakon*.

Commands were shouted. The studdingsails unfurled and were sheeted home. The leadsman's regular calls told Philippe there was ample water under the hull, and he had a fleeting idle thought to the effect that this vast natural harbour, this Scapa Flow, could hold many thousands of ships in perfect safety. The English and French navies in their entireties could be accommodated within it, probably many times over. But why would great fleets ever have cause to come to such a remote, insignificant place?

Before the corsair cleared the last headland and reached the open sea, Philippe allowed himself a quick backward glance instead of keeping all his attention focused on the oncoming *Drakon*. He had one last sight of Fava, and wondered how the lives of Anne-Catherine Heinrich and Thorfinn Rendall would play out. Somehow, he knew their love would overcome every obstacle, even another attempt by Antoine Heinrich to recapture his lost wife, if the Switzer was deranged enough to make one. Philippe had known such love once, ached to know it again, and envied them. Then he turned back to focus solely on the Russian frigate.

For perhaps half an hour, the outcome was in the balance. The corsair and Komarov's command were on convergent courses, but Philippe's freedom of manoeuvre was constrained by the need to sail well clear of the headlands where the local volunteers might have set up batteries. One lucky shot from one of those, one hit that slowed the faster corsair, and *La Verité* might indeed give the arrogant, erratic Komarov the honour of the first victory by a Russian warship during the war. Philippe said little, leaving the minute-by-minute commands to Ugarte, who was more than competent for the task. Instead, Philippe kept his telescope trained on the familiar lines and black-and-gold painted hull of *Drakon*, switching frequently between her and the headlands. There was a battery on the promontory Rendall had identified as Hoxa Head, the red-uniformed troops manning it standing and watching the sea-chase playing out before them, but the corsair was already out of their range. That left *Drakon*, still coming down the Flow upon the wind. Komarov would not know who his opponent was, but he was not a man who would be sentimental over past acquaintances. Probably the opposite: Pavel Nickolaiovich Komarov was not a man who cared much for foreigners not born on the holy soil of Mother Russia, and to whom Philippe Kermorvant would also be a traitor who preferred the cause of an atheist, regicide republic to that of monarchy and the Church. No, if anything Komarov would relish the prospect of blasting his former comrade-in-arms to the hell proclaimed by the Holy Orthodox Church.

There were more agonising minutes. Another turn of the ship's glass. Another eternity of staring through the telescope. But slowly, so very slowly, *La Verité* began to pull ahead of the straining *Drakon*, still out of range astern. Every minute, the corsair's bow edged a little further into open water. Komarov would keep up the pursuit if only for form's sake, but he would already know it was futile. He was stretching every inch of canvas to the very limit, but to no avail. By nightfall, or rather the half-gloom that prevailed in that latitude at midsummer, the Russian frigate was a long way astern, *La Verité* already well clear of the Pentland Firth and out into the broad expanse of the North Sea. Before dawn, with the Russian frigate no longer in sight, Philippe would give the order to alter course toward their destination. First, though, he had to decide on where that destination would be.

PART THREE

CHAPTER TWENTY-SEVEN

La Verité, under topsails alone, glided upon the waters of the Texel seagate on a bright and calm summer's morning. The large, flat island of Texel itself lay immediately to the north, the first and largest in the string of Frisian Islands that fringed the coasts of Germany and The Netherlands like a necklace. On the south side of the broad channel was the small town and naval depot called The Helder, which stood upon the northernmost tip of the sometime province of Holland. Philippe could make out half-formed hulls upon the stocks, and behind them the masts of men-of-war already in commission. The Helder was protected by a barrier of forts that stretched across the low-lying peninsula, and from these flew the flag of the newborn Batavian Republic. Philippe studied this through his telescope. It was identical to the old flag of the former state, the United Provinces of the Netherlands: three horizontal strips, red, white and blue. But now there was a new addition, an allegorical fantasy portraying a maiden, a lion and a cap of liberty. The republic was only a few months old, having been born in the most unlikely of circumstances. A revolution in Amsterdam was hardly unexpected, for there had always been enthusiasm for France's revolution in the Netherlands and Amsterdam was always a hotbed of every kind of fervour as well as being implacably hostile to the Princes of Orange.

Indeed, since the traumatic experience of the reign of terror that had shaken France to its very core, it was quite probable that the Dutch were now more enthusiastic and committed revolutionaries than the French. Meanwhile the Dutch navy, once the most vaunted and feared on the world's oceans, had fallen to the new regime in the most unlikely and embarrassing of circumstances: frozen into this very anchorage during a bitterly cold January, the entire fleet surrendered to a regiment of French cavalry that approached it over the thick ice. The news of a navy capitulating so ignominiously to mere *soldiers* made sailors of every other nation laugh themselves into paroxysms.

Past the seagate and in the lee of Texel was the southerly reach of the Frisian Sea, the anchorage long used by seamen of all nations while awaiting favourable winds and tides to carry them up to Amsterdam and the other ports on the shores of the Zuider Zee, or else out to the North Sea, the Baltic and all the oceans of the world. As *La Verité* came to an anchor, she was in the midst of a throng of perhaps two or three hundred ships flying an extraordinary array of flags, some of which might even have been their true colours. There were hulls of all sorts and sizes, big modern ships that were probably Indiamen or Levanters, broad-hulled Dutch *fluyts*, an old style no longer in favour among shipowners, luggers, brigs, all either at anchor or trying to catch a favourable wind that would carry them to their destinations. The shouts exchanged between the ships in the crowded anchorage were in a babel of languages, many that Philippe recognised but some that were utterly alien to him. The corsair came to an anchor in the heart of the throng, closer to The Helder than to the island of Texel itself.

This was where Philippe should have delivered Anne-Catherine Heinrich back into the embraces of her supposedly loving husband. But now he knew that was a monstrous lie, just as Augustin Heinrich's dream of landing here with his stepmother and riding off with her into a future of unalloyed bliss somewhere beyond his father's reach was nothing but a delusional fantasy. Philippe and the crew now had no purpose, but the Texel anchorage afforded the opportunity to lie up in a friendly haven while he made contact with Antoine Heinrich or his agents. Perhaps the *armateur* would forgive Philippe for the death of his son and the failure to return his wife. Perhaps the crew of *La Verité* would receive orders to follow their original instructions and undertake a cruise against enemy shipping in the North Sea and Baltic. He thought that unlikely, but if Antoine Heinrich washed his hands of Philippe Kermorvant and his entire crew, as Philippe suspected he would, then at least they were in the best place in Europe to either find a new employer or else to sell the ship and pay off the crew with the proceeds. The other possibility, the one he preferred not to think of at all, was that Antoine Heinrich would want to exact revenge, immediate and brutal revenge, on Philippe, his crew and anyone else within his orbit.

Ugarte joined him on the quarterdeck.

'Some of the men are asking about shore leave, *mon Capitaine*.'

Philippe nodded and considered the request. The men had been restless and uneasy since the episode on Fara, and it had not taken long for rumours to spread. Although they had no idea of the real reason why their *armateur* had sent them to Orkney, there had been several witnesses among the crew to what was said in Fara House and to the fates of Marcus Drever and Augustin Heinrich. Seamen always wanted to know where they were bound and who would pay them, and although Philippe had been as honest with them all as he thought he could be, he could hardly blame them for feeling anxious.

'Will many run, d'you think?' he asked Ugarte.

'No doubt of it. Look at all those hulls around us, all those berths needing to be filled. And if they can't find a ship here, it's not too far to Amsterdam. So aye, they'll desert all right. But deny 'em leave, Captain, and they'll cut your throat first, then run anyway.'

Philippe considered the matter. It was the antithesis of naval discipline, although even in the Marine Nationale, a situation such as that which faced the men of *La Verité* might be ample cause for mutiny. But the men of the corsair had been misled about the true purpose of their mission as entirely as Philippe had, and his sympathies were wholly with them.

'Very well. Organise leave parties from tomorrow onwards, Lieutenant, and inform the men of it. We'll have to trust that we're still left a shipkeeping crew at least.'

'*Commande, mon Capitaine.*'

La Verité lay at anchor that afternoon and into the evening, the crew making at least a pretence of going about their harbour duties. It was gone ten when one of the countless rowing boats that plied between the shore and the ships in the anchorage approached and hailed the corsair. Philippe, who had been snatching an hour's sleep, was summoned back on deck to meet its passenger, a stocky and stern-faced young Dutchman, probably in his early twenties, wearing the sort of costume that might from a distance have appeared to belong to a customs official or some sort of naval officer, but which was nothing of the sort. He wore a leather pouch over his left shoulder. The newcomer left his companions, a rough-looking crew of a dozen, in the boat as he hauled himself aboard *La Verité*.

'Willem Engelbrecht at your service, Captain,' said the Dutchman in good French as he presented himself before Philippe. 'I have the honour to be the agent in this haven and the whole of North Holland for your *armateur*, Citizen Antoine Heinrich. I was informed of your arrival by the port officials. I have instructions to receive from you two passengers, Citizen Heinrich's wife and son, and to see they are conveyed to him as expeditiously as possible. These instructions are in writing, and I will show them to you if you doubt my credentials.'

'I don't doubt you, Meinheer Engelbrecht. But I think we should speak in my cabin.'

'No need, Captain. Simply deliver them to me and I will be about my business, while you will be free to return to your privateering voyage at your convenience.'

'There is no one to deliver, Meinheer.'

This intelligence seemingly came as no surprise to Engelbrecht.

'And that is because?'

'To be blunt, Meinheer Engelbrecht, Citizeness Heinrich refused to accompany us. Contrary to the story I was told, she loves the Scot, Rendall, and despises your employer.'

Engelbrecht frowned.

'And you did not compel her? Citizen Heinrich will be displeased. Most displeased. But what of his son, Meinheer Augustin? Surely he is with you? I wish to hear his account of these proceedings.'

'Augustin Heinrich is dead by his own hand.'

'Suicide? And Madame Heinrich not secured? I have to report *this*, this calamity, to Citizen Heinrich. You will not have had as many dealings with him as I have, Captain. I assure you he will be furious. Furious with you most certainly, but also with me for addressing such tidings to him.'

'Report what you will, Citizen. My concern is only to obtain the monies rightfully due to all of us aboard this ship. You can do that?'

Engelbrecht had still barely digested the news which had been presented to him, and waved a hand to dismiss Philippe's concerns.

'I must seek instructions from Citizen Heinrich.'

'That may take weeks, man! Are we meant to fester here all that time, with no certainty of recompense at the end of it? Do you think there will be any men left in the crew?'

Engelbrecht shrugged. 'I have the authority to pay allowances and provide victuals for as long as the ship is in Dutch waters. Anything further will be set out in Citizen Heinrich's letter to you.'

'A letter, Meinheer? What letter is that?'

Engelbrecht removed the leather bag from his shoulder, opened it and produced a cache of half a dozen letters bound together by twine. He removed them from the twine, thumbed through them and produced one that was superscribed with a large number five.

'I think this one best corresponds to the tale you have told me, Captain. Citizen Heinrich is a meticulous man, as you know as well as I. He anticipated as far as he could all the possible outcomes of your mission, no matter how unpalatable some of them were to him, and drafted different sets of orders to you. So yes, number five applies in this case, I think. I will leave you to read it and consider your response, Captain. Should you need to speak further to me, I can usually be found at the Sign of the Black Boar in Den Helder, or else messages can be left there for me.'

The clearly unhappy Willem Engelbrecht took his leave. As the evening's gloom descended, Philippe watched his boat's crew row him back toward the shore. The vessel disappeared behind the hulls of several anchored ships, and Philippe returned below to read Antoine Heinrich's letter.

Captain Kermorvant.

If you are reading this letter, it means that you have failed to secure the person of my wife. It means also that my son has betrayed me and tried to take her for himself.

Perhaps you are surprised that I am aware of my son's true feelings for my wife, and of the possibility that he will try to take her away. In truth, Captain Kermorvant, Augustin has never been able to conceal his emotions. He thinks he has hidden his feelings for her from me, but in that he has failed utterly. Of course, I do not wish to hurt my son, but he cannot be with her. She is mine, and that is an end to the matter. I don't doubt that he will try to persuade you to let them go, but you must reject his entreaties and deliver her to the bearer of this letter, Citizen Engelbrecht, who will ensure she is delivered to me. As for my son, if he chooses to oppose this course then this letter is my authority to you to kill him. I will mourn my son most grievously, but nothing, not even his life, can be permitted to stand in the way of her returning to me.

It is possible that she has refused to part from the Scot, Rendall, and you may have heard tales told of me from her or them that run counter to the previous understanding you had from me. I believe I do not misjudge you, the son of the noble Verité, when I say that you will not be taken in by such lies. She is my life, my essence, and I must have her back at all costs. But, Monsieur le Vicomte, believe me when I say that if you have fallen for the lies and delusions peddled by Rendall, and if you have believed my wife if she says she wants to be with him, or my son, and not with me, and if you give credence to any malicious tales about me – I will say only that to do so would be to place you and those dear to you in the utmost peril. I am not a forgiving man, Captain Kermorvant, and any person who stands in the way of my wife returning to me will pay the highest price.

I have given Citizen Engelbrecht discretion to act as he sees fit in this and all other eventualities.

Philippe reread the letter. Such seemingly reasonable words, but what reasonable man gave sanction to another to murder his own son? Antoine Heinrich was a madman. Philippe, the entire crew of the corsair, anyone associated in any way with the Vicomte de Saint-Victor or the voyage of *La Verité*… all stood in mortal danger. He had no concern for himself and would confront whatever vengeance Heinrich sought to exact on him. But there were others, one other above all, who would not be so prepared and who needed to be warned.

Philippe sat down at the small writing table in his cabin and wrote one letter. He had no idea whether it would reach its intended recipient in time, given the uncertainties of the post in France, but it would probably take any report of Engelbrecht's roughly the same interval to reach his employer, so the attempt had to be made. He applied his seal to the letter, then did something he had not even contemplated for many years.

Philippe Kermorvant, Vicomte de Saint-Victor, committed republican, son of a man renowned for a philosophy that held atheism at its core, offered up a heartfelt prayer to God and the Virgin. Then he sent for Juan Ugarte.

CHAPTER TWENTY-EIGHT

The attack came the next night.

The day had been spent in taking on water and victuals, Philippe calling on his own credit to obtain the necessary supplies. Of course, it was entirely possible that the reprovisioning of the ship would prove unnecessary and a waste of Philippe's limited money, but he considered it better to prepare for all eventualities, including the admittedly unlikely resumption of her original mission. But the crew of *La Verité* were restless. He saw the looks, he heard the murmurs, and he knew that he could hold the men's confidence for no more than a day or two longer. He knew that despite the persistent drizzle of a tedious grey day, they would be looking out over the anchorage to the hundreds of ships crowding the Texel haven. Ships bound on lucrative voyages, ships with owners and captains whose credit was certain, ships where the owner's son had not died by his own hand. He knew there were whispers below deck that the ship was cursed, that they were all cursed with it, that they should never have gone anywhere near the pagan, fatal isles of Orkney. Somehow Marcus Drever's malevolent presence seemed still to permeate the timbers, ropes and the very bones of the corsair and her men. As yet there had been no desertions, but it was only a matter of time.

As the day wore on, there was no sign of Willem Engelbrecht nor anyone acting in his name. Through his telescope Philippe could see Dutchmen on the shore and ramparts of The Helder, some of them wearing the blue and red uniform of the Batavian Republic. He imagined that fingers were being pointed at *La Verité*, but no boat approached. That in itself was strange. By now they should surely have had a visitation from an official of the customs or some other functionary of the newly fledged republic, but while boats plied between the shore and many of the other ships in the anchorage, the corsair was left alone. It was as if word of a curse on *La Verité* had spread through the length and breadth of Holland, and every man ashore or afloat was shunning the ill-starred, doomed corsair.

He and Ugarte took turns on watch, each snatching some sleep as and when they could. He would not trust the harbour watch on deck to any of the others, even the likes of Ar Braz, Vuillermoz and Madec, who had all proved themselves to be good and steady men, for he knew how easily even the firmest and most loyal mariner might be seduced by the potential rewards on offer elsewhere in the Texel anchorage. Darkness fell halfway through the First Watch, although there was little difference between nighttime and the oppressive grey murk that had prevailed all day. A damp mist settled heavily over the anchorage, turning the ships at anchor nearby into spectral hulks. Apart from the intermittent tolling of ships' bells and the light spilling from stern lanterns and a few captains' cabins, there was no sign of life within hailing distance of *La Verité*.

It was Teschow, the German, who sighted them first.

'There, Captain!'

Teschow was pointing to splashes in the water that betrayed the movement of rowing craft. After a few moments it was possible to make out the dark silhouettes of the approaching hulls.

'I see them. Lieutenant Ugarte!'

'*Mon Capitaine?*'

'Pass the word to all quarters!'

'*Commande!*'

As they drew nearer, Philippe made out four small boats, *jachts* as the Dutch called them, approaching *La Verité* under oars alone and from different quarters, each crammed with perhaps twenty or thirty men. Philippe recognised Engelbrecht, standing in the bows of the nearest vessel. He readied his pistols.

'Now!' he shouted, and the man at the belfry began furiously to ring the ship's bell.

Men concealed behind the gunwales stood and levelled muskets at the attacking boats. Others emerged from below armed with a variety of guns, dirks and cutlasses. Engelbrecht and his crew opened fire as two of his men threw a hooked line to try to grapple onto the starboard quarter of *La Verité*. Philippe fired both of his pistols and reloaded as the men along the starboard rail took up the fire, followed by the men to port as the enemy boats on that beam closed the hull of the corsair. Ugarte paced for'ard and aft, yelling encouragement at the men, discharging his own pistols when he sighted a likely target.

Despite the defence put up by Philippe's crew, a few of Engelbrecht's men managed to secure to the starboard bow and scrambled up into the beakhead, then onto the fo'c'sle itself. A couple of the corsair's men fell before the ferocious onslaught, and Ugarte, his cutlass in hand, drew a half-dozen men to himself and rushed forward to repel the enemy's bridgehead.

There were other Dutchmen on deck...

Philippe looked over the side and saw that a boat had secured right under the stern, her men scrambling up grappling ropes to enter the ship through a couple of shattered windows of his own cabin. One of the invaders ran at him, screaming and brandishing a cutlass already stained with French blood, but Philippe levelled his only loaded pistol and shot him dead at point blank range.

There was no more time to reload. Philippe drew his own cutlass and strode forward, slashing and cutting as he went. A dozen of his men formed around him, pushing the enemy back toward the stern ladder. Philippe managed a glance for'ard and saw Ugarte fighting like one of the berserkers of ancient legend. He and the men around him were holding their own, but in the ship's waist matters seemed to be in the balance as more and more of the enemy managed to board the ship.

Engelbrecht. He had to get to Engelbrecht. Kill the leader and the attack would surely fail. But where was he?

'Captain!'

He swung round and saw Lavigne, one of the youngest lads in the crew, adopted almost as a mascot by his fellow Bretons.

'Lavigne?'

'Below, sir! The magazine! Their leader's down there! I think he's going to blow it!'

Philippe did not hesitate. He fought his way to the ladder, exchanging sword cuts with a couple of the enemy. But Lavigne's words were barely believable. Surely Engelbrecht couldn't intend to blow up the ship, killing dozens of his own men?

Below decks, *La Verité* was eerily silent. The battle was above, on the upper deck, and there seemed to be nobody at all below.

Down into the depths of the ship, into its very bowels.

There, lit only by a single dim lantern suspended from a beam, was Willem Engelbrecht, entirely oblivious to the fact that he was no longer alone, laying a trail of powder from the barrels that formed the corsair's magazine. All bought at the expense of the *armateur* Antoine Heinrich, and now they would be the means by which his creature Engelbrecht would destroy the crew and captain who had failed to return with Heinrich's wife.

But Engelbrecht would not want to destroy himself, even if he was prepared to sacrifice most of the men fighting on his behalf. He was laying a long fuse and would presumably then escape the blast by leaving through the stern windows. Philippe had managed to reload one pistol and could easily shoot Engelbrecht while the Dutchman was still oblivious to his presence and had his back turned, but a shot so close to the powder could set off the magazine just as surely as if Engelbrecht lit the fuse.

Philippe put the pistol back in his belt.

'Engelbrecht!' he cried.

The Dutchman turned and drew his dirk in the same movement, rushing for Philippe and striking for the heart. The confined space made it difficult for Philippe to bring his cutlass through its usual arc to parry the onslaught, but steel struck steel a moment before Engelbrecht's blade would have buried itself in his chest. The Dutchman adopted the crouching stance of a knifeman, daring Philippe to come at him. Philippe made a thrust but Engelbrecht parried, proving unexpectedly nimble on his feet. His relative youth was deceptive. Willem Engelbrecht was a fighter, and a capable one.

They exchanged attacks again, but Philippe had the advantages of the longer, more potent weapon and the position, standing between Engelbrecht and the route he had to take to escape the blast. The Dutchman feinted left but thrust right, almost catching Philippe by surprise, but he countered and caught Engelbrecht's left forearm, which started bleeding copiously. Philippe's adversary looked at the wound in astonishment, as if it was the first time he had seen his own blood. But he used the same arm to draw a small concealed pistol from his belt and aim it directly at Philippe's eyes.

'Fire it,' said Philippe. 'Fire it, Engelbrecht, and you know the consequences! I die, but so will you.'

'Too late for me now,' said Engelbrecht. 'As you now know, Citizen Heinrich doesn't tolerate failure.'

He began to turn, swinging the pistol around in his hand. The Dutchman was going to fire and blow the magazine. He was going to kill them both and destroy the ship. That thought was barely half formed when Philippe acted. There was no headroom to raise his arm and throw as his friend Opechancanough of the Powhatan of Virginia had once taught him with a tomahawk, but instead he flung his cutlass underarm with minimal backlift, a move entirely of his own devising. The blade pierced Engelbrecht's side below the ribcage. As the Dutchman reeled from the shock, Philippe leapt forward and grabbed his already damaged left arm, forcing the pistol from it. The weapon fell to the deck. Surely it would fire on impact –

But it did not. Philippe kicked it away with his left foot while his right hand drove the cutlass deeper into

Engelbrecht's innards, then withdrew the blade. The Dutchman staggered then fell backwards, his dead eyes seemingly staring accusingly at Philippe as he dropped to the deck.

Philippe bent over, took two deep breaths, then scuffed away the makeshift powder fuse. Once again he gripped his cutlass, now stained with the blood of Willem Engelbrecht, and made his way back up to the upper deck. The clammy air was a relief from the stench below, and he was greeted by the sight of his men, the corsairs of *La Verité*, cheering and firing a few parting shots from muskets and pistols as the last of the defeated attackers made off in their boats.

Ugarte, his face dripping with sweat, presented himself and saluted with his sword in the naval fashion.

'*Mon Capitaine*,' he said, 'I beg to report that the ship has been cleared of the enemy and is secure once again.'

'Well done, Lieutenant, and well done all hands! Shore leave from dawn, messes to draw lots for the order of going ashore.'

A few ragged cheers greeted Philippe's announcement, but most of the men on deck seemed too exhausted to react with more than tired smiles.

'And then, Captain?' said Ugarte in a lower voice.

'And then, Lieutenant, we see if we can find papers containing Citizen Engelbrecht's credentials from Citizen Heinrich, and see how far Citizen Heinrich's credit extends in this Batavian Republic before he learns what we're about. Pay off the ship, the crew and ourselves. Then, *mon ami*, it'll be time to go home.'

CHAPTER TWENTY-NINE

'*Encore!*' bawled the drill master, a grizzled old sergeant of the *emigré* Regiment du Dresnay. '*Oblique a droite – marche!*'

It was the day before the scheduled requiem mass for King Louis the Seventeenth, and Hervilly was taking advantage of the brief intermission in the campaign to embark on the vital task, as he saw it, of turning the Chouans into proper soldiers. Now, at Sergeant Lafontaine's command, the troops of the newly designated Regiment du Cozanet stepped forward to make their fourth attempt at the manoeuvre, watched by their commanding officer. Like all his men, Georges Cozanet was wearing a newly issued red uniform and British regulation boots. Again, like all his men, he found the outfit uncomfortable and impractical, the boots being particularly excruciating. What was more, England had attacked Brittany many times, and the folk memories of the Bretons ran very deep indeed. No words of reassurance from Puisaye or anyone else would ever convince the Bretons that red was not the uniform of their eternal enemy. He had asked why the Catholic and Royal Army had not been outfitted in white, the traditional uniform of French armies in the great days of the Bourbon kings and the mighty victories they had won, and had been informed there was no white dye in England. The

Chouans refused to believe it, muttering instead about a deal with the devil hatched in Whitehall by which Pitt and his minions would dress the French royalist forces in English colours. All things considered, then, it had hardly been a surprise when two men of the Regiment de Cozanet had discarded their red uniforms and boots almost immediately, proclaiming angrily that the Chouans knew how to kill republicans much better than the battle-virgin *emigrés* fresh off the British ships in Quiberon Bay and that they did not need to wear scratchy English cloth of hated English red and boots of inflexible English leather to do it. That night the two slipped away into the darkness, bound for their homes or perhaps for other groups of Chouans who still fought in their accustomed and brutally effective manner while wearing whatever they pleased. The next night, five more men disappeared, leaving their hated boots and uniforms behind them. Now, on the third day, Cozanet fully expected the arrival of the unforgiving Sergeant Lafontaine and the men's abrupt introduction to the intricacies of parade ground drill to trigger another round of desertions.

Unlike his men, Cozanet did not have to attempt to execute the textbook drill manoeuvres upon which Hervilly insisted. He was present only to add their commanding officer's authority to the proceedings and, in practice, to stop his men turning on Lafontaine, who had taken only a few minutes to become universally hated.

The sergeant's latest order quickly produced a calamity. The first step was perhaps passable, the second unsatisfactory, the third a catastrophe. The manoeuvre required the entire formation to move off by stepping off straight on the left foot while the right went at a forty-five degree angle. The sergeant had spent the best part of an hour describing what a forty-five degree angle looked like, and in the cases of a gratifyingly few men, explaining the difference between left and right. It was probably inevitable that when the regiment came to attempt the manoeuvre, it would be a wholly predictable disaster. Some men set off on the right foot rather than the left. Some brought their other foot to a position perhaps ninety degrees from straight. Others, for some reason known only to themselves, attempted to wheel around completely. A few of the brighter men realised their mistakes, observed what their betters were doing and attempted to shuffle back into line and step.

'*Quelle bande de connards*,' said Sergeant Lafontaine to himself. What a bunch of shitheads. Suddenly remembering the identity of his neighbour, he quickly added, 'Begging your pardon, Colonel.'

Cozanet felt for the man. It was not his fault, just as it was not his men's fault. It was the fault of one man alone, and after some placatory words to the drill sergeant, Cozanet set off in search of him. It would do no good, other than for the condition of Georges Cozanet's conscience, but at least a protest would be registered.

He found Hervilly in his makeshift headquarters, a small tented encampment between the beach and Carnac itself. The general was sitting at a table, poring over maps of the region, speaking animatedly about potential locations for further defensive dispositions. His staff officers buzzed around him, all conveying rather too overt a sense of urgency and self-importance. One of them, Cozanet noted with bemusement but no real surprise, was his former second in command, Yves, Marquis de Montargis, evidently much more comfortable in his new and immaculate red uniform than Cozanet felt in his.

Several minutes passed before Hervilly deigned even to notice Cozanet, several more before he beckoned him to come forward.

'Cozanet, isn't it? One of Puisaye's acolytes. Well, what is it? We are busy. I am busy. Losing a day for the requiem makes it all so much more difficult, you understand. So speak, Colonel. I am all ears. Tell us what concerns you.'

'General, my men are restive. We have already had desertions, and I anticipate more. The cause, sir—'

'Restive? Desertions? What is this, Cozanet? This is a matter for the regimental officers, the colonel of the regiment in particular. If men are restive, the colonel must calm them. If men desert, the colonel must catch them and hang them. You are the colonel, are you not? So it is entirely your responsibility, *mon cher* Colonel Cozanet. *Voila.*'

A couple of the staff officers laughed out loud, while most of the others smirked. Montargis was one of the few who kept a straight face.

Cozanet pressed on. The men deserved that of him, at least, even if he championed a lost cause.

'It is the uniforms, General. The men do not like them, especially the boots. Chouans, Bretons, are not accustomed to such things. Nor do they take to drill. They have been fighting the Blues their way for two years, but now they are expected to drill as if they were on the parade ground at Versailles. What explanation can I give to them, General Hervilly?'

Hervilly shook his head, sighing as though he was dealing with a particularly recalcitrant four-year-old.

'Officers do not give explanations to the men, Colonel. The men serve unquestioningly. The men obey orders. Anything less than that and we unleash the forces that brought about the revolution. All becomes anarchy. So to ensure obedience to orders men must act in a soldierly manner. Uniforms give men a common identity, drill teaches unthinking obedience to command and builds a sense of common purpose. It is really all very simple, Colonel Cozanet.'

The staff officers nodded at what they took to be the sage wisdom of their commander.

'But, General,' said Cozanet, 'the Chouans already have the strongest common identity imaginable. They are Bretons, fighting for their fatherland—'

'Frenchmen, fighting for the King of France.'

Cozanet took a breath. He could not, dare not, lose his temper.

'Their sense of purpose is matchless, General, and requires no uniform to show it, least of all a red uniform. Nor English boots either.'

'An army is not an army without a uniform. Yes, without boots! Soldiers, proper soldiers that is, march in step and drill. I know the Chouans have been accustomed to a different dispensation, and that men like the Comte de Puisaye and yourself have permitted it, Colonel. But without training and discipline, without unquestioning obedience to the orders of their superiors, your Chouans are nothing but a rabble. They cannot possibly stand alongside the *emigré* regiments in a line of battle against the Blues. They cannot campaign. As the commanding general, I must know that I can rely on every single one of my regiments, and to be blunt, Colonel Cozanet, I cannot rely on yours if your men quibble about such little matters as boots and the merest taste of proper drill.'

Georges Cozanet felt the rage rising within him, and struggled to keep his emotions in check.

'Every one of my men is loyal unto death to the cause of the King and Holy Church. Can that be said of your beloved *emigré* regiments, General?'

Cozanet's allusion to this awkward truth, that many of the rank and file recruited in England had come from prison camps, having previously fought for the Republic, enraged the volatile Hervilly. He stood abruptly and slammed his fists on the table.

'Damn your insolence, Cozanet! Damn your Breton pride! I will have satisfaction!'

Montargis stepped between his former commanding officer and his new one.

'*Messieurs*,' he said evenly, 'we are all mourning our king. Let us not stain his memory with the needless blood of loyal men.'

Cozanet was ready to continue the quarrel with Hervilly, to the extent of being ready to give up his commission or even to satisfy the general's demand for satisfaction in a duel, although a contest between a Breton blacksmith's son and a professional army officer of noble birth would undoubtedly have only one outcome. But Montargis's words gave him pause. Yes, he would respect the memory of Louis the Seventeenth until the moment the requiem mass concluded. Then he would resume his argument, reinforced by a fair measure of Chouan bewilderment at the failure of the Catholic and Royal Army to advance one step beyond the defensive perimeter it had established. So despite the rage he felt within, Georges Cozanet kept his counsel, saluted Hervilly, nodded to Montargis, and returned to his men.

Morning in the rough encampment of the Regiment de Cozanet brought the sight of six more red uniforms and six more pairs of English boots neatly arranged where their wearers left them when they slipped away during the night. Cozanet's anger, which he had managed to suppress since the meeting with Hervilly on the previous day, returned with a vengeance. There was no doubt of it: the royalists' own general was causing a far greater attrition rate among the ranks of the Chouans than General Hoche, commander of the Blue army known to be coming against them.

Kerouac, the sturdy captain and sometime locksmith of Morlaix serving as second in command of the regiment since Montargis's departure, stepped before Cozanet, glanced at the piles of discarded clothing, then saluted his colonel. There was no need for words. Kerouac knew as well as Cozanet that the steady trickle of desertions would soon become a flood.

'Your orders, Colonel?' Kerouac asked.

'Another day of drill, Captain. The general insists on as much as possible before we resume operations against the Blues. Fall the men in and await further direction from Sergeant Lafontaine.'

Kerouac looked as though he would rather be flogged raw, but he saluted and turned away to execute his colonel's order. Cozanet would rejoin his men later, but meanwhile he intended to write a letter to the Comte de Puisaye to protest against the ridiculous insistence on rigid drill for the Chouan regiments. Perhaps a letter to the Comte d'Artois, too. It would do no good, of course. It would probably be better to direct any letter to the pale Englishman, Wilden, the representative of the Catholic and Royal Army's undoubted paymaster, but such an action would almost certainly cost him his commission. The letter he would much prefer to write would be addressed to Leonore Kermorvant, but he chided himself for the thought. She had been one fleeting moment of his life, one unattainable dream, one destined to be with another, and he needed to dismiss her from his mind.

Cozanet returned to his bivouac, unfolded his campaign table and sat down to compose the letter to Puisaye. He was still struggling to find the right tone for it several minutes later when Kerouac returned, his expression particularly foul even for a man who was rarely seen to smile.

'Well, Captain? Are the men formed up?'

'The men, aye, they're formed all right. But there's no sign of Sergeant Lafontaine. The Regiment de Dresnay are encamped close to us so I went over there and no man's seen him. He missed the muster this morning.'

'Have they searched for him?'

Cozanet had a vision of the lifeless corpse of Lafontaine lying in a ditch drenched in the blood from several dozen stab wounds, the vengeance of the Chouans – *his* Chouans – for daring to inflict on them the detested English boots and the most nitpicking kinds of parade ground drill.

'No, Colonel. It's presumed he's deserted. Seems scores have run from the *emigré* regiments, just as they have from the Chouans. Their officers don't want it proclaimed from every rooftop, naturally. But it seems that Sergeant Lafontaine had fought for the Blue army before he was taken prisoner. The fellow I spoke to in de Dresnay's reckoned all the men they'd lost were just like Lafontaine.'

Cozanet nodded at the intelligence, but he was not entirely convinced. Lafontaine had seemed firm enough in the royal cause, but perhaps he was a good actor.

Cozanet could still not drive out the thought that his men had dealt with the despised drill sergeant during the night, but if they had, it was very unlikely that any trace of Sergeant Lafontaine would ever be discovered. Almost all the Chouans were men of the land, and they knew very well indeed just how voracious Breton pigs could be.

No, Lafontaine's fate was not worth a second thought. But the broader truth revealed by Kerouac's account struck Cozanet at once. The desertions from the Chouan ranks were increasing rapidly, fuelled not just by the debacle of the boots and uniforms but by the arrogant disdain and outright contempt of the *emigrés* and disillusionment with Hervilly's overly cautious defensive tactics. But if there were also mass desertions from the *emigré* rank and file, the former republicans who had been recruited from prison camps with double-edged promises of freedom, then what chance would the Catholic and Royal Army stand when it eventually went up against the ever-strengthening ranks of General Hoche's Blue army?

CHAPTER THIRTY

Objectively, Lord Wilden judged, the death of the boy-king was an utter disaster for the Quiberon expedition's prospects and for the entire royalist cause in France. It was easy to win sympathy for a ten-year-old child whose parents had been brutally executed and who existed entirely at the mercy of unscrupulous gaolers and the foul condition of a Paris prison. Louis the Seventeenth had been an ideal, a fantasy to be idolised, a blank slate upon which all the royalist factions, as well as those who wavered between support for a monarchy and a republic, might draw any image they liked of the sort of man and king he might grow into. But the Comte de Provence, now King Louis the Eighteenth in name, was thirty-nine years old. He was a known quantity, irrevocably associated with the Bourbon arrogance and extravagance that had characterised the reign of his guillotined elder brother. The waverers would consider him a man incapable of changing his ways, the *emigrés* and Chouans alike would pray he was exactly that.

Nonetheless, the appropriate formalities had to be observed. The requiem mass for the *soi-disant* Louis the Seventeenth, nominally King of France for two years, was ordered to be held on the beach at Carnac and conducted by the Bishop of Dol, the expedition's de facto chaplain. That, at least, was the order that came down from the Comte de Puisaye. As it was, only the Loyal Emigrant Regiment, the one most closely attached to Puisaye, attended the service he ordered. The other troops that could be spared from immediate duty crowded instead into the church at Carnac by order of Hervilly, who found a nearly senile old local priest, so decrepit the local revolutionaries must have thought him unworthy of even their righteous republican wrath, to conduct a competing requiem. Two rival services in two different locations, presided over by two different priests at the behest of the two different generals who claimed to be the rightful commander-in-chief of the Catholic and Royal Army of France.

Such division reminded Wilden of the Welsh.

As a good Anglican, of course, he did not intend to attend either service. Instead he saw a sudden window of opportunity to do something that had been at the back of his mind since that day in Downing Street when William Pitt ordered him to accompany the invasion of France. Despite Wilden's horrified reaction to the prospect, he had pored over maps and charts of Quiberon Bay and the regions adjacent when he returned to his quarters in Hill Street. One place name caught Ned Wilden's attention, one that he had first heard in his childhood and had always intrigued him, one that could provide some consolation for being ordered from the comfort of his hearth to the manifold discomforts and perils of a full-scale invasion of France. There was an element of danger to it, but the French officers to whom he spoke in the days before the requiems for the dead king were held were categorical. The entire area was safe, they said. It had been wholly cleared of the Blue scum, they said. That being so, and with no significant military moves in prospect, what harm could there be in a brief diversion of antiquarian interest?

He broached the subject with Sir John Borlase Warren, who was aghast.

'An excursion, my lord? To view *stones*?'

'They are vast alignments, Sir John! They are said to be so considerable that they make our Stonehenge appear akin to mere children's building blocks.'

Warren raised an eyebrow, and Wilden suddenly wondered whether the commodore had ever seen Stonehenge, or even heard of it. He was a sailor, after all, and sailors were not as other men.

'I understand your interest, my lord,' said Warren, his expression suggesting the opposite. 'But really? You'd endanger yourself just for some stones?'

'Our French friends will be making no moves while they hold their requiem, nor for some days to come, I think. The solemnity of the occasion has even brought a kind of truce between Hervilly and Puisaye, leaving aside the matter of the rival requiems. We have assurances from all of the *emigrés* and the Chouans that the countryside as far inland as Auray and Landévant is entirely clear of the enemy. General Hoche and the army he is assembling is no nearer than Vannes. Besides, Sir John, I will have my two splendid Marines to watch over me, so I will be perfectly safe.'

Warren shook his head.

'I still advise against it, my lord.'

'I'm told that the stones are no more than a mile from the landing beaches, Sir John! How can I be in any danger so near to the royal army and our own squadron, in countryside entirely royalist in sentiment and controlled by our Chouan friends? I pray you, Sir John, indulge me in this. I have a passion for all things antiquarian, and I cannot be so near such a unique and famous landmark without indulging my interest! I grant, Sir John, that you are the commodore of the British and naval elements of this expedition and if you wish to prevent me, you have ample force at your disposal. But you would have to clap me in irons to stop me going ashore!'

Warren inclined his head.

'Far be it from me to deny the wishes of a lord of the Admiralty, my lord. We shall put you ashore again on the next boat.'

Edward, Lord Wilden was not easily moved, and despite his uncharacteristic sorrow over the death of Jack Kenton he would certainly not have counted himself an emotional man. But the age, the beauty, the sheer scale of the stones of Carnac moved him more than many of the human interactions he had experienced in his life. He walked through the silent rows, his thoughts running wild. Here were the mysteries of the ages, making the conflicts of his own time seem utterly insignificant. When a similar passage of time separated the moment he was experiencing from that new age, far off in the future, would men still remember the expedition of which he was part? Or would only these stones still endure, and he and Pitt, Puisaye and Hervilly, all be wholly forgotten? Would they long outlast the poisonous legacies of France's bloody revolution, until some far distant day when that colossal upheaval of his own time no longer merited even one sentence in the histories? Would there even be men at all to look upon the stones, and to remember or forget everything that was playing out at Quiberon?

Marine Lynch turned sharply, raising his musket, and Jardine imitated him.

'Get down, my lord!' shouted Lynch, and Wilden fell to the ground.

But it was only some roughly dressed peasant children, two boys and a girl, intently watching the three Britons from several hundred yards away. The two Marines relaxed, lowering their weapons. Wilden stood, waved to the children, and continued his perambulation of the stones, aware of the curious gaze of the silent youngsters. Every few minutes he took a sketchbook from the satchel he carried and quickly attempted to capture a scene or a notable feature that took his eye. He knew he was no Canaletto, but he flattered himself that he had a reasonable eye for proportion and perspective. Quite what his two Marine guards, or even the silent, staring Breton children, made of the English nobleman making sketches of old stones during a war was altogether a different matter.

He had little awareness of the passage of time. He could see *Pomone*'s topmasts in the distance, out in Quiberon Bay, and he knew he would have to return to her at some point, but there, amid the ancient stones of Carnac, it was as though time had simply stopped. His life was frantic. He stood on foreign soil – enemy soil – in the midst of a great war between religion, order and sheer *decency* on his side against fanaticism, atheism and mass murder on the other, yet here, at the heart of a mysterious landscape shaped by many millennia—

The peace was shattered by the sudden, unexpected, shocking sound of musket fire from the trees fringing the open ground where the stones stood. The first bullet struck Lynch in the shoulder, spinning him round. The second and third struck the Irishman's torso at the same moment that the fourth blew off the left side of Jardine's skull. Instinct made Ned Wilden throw himself to the ground once again. He was only a few feet from one of the stones. He had to reach it, to take cover behind it. If he stayed in the open he would surely die in the next few moments.

He used his elbows to haul himself across the ground. A peer of the realm impersonating a caterpillar – it was surely a ludicrous sight. But it was no time to worry about appearances. The enemy was still out there, and although there was a respite in their fire, they would surely be closing in.

He propped himself up behind the nearest stone, which provided him with at least a semblance of cover from the Blue troops who had to be somewhere in the woods. Wilden had no weapon other than a rapier that was largely for show and had never been drawn in anger. Warren had suggested he take pistols, but he had disregarded the advice. He had the protection of two sturdy Marines, he said, so what need had he of more? He did not betray the less confident truth behind his words, that he detested guns and was an appalling shot. But now his insouciance and unmartial inclinations would surely end in his death, kissing foreign soil like the nearby corpses of Jardine and Lynch.

There were no more shots, so he risked a glance toward the woods. No movement. No sign of the enemy. He thought of running, of making a dash for the safety of the beachhead and *Pomone*. No, Ned, he chided himself, patience *mon brave*. Perhaps in an hour or two, but the enemy would surely be watching and waiting for him to make exactly such a move. He imagined breaking cover, and the crack of musket fire being the last sound he would ever hear. But if he stayed, surely they would discover him anyway? All that would differ would be the means of his death. Every moment might bring a flash of blue around the side of the stone, then the fatal glint of a bayonet or a rapier—

'*Bonjour, monsieur,*' said a childish, seemingly amused voice to his left.

He turned in terror, expecting to see his nemesis and to meet his death. But it was not some burly republican infantryman with a bayonet fixed to his musket, about to plunge it into his throat. It was the girl who had been watching him from across the field. She was very small, grubby but round-faced and bright-eyed. She looked entirely different and belonged to a different sex, but somehow she reminded him of poor Midshipman Jack Kenton.

Careful, Ned. She may have appeared no more than an innocent child, but she was French. She could yet betray him to the republicans. On the other hand...

'*Bonjour, mademoiselle,*' he whispered.

'*Je suis Melanie, monsieur.* It's all right, Englishman, the Blue soldiers have gone. They were only a small patrol, and they've gone to scout down toward the beach.'

Gone? But they must have seen that he was alone, the easiest target imaginable. It made no sense – no, of course, it made all the sense in the world. An outlying patrol deep in enemy-held territory... the Blues would surely expect to be surrounded and destroyed by *emigré* forces at any moment unless they kept moving and kept under cover. Kill the two heavily armed British Marines, most certainly, but an insignificant civilian making sketches was not worth a moment's further risk.

'You can't sit behind this stone all day, Englishman,' said the girl, and Ned Wilden felt a pang of shame. He was being lectured in courage by a child, and a girl child at that. 'We'll lead you back down to your positions. We know all the tracks, *monsieur*.'

It could still be a trap. These children could be a ploy to get him to show himself, to put him in the sights of the Blue patrol or to betray him to them. He knew he could not endure a French prison, a worse fate in his mind than the prospect of a bullet shattering his skull as it had poor, loyal, valiant Jardine's.

But the girl's features seemed wholly ingenuous, and he undoubtedly stood a better chance with these children than any adults who might come that way. He got to his feet once again, brushing the dust off his clothes as best he could. The girl beckoned her two reluctant-looking companions to join them.

'This is Vincent,' she said, 'and this is Thierry. They're ignorant fellows so they can only speak Breton.'

Wilden blinked. He was standing in a field in Brittany next to the still warm bodies of his Marine guards, yet this precocious child was making introductions as formally as a dowager at a palace ball and the two boys were executing bows so deep they might have been genuflecting before some exotic and mighty eastern potentate. Even so, introducing himself by his title seemed wildly inappropriate in that time and place.

'*Je suis Ned*,' he said.

The three children grinned and immediately formed a conspiratorial huddle, whispering to each other excitedly in a language that Wilden had never heard before. Then the girl, Melanie, turned to him again and said gravely,

'By your pardon, monsieur, but just what sort of a name is Ned?'

'Short for Edward,' he said. 'Edouard in this country.'

'*Très bon, Monsieur Edouard.*' She translated for the boys, then turned back to him. 'But come, we'll get you back to your people. Briskly now, Monsieur Edouard!'

The fifth Baron Wilden, Lord of His Britannic Majesty's Admiralty, followed meekly as three unwashed and ragged Breton children captained by a small girl led him through the silent rows of ancient stones toward the distant mastheads of the British squadron.

CHAPTER THIRTY-ONE

At Wilden's insistence, the emergency council of war was held in Warren's cabin aboard *Pomone*. He sat in the centre of the table with a view out of the stern window toward Fort Penthièvre, the preferred venue of the French that he had, with uncharacteristic vehemence, categorically rejected in favour of this floating manifestation of the power of the British state. Warren sat opposite him, Puisaye and Hervilly at each end, four of the other senior *emigré* officers and the same number of their Chouan counterparts arrayed along each side. Cozanet had the place immediately to Wilden's left.

The atmosphere in the cabin was tense, the mood sombre. Sir John Borlase Warren looked as though he wished to be a very long way away. The royalists babbled among themselves but several of them stole nervous glances at Wilden, who sat impassively and waited for the ship's bell to toll the hour appointed for the council. Warren checked his pocket watch and continued to look at it, avoiding any chance of making eye contact with Wilden, until he and the others in the cabin heard the familiar ring marking the changeover of the ship's watches. Even the most garrulous of the Frenchmen fell silent and waited for Ned Wilden to speak.

He hated being the centre of attention, but he hated brushes with death even more. When he spoke, it was very quietly but angrily.

'I had assurances,' he said. 'I was told by many of you – *no, all of you* – that the country was secure. There were no enemy troops this side of the Rivière d'Auray. None closer than Landévant. But two good men lie dead, and I might have joined them but for the hand of fate. Now you tell me that at this very moment there are Blue patrols ranging as far as the shore opposite us. You tell me that the enemy has units at this place, and also at that place, and then at another, all well this side of the Rivière d'Auray. You tell me that General Hoche has already assembled thirteen thousand men of the Army of Cherbourg at Vannes. Intelligence you chose to keep not only from me, but also from Sir John, here, and your other British friends and allies. How can this be so, *messieurs*?'

Hervilly looked entirely unabashed. He raised his hands expansively and inclined his head slightly toward Wilden.

'My lord, naturally I rejoice in your deliverance from the brutal intent of our enemies. I regret that the Catholic and Royal cause should have been disgraced by the failings of those upon whom we depended.'

The Chouan officers were immediately outraged, Puisaye taking their side at once. It was perfectly obvious who Hervilly meant.

'Failings?' roared Tinténiac, one of the most influential Chouan leaders. 'You mean by us, Hervilly?'

Hervilly spread his hands wide once again, assuming the pose of a crucified messiah. The frequency of the gesture had irritated Wilden at their many meetings in

London while the expedition was being prepared, and it infuriated him now.

'My dear Tinténiac,' said Hervilly smoothly, 'since we landed, you Chouans have never ceased telling us how well you know the land, how all the people are for our cause, how you will provide seventy, eighty, ninety thousand men – but where are they, sir? You have provided only a fraction of that number. And as Lord Wilden's experience demonstrates all too plainly, you do not have control of the land, for all your bluster!'

'*Bluster?*' interjected Cozanet, his face reddening. 'Be careful of your words, General. Challenges have been issued for less!'

Wilden was about to intervene but Puisaye forestalled him.

'If we adopted my strategy, none of this would matter! We should be breaking out of this bridgehead, striking fast for Rennes and Lorient, not festering here on the beaches waiting for Hoche to muster sufficient strength to attack us!'

'I dictate strategy,' said Hervilly pompously. 'I dictate the terms of the campaign. Is that not so, Lord Wilden?'

It could not be denied. Wilden and Pitt between them had devised the dual command reckoning that Hervilly's greater military experience should be given precedence over Puisaye's credibility among the Chouans. Wilden nodded reluctantly.

'And I continue to say we should consolidate,' Hervilly continued. 'Dig in. Advance the perimeter slowly and cautiously. At all costs, keep open our connection to the sea. Reinforcements are coming from England. Who knows, our Chouan friends might indeed prove able to conjure mighty but as yet unseen legions from the forests of Brittany. But if we advance too quickly, before we have our full strength, we will undoubtedly be cut off from the rear. Cut off from fresh supplies from England. Cut off from reinforcements, and remember, *messieurs*, Sombreuil and the second division of the *emigré* army are due here any day. Cut off, moreover, from Sir John's squadron and any prospect of Lord Bridport's fleet coming to our aid.'

Wilden listened to Hervilly's words and felt the same tightening of his gut, the same tension in his muscles, that he had experienced when he was hiding among the stones of Carnac in sight of his two dead Marine guards. He knew this was how fear felt.

He and Pitt and all the others involved in the decision had decided to give Hervilly the command of the active military element of the expedition because he was a more experienced soldier than Puisaye. They had assumed – at least, Wilden had – that this experience would mean Hervilly would pursue the agreed strategy boldly and above all quickly.

'And all the while our enemy will mass his forces against us,' said Puisaye angrily. 'We already have good intelligence that General Hoche is at Vannes with reinforcements pouring in to him every day. He will only get stronger and become so faster than we can. We must strike, and strike now! Not another day's delay. We must march on Rennes and take it! That will encourage the rest of the Chouans, and those in the rest of France who wait only for a signal from the west!'

'Monsieur le Comte de Puisaye is right,' snapped Cozanet. 'Such an advance will light a flame that will inspire all well-intentioned Bretons and Frenchmen. But I will tell you what will discourage them, General Hervilly. What discourages them today, and has done since the day you landed. You do not trust us. Oh, you may shake your head, *monsieur*, but you make it very obvious! You refuse to join Chouan units with your own. You give us modern arms only grudgingly. You insist that we wear uniforms and learn drill as if such formalities are essential in war. You seek pride of place for your troops, not ours. You openly sneer at us, all you *emigrés*, but we stayed in France these last years, fighting the republican scum every day and in every field, while you warmed your arses in comfortable quarters in England!'

Hervilly made to rise from his chair, but Wilden raised a hand and the general reluctantly sat down again, staring furiously at Cozanet as he did so.

'You all ran at the very first whisper of the guillotine,' Cozanet continued, 'whereas we, and all the nobility who dared to stay in France to fight with us – whereas we, sir, put our lives at risk for our king every moment of every day!'

'*Messieurs*,' said Wilden, his body still tense and his thoughts running wild, 'we are all united in the same cause. No good will come of one party claiming greater virtue than the other.'

There were a few growls at that from the Chouans, who plainly thought that they, who had fought the Republic from the beginning, possessed precisely such virtue.

'Now, sirs, I am not a military man. In truth, I am not a naval man either, despite the position in His Majesty's government that I have the honour to hold. But it seems to me that we ought to be striking for Lorient as soon as possible. You concur, Sir John?'

Warren, who had been plainly embarrassed at having such discord mar a council he was nominally hosting, nodded and spoke, somewhat reluctantly and hesitantly at first, then with greater confidence.

'As you say, my lord. We know for certain that after the battle with Lord Bridport's fleet, Villaret withdrew to Lorient and remains there, wary of coming back round to Brest while we are here and our fleet is at sea. So, as I see it, taking Lorient would serve a dual purpose, giving this expedition a great victory to hold up as an example to all those in France who only pay lip service to the Republic while also knocking the enemy's Brest fleet out of the war.'

'Taking Rennes sends a more powerful signal to the rest of France and the whole world,' protested Puisaye. Hervilly, visibly furious at the criticism of his strategy, shook his head but did not interject. 'With respect, Lord Wilden,' Puisaye continued, 'disabling the Brest fleet serves only England's purposes.'

'And taking Rennes serves only yours,' said Hervilly.

'Staying here and waiting for the Blues to slaughter us serves nobody's!' cried the exasperated Puisaye.

The comment caused uproar. Hervilly glowered, half rose and began to reach for the hit of his sword, but Wilden glared at him and the *emigré* general sat down. The Chouans began to all talk at once, while Puisaye, at the other end of the table, smiled. Wilden caught Warren's expression. The commodore's face was white, his eyes raised to the beam over their heads.

The bitter arguments among the French showed no sign of receding, and Lord Wilden felt a terrible new certainty come over him. The Quiberon expedition was a fiasco, and it would be a fiasco for which he bore some responsibility. Even if he did not bear it for the conception and planning, he certainly did bear a substantial amount for the fatal decision to supplant Puisaye with Hervilly.

The whole episode would surely end in utter disaster, if not the slaughter of most of the men in the captain's cabin of *Pomone* and many hundreds, or even thousands, of valiant, loyal French royalists. Their blood would be on his hands.

He chided himself for his equal measures of hubris and self-pity. Of course it was not entirely his fault, just as it was not Hervilly's. He remembered the extraordinary scenes at Carnac when the expedition landed, and the unbridled joy of the Bretons as the *emigrés* came ashore. How swiftly that enthusiasm had died, giving way to disillusionment and resentment as the Bretons realised that the promised prince of the blood, Artois, did not accompany the expedition, then the falling out of Chouans with *emigrés* and the different factions within each group giving vent to their peevish jealousies of each other. The affair of the boots and red uniforms symbolised the whole calamitous episode, and the death of the nominal King of France at the very beginning of the campaign could be seen as a terrible omen by those, including virtually all the notoriously superstitious Bretons as far as he could judge, who believed in such things. No, Ned Wilden decided as the French assembled in the captain's cabin of *Pomone* continued to squabble viciously among themselves, this was a fiasco with many roots. What could have been a triumphant destiny had somehow been refashioned as the bleakest of comedies.

He knew there would be those who would say he should stay, that he should do his utmost to knock stubborn French heads together, that he should see the whole affair through to its conclusion. He was no coward, and he was too self-aware to imagine himself indispensable. He knew that if he died on the cursed shore of Quiberon,

Pitt would easily find a new Lord of the Admiralty to take his place. He would also, if less easily, find someone else capable of taking over the shadowy intelligence activities over which Wilden presided. But he did not believe he was deluding himself when he conceived that the prime minister would prefer not to have to undertake those two tasks and would much rather that Ned Wilden lived.

The expedition had already nearly cost Wilden his life, and he was certain that if he stayed with it death would surely make no mistake a second time. Better to die for a purpose, his old servant and mentor, Augustus Jenkins, always said, than to live with none. Remaining to see the inevitable tragedy unfold would serve no purpose, whereas preserving himself would achieve not just the saving of a life that could still give uniquely valuable service to his king and country. If he remained with the expedition, there was every chance that in years to come French politicians and historians would seize upon his presence as proof that the calamity at Quiberon was caused by the Frenchman's eternal scapegoat of choice.

Les rosbifs.

La perfide Albion.

Lord Wilden would not give them that opportunity. Instead, he would speak to Commodore Sir John Borlase Warren and obtain a place on the first ship returning to England.

CHAPTER THIRTY-TWO

From the papers of Leonore Kermorvant.

It is a dangerous time to be a woman in France.

Then again, when is it not a dangerous time to be a woman in any land? Marriage is a lottery. I have known couples who have been loving and faithful to each other for fifty years, and bon chance *to them. Or one may marry and find oneself shackled to an abusive brute, as I was. Then again, childbirth is a lottery. Two of my sisters died in that condition. One may avoid both outcomes by never marrying or being with a man at all, as Sandrine Cadoudal has done. But even then there is the constant peril of rape and the utter certainty of being ignored by men who think an unmarried, childless woman, especially one who dares to think, is an offence to every natural law. Every heavenly law, if one believes in a heaven. So yes, womankind lives in perpetual fear.*

But add to that already potent concoction the upheaval of the present times. We have witnessed a revolution unprecedented in the history of France, and perhaps of any nation since the fall of ancient Rome or Byzantium. All the certainties upon which life was built for countless centuries, king, Church, nobility, have been swept away almost overnight in a tempest of bloodletting. Even the names for days of the week, months and years have changed to new dispensations. Loved ones have been sent to the guillotine by the thousand, or else have simply disappeared from the face of the earth. Women could be presented with impossible choices, such as whether or not to denounce and send to the guillotine their abusive husbands to save the life of the said husband's infinitely more worthy brother. The revolution also meant war against the other nations of Europe, and that meant many of the men were summoned to fight and sent away to far distant campaigns, many never to be seen again. For the women of France, just as for the women of Austria and England and Prussia, that meant months or years of being suspended in a kind of half-life, not knowing whether loved ones lived or had been dead for many weeks or months.

War has also brought suspicion. This is doubly true here in Brittany, where a neighbour or a servant or even a loved one might prove to be a secret supporter of the enemy's cause. Worse, one day might bring a Blue regiment to one's door, the next a column of Chouans. We have seen both here at the Chateau de Brechelean over the course of the last year or so, most recently the extended recuperation of the memorable Colonel Georges Cozanet.

Strangers are especially unwelcome, for who knows what they might prove to be? So when Jacques Penhouet comes to tell me that a bourgeois of obvious rank but not necessarily good breeding, albeit foreign and unspeakably ugly, is at the door of the chateau, I am immediately on my guard. More so when I learn that the gentlemen gives his name as Citizen Antoine Heinrich of Rennes, claims prior acquaintance with me, and insists that he speak to me in person. Jacques presses him further, or so he says, and the man claiming to be Heinrich says that he is well acquainted with my brother-in-law, Philippe, the vicomte. He knows, as do I, that invoking the name of the chateau's owner, essentially my landlord, and claiming him for an acquaintance, makes it impossible for Jacques to refuse him admittance.

I make myself presentable, ensure I have made ready all I need to meet my unexpected guest, and then go down. In the time before the guillotine appeared in France, of course, the chatelaine of an estate would never have dreamed of appearing at her own door. But most footmen have gone to the army or the grave, even housemaids to the mills or the brothels. Like so much else in France, genteel civilities have become as dust.

When I appear, Antoine Heinrich bows rather too low. I could swear the top of his head is so bright it must have been polished with furniture wax.

'I must crave your forgiveness for my uninvited intrusion, Citizeness,' he says, 'but I have news of your brother-in-law, the vicomte, that I thought it best to convey in person.'

I cover my mouth, the reaction of one in shock.

'News, Citizen? Bad news? Has Philippe – has he been killed? Oh sir, tell me, I beg you!'

'Perhaps, Citizeness, it would be better if we discuss my news inside?'

'Why of course, Citizen Heinrich! No matter what your tidings are, you must consider me unforgivably inhospitable!'

I take him through to the drawing room but do not invite him to sit. To ensure that propriety is maintained, Jacques Penhouet stands by the door. His age makes standing for any amount of time difficult, so I allow him to lean on the oak cabinet that stands by the wall.

'Well, sir,' I say to Heinrich, an urgency to my words, 'what is your news of Philippe? This news that brings you here in person?'

Heinrich takes a long pause before replying. He seems to be studying the furniture and fittings of the room, especially the paintings of long-dead members of Philippe's family.

'Your brother-in-law captains a ship I own. One can dress this up in all sorts of legal nicety, but the simple truth is it puts him in my employ. He is my servant. He is beholden to me.'

'I cannot imagine the vicomte would agree with you, sir. But your opinion of his relations with you is hardly news urgent enough to bring you to my door.'

As I witnessed at Rennes, Heinrich is a man who resents being interrupted, especially by a woman. Once again I think that in terms of both his manners and his appearance he is one of the most repulsive men I have ever encountered.

'My servant,' he repeats, his tone becoming ever angrier, 'and as such, I gave him instructions that I expected to be obeyed. Orders, indeed. But he has failed me, madame, failed me most grievously. I commanded him to obtain a piece of property of mine that had been wrongly separated from me. I had confidence in his ability to perform this task. But I say again, he has failed me, madame! Failed me grievously! Worse, he has connived in keeping the property of which I speak apart from me!'

'I sympathise with your loss, sir,' I say, feeling no sympathy whatsoever. 'But I still cannot comprehend what any of this has to do with me, and why you have come here to tell me this.'

Heinrich's thoughts seem to be far away. Slowly, though, his gaze settles on me once again, and now there is a fierce look in his eyes.

'I will have restitution! I will have something of his to compensate for my loss!'

'Your tone is frightening me, Citizen.'

He seems not to hear. There is a mania about him now, a wild ferocity to his expression and a tension about his entire posture.

'I read your letter to him,' he says. I blink, but not in surprise. Part of me always expected Antoine Heinrich to open the letter I entrusted to him. 'Such passion. Such humility. Emotion that I would not have believed possible in such a demure widow as yourself. These are qualities I value in a woman.'

'You had no right to open—'

'I have secured this chateau, madame,' he says triumphantly, entirely ignoring my protest. *'By now my men will have rounded up all your servants. So you will do my will now, Madame Leonore Kermorvant. You will do it for all time to come.'*

I try to remain calm, but my voice trembles.

'Your will, Citizen? And what is your will, pray?'

His jowly features flush with anticipation.

'I have certain tastes, madame. Certain inclinations. I have – have had – a wife who I made to indulge these tastes, but she was snatched from me by a very devil. Your precious vicomte has failed to reclaim her for me as I ordered him to. So I will have you in her stead.'

I stare at him. I hope I do not give the impression of fear and weakness. Jacques still stands by the cabinet, his dear old face creased with fury. He takes a step forward, but Heinrich draws a knife from inside his tunic coat and holds it out before him.

'Stay where you are, old man. Another step and I'll slice your belly open. Try for the door and you'll find a dozen of my men beyond it.'

He is deranged. He should be locked away and chained up in an asylum. But ancient Jacques, dear Jacques, seems genuinely disturbed by the threat from the lunatic before us. It is time to end the charade.

'A dozen of your men,' I say. *'These would be the dozen men who are now locked in my cellars?'*

For the first time, Heinrich looks confused and unsure of himself.

'Blum!' he shouts. *'Itten! Belocien! Renaudie!'*

There is no answer. There is perfect silence apart from the ticking of the Boulle mantel clock. I smile.

'I regret to have to tell you, Citizen Heinrich, that your arrival was anticipated.'

For once, the supremely arrogant Antoine Heinrich has no words.

The post-haste letter from Philippe had arrived only three days before, following a minor miracle of rare efficiency from the post offices. The letter, which must have crossed my compromised letter to him, set out what had transpired in the isles of Orkney and at The Helder along with his warning that Heinrich might attempt to take revenge on him by striking at me. A small regiment was swiftly assembled from the nearest tenants of Brechelean, men who were entirely willing to spend a few days billeted in the chateau in return for ample victuals and unlimited cider.

Jacques turns and opens the largest compartment of the cabinet. He draws out the musket that I always keep primed and loaded and have placed in the cabinet for this specific purpose, and hands it to me. I raise it and level it at Citizen Antoine Heinrich.

He cannot comprehend what is happening. His eyes are wide but blank, staring at some remote distance that he cannot see. Then he reaches down suddenly. I see the butt of a small concealed pistol in his right riding boot.

Jacques calls out – 'Madame!'

But I have already pulled the trigger. The range is so short that the ball goes straight through Antoine Heinrich and shatters the face of the Boulle clock. Its ticking stops for ever. The Swiss, the monster of the most depraved perversions, lies dead on the floor, the blood slowly seeping onto the venerable mosaic of parquet.

I stare at what I have done. I am barely aware of Jacques at my side, murmuring words of reassurance. I do not yet feel shock, but that will come. Indeed, I felt more emotion when Philippe's letter from The Helder in Holland arrived at the chateau. As well as warning me of the likely appearance of the vengeful Antoine Heinrich and apologising for what he termed his unforgivable curtness toward me over the matter of Colonel

Cozanet, he also expressed certain sentiments that I never knew him to possess. Sentiments expressed toward me, sentiments that finally addressed that elusive, long-evaded question of the feelings between us. Sentiments almost identical to those I had addressed to him in the letter I had foolishly entrusted for onward forwarding to the safekeeping of Antoine Heinrich, unaware then of the sort of man he was. The sort of man who opens private correspondence, reads what is within, and thus discovers expressions of emotion that, to his warped mind, could give him power over another human being. Over me.

In his letter, Philippe also made a proposition that I had not expected from him, especially considering the circumstances of our parting. A proposition that changes everything.

Those words, those sentiments, that proposition, gave me the most profound shock imaginable. The killing of Antoine Heinrich does not.

Olivier arrives with a couple of the lads from the village, and they carry away the corpse of the monster. Martha Penhouet arrives to scrub his blood from the floor.

Yes, it is a dangerous time to be a woman in France. But it can be more dangerous for others.

CHAPTER THIRTY-THREE

Relieved to be out at last of the noise and bustle of the City of Westminster, Lord Wilden crossed the familiar threshold of the five-storeyed building on Saint James's Street, handed his coat and hat to a footman, and followed the directions given by the major-domo. He found his quarry in the library, as he had expected. Equally expected was the emptiness of that particular room. At that time of day most of the members of White's would be found in the dining room or, more likely, the card room. Even when those locations were empty, few members ever found their way to the library. A thirst for intellectual enrichment was not high on the list of qualities expected of members in any London club, perhaps especially so at White's. But the prime minister's inclinations were very much in tune with Wilden's own, and he found William Pitt seated in an alcove reading a volume of Cicero, a glass of port and the decanter from which it was drawn nestling on the small side table. Later that day the prime minister would have to host a Cabinet meeting to discuss the continuing wave of bread riots taking place across the length and breadth of Britain. For the moment, though, the long parliamentary summer recess meant that Pitt could take advantage of a few precious hours of relative leisure.

'Good afternoon, Ned,' said the prime minister, gesturing for Wilden to take the chair opposite his. Pitt reached at once for the adjacent decanter. 'Port?'

'Thank you but no, Prime Minister. I regret that my digestion has been a little erratic since I returned from Quiberon.'

'Understandable, that,' said Pitt, pouring himself a glass and devouring a few more lines of text before closing the book and placing it on the table alongside the port. 'A forgettable business altogether. You've heard that Fort Penthièvre has fallen to the enemy, of course?' Wilden nodded. 'Thank God we had time to recall Lord Moira's division before they got there. No English blood spilled, at least. So you got out of there in the nick of time, Ned. Warren evacuated as many as he could, of course, but God knows how many hundreds – thousands, maybe – drowned trying to get out to his ships. The rest accepted terms and surrendered, I'm told, so one can only hope those terms are honoured. Puisaye and Hervilly got out, naturally.'

Wilden grimaced.

'I hear they're both back in London, blaming each other. Blaming us, too.'

'Everyone to blame apart from themselves, eh? That's the way of the world, Ned. But Hervilly won't live much longer to blame anyone ever again, or so I gather.'

Wilden nodded. Hervilly had been mortally wounded in the chest during the final republican attacks, and it was a miracle that he had been somehow kept alive throughout the voyage back to England and the subsequent return to London. But the consensus of the doctors was unanimous, and there was no hope of the opinionated *emigré* general seeing in 1796.

The prime minister had fallen silent, seemingly intent on inspecting the dregs of his glass of port. Wilden's eyes wandered to the titles on the adjacent shelves. Time for a little frankness, perchance. Pitt seemed to be in a frame of mind that could accommodate a little candour.

'We did back the wrong horse, Prime Minister. Hervilly, I mean. I'm no general, but dear God, the things I witnessed – his insistence that they could not advance until Sombreuil's troops had arrived, and then when they do arrive, he attacks before they can disembark, by which time General Hoche has a vastly larger army cutting off the peninsula and the attack Hervilly orders is hopeless. And that was by no means his only error of judgement, sir. I take responsibility, of course. I advised the course we adopted, and I made every effort I could to reconcile Hervilly and Puisaye to it. But I failed.'

Pitt sniffed. The distinct odours of recently taken snuff and fine old port wine hung in the air between them.

'Oh, undoubtedly the wrong horse, Ned, although I'll never admit that in the Commons, needless to say, and have Fox eviscerate me yet again.' Charles James Fox, the ever-belligerent leader of the opposition, had been vocal in denouncing the perceived failure of the Quiberon expedition. 'Nor will I admit it to the king, come to that. And I don't blame you, Ned, have no fear on that score. Rest assured it will not be counted as your failure. One of the inescapable truths of being prime minister is that ultimately, responsibility for success and failure, victory and defeat alike is always mine. But would it have made any difference if we'd gone the other way and backed Puisaye, eh? You were there, Ned, so what say you?'

'The truth, Prime Minister?' Pitt nodded. An accommodating frame of mind indeed. 'I think if we'd given

Puisaye his head, he'd have led the expedition to disaster in four days instead of four weeks, even assuming the *emigrés* would have obeyed him, which I very much doubt. If Artois had been there… but that's spilled milk now. In his absence we should have insisted on a British general, sir. Given the supreme command to Lord Moira, for example.'

Pitt looked sharply at him.

'A French army under the command of an Englishman. As if that would have ended well either, eh? As it is, the king, who's unexpectedly sanguine about the whole business, tells me daily that we've suffered no great loss by it. Our own army thankfully remains intact because Moira's division couldn't get there in time, Bridport's victory brought us three more ships of the line, so all's well, he says. I humour His Majesty, of course, but I fear he isn't quite as mindful of our reputation with our allies – our credibility upon the international stage, if you prefer – as you and I have to be, Ned.'

Wilden had seen partial proof of the king's somewhat rose-coloured opinion of the outcome of the expedition from a purely British point of view when the frigate bringing him back from Quiberon came into Portsmouth harbour and Wilden saw the three prizes taken by Lord Bridport's fleet with his own eyes, now HMS *Alexander*, HMS *Tigre* and HMS *Belleisle*, formerly *Le Formidable*, all now refitting for service in the Royal Navy. They were a cheering sight, despite bringing back memories of gallant Midshipman Kenton and all the other brave men who died to win that battle and secure those three ships. But having been in Brittany and having also known many of the brave French royalists who, unlike Jack Kenton, had perished in an utterly hopeless cause, Wilden could not see the degree of equivalence that the king apparently perceived. But he would certainly not argue the point with William Pitt, let alone with King George himself.

'As you say, Prime Minister.'

Pitt took a sip of his glass of port, looked out of the library window for several seconds, and then seemed to banish from his mind both difficult thoughts of King George's veritable multitude of idiosyncrasies and the undoubted fiasco of the Quiberon expedition.

'Speaking of reputations, Ned, I hear tales that since your return you've been paying much court to a widow in Oxfordshire. A dead midshipman's mother, I believe? And you're said to have arranged a pension for her from your own funds? Tongues are wagging around the gaming tables, my Lord Wilden.'

Pitt's odd expression was probably the closest the prime minister could come to a mischievous mocking smile. Wilden knew he was blushing, a strange reaction considering that his dealings with Mrs Kenton were entirely appropriate and quite beyond reproach. But Jack Kenton's mother had been markedly grateful for a first-hand account of her son's death, and her home lay just off one of the best roads between London and his Shropshire estate. An easy detour to make again, should he wish to do so and if she would deign to receive him. Which she undoubtedly would.

Yes, entirely appropriate and beyond reproach.

'Prime Minister, I—'

The door of the library opened abruptly. An elderly club member whom Wilden vaguely recognised, an obscure Irish peer if he recalled aright, made for the shelves devoted to Roman history, his thoughts seemingly far away. Then, with a start, he noticed the prime minister and a famously enigmatic lord of the Admiralty deep in conference. The ancient earl muttered apologies and scuttled off as though an unbreachable curtain wall surrounded the two men.

The interruption was fortuitous, as it deflected William Pitt back to the principal matter in both their minds from any further inquisitiveness about Ned Wilden's tentative dealings with Mrs Kenton.

'No, Ned,' said Pitt reflectively, 'enough of the whole cursed business of Quiberon. We are done with expeditions to France, I think, for some years at any rate. But there are other fronts, eh? Other potential allies who may yet tip the scales in our favour, the Empress Catherine for one. Other schemes to devise, other plans to set in motion. God willing, Ned, victory will be ours one day. Perhaps we shall even live to see it.'

Ignoring Wilden's protests about his digestion, the prime minister filled a glass and handed it to Ned while also refilling his own. He raised it for a toast.

'To victory, my Lord Wilden.'

Ned raised his own glass.

'To victory, Prime Minister.'

CHAPTER THIRTY-FOUR

They had been promised pardon and safe conduct.

Georges Cozanet had heard it himself. Within his earshot General Lazare Hoche, the young commanding officer of the victorious Blue army in the Quiberon campaign, had promised that all the royalist prisoners, both *emigré* and Chouan, would live. But either Hoche had lied or, more likely, other counsels had prevailed in Paris and other orders had been sent to the west. There had been military tribunals, mere pretences with only one inevitable verdict. Many good men, many loyal Chouans, had already been summarily shot. The young and valiant Marquis de Sombreuil, come too late to the campaign to do anything but die, was gone. Cozanet's old second in command, Yves de Montargis, was gone too. Both had acquitted themselves bravely before the firing squad, as had every Chouan who had met the same fate. Now it was to be Cozanet's turn. Not for him the more eminent place of execution at Vannes, where some of the other Chouan and *emigré* leaders had gone and both Sombreuil and Montargis had met their ends. No, Cozanet would die with the common men of the *Chouanerrie* here at Auray, and he was proud that it would be so. These were his people, the stock from which he had sprung, and he preferred to die with them than with the strutting, arrogant *emigrés*.

He had faced a military tribunal of sorts, held in the redundant chapel of a former convent in the small town of Auray. They were an unimpressive court, half a dozen evidently bored scrapings of the Blue army ranging from a fat, drunken captain down to a mere corporal. But they could have been the old *Parlement de Paris* itself for the difference it might have made. The evidence against him was overwhelming and he could not, would not dispute it. He could not deny that he had been a colonel in the Catholic and Royal Army and that he had been in arms against their so-called French Republic, supposedly one and allegedly indivisible, for the best part of three years. He could not deny that most recently he had been in arms in the hated red uniform of France's eternal enemy, disembarked from British warships, to fight in an expedition instigated by the British prime minister and accompanied in person by a British lord of the Admiralty. The verdict was never in doubt and undoubtedly justified by any standards, let alone those of the revolutionary republic. Instead, Georges Cozanet reconciled himself to dying for his king and a better France, and in the hope that death would bring the blessed reunion with lost loved ones that Holy Church promised.

Three lots of prisoners had already been led out by small detachments of Blue troops, and after a few minutes in each case, those left in the cells had heard distant volleys of musket fire. Now it was the term for Georges Cozanet and his brothers-in-arms. As he and a dozen others were herded together by the guards, ready for their final journey, Georges thought of his fleeting but charged encounter with Leonore Kermorvant at the Chateau de Brechelean. Would that remarkable woman weep for him when she learned of his death? He hoped so. She was so different to his dead love, his wife, Thérèse, yet perhaps in another time, in another world...

But he had seen the looks exchanged between her and her brother-in-law, the Vicomte de Saint-Victor, and knew his dreams could never have been. Another world indeed. So be it. Dawn was not long past. Birds were singing, the late summer sun was shining. It was a beautiful day to die.

Only a few minutes passed, then another detachment of Blue troops arrived to escort the next batch of prisoners, the batch including Georges Cozanet, from their prison quarters in the dormitories of the old convent out to the execution ground, a rough meadow on the edge of town. He walked with his erstwhile captain, Kerouac, who was still fulminating bitterly over the calamitous outcome of the campaign.

'Damn the English,' said Kerouac. 'They brought us to this. Made all sorts of promises, but did they send any of their own troops? Ha. *Merde*. Made us fight in their fucking red uniforms, then abandoned us to the Blues. Betrayed us. Pitt, that weasel Wilden, every damn one of 'em. Fuck 'em all.'

Georges knew the Quiberon expedition had failed for many other reasons, but he sensed that when the French histories of the debacle were written, it would be Kerouac's view that would prevail. England had always provided a very convenient scapegoat for Frenchmen's own failings. The red uniforms would serve for all eternity as the emblem for the utter fiasco that had been the affair of Quiberon, and the presence of the English envoy, Lord Wilden, would be another.

'Let it pass,' he said to Kerouac as they entered the meadow where the sentence of the military tribunals would be carried out. 'Think of nothing but prayers now.'

'Prayers, Colonel? Look at who commands the firing squad, then tell me prayers do any fucking good.'

Cozanet looked in the direction where Kerouac was pointing. The commander of the firing squad saw him and grinned brazenly. It was Lafontaine, sometime drill sergeant of the Regiment de Dresnay of the Catholic and Royal Army, formerly attached to the Regiment de Cozanet to teach it proper drill. He was back in the blue uniform that he evidently found far more comfortable than the red one he had abandoned. The one consolation in the appearance of the man who had turned his coat so many times was that it exonerated Georges' own Chouans, who had not, after all, silently slit the detested sergeant's throat and fed him to the pigs.

Perhaps there was a lesson to be drawn from Lafontaine's triumphant smile. The men of loyalty to their causes, the men of valour and worth, were being slaughtered on the killing grounds of Vannes and Auray, or in the case of the Blues, on the battlefields of the Rhine and Italy. Somehow, though, the Sergeant Lafontaines of the world would always survive. One day, theirs would be the victory.

As they bundled him into position and the sentences of the military tribunal were read aloud, Cozanet was able to study the crowd of onlookers standing at the edges of the meadow, a substantial crowd being held back by blue-uniformed National Guardsmen. Most were women and children, the menfolk probably dead or else away fighting for one allegiance or the other. As he scanned the faces, Georges saw every emotion depending on the sentiments of each individual spectator: grief, weeping, frozen disbelief, revulsion, indifference, exultation, delirious happiness. Some were chattering excitedly to each other, no hint of solemnity in their demeanour. These were the people he had tried to fight for, the people and the world he was about to leave. He and his comrades were being shot to death as an example to these people, but what example would that be? A warning of the fate that befell those who fought against the Republic, the lesson that the Blue officers and their principals in Paris undoubtedly wished to be drawn? Or the legacy of a glorious martyrdom in the cause of the rightful King of France, who would surely one day return to his own? But the world of the future no longer held any relevance at all for Georges Cozanet. He took a deep breath to compose himself.

One of the others, at the far end of the line of doomed royalists, began reciting the mass for the dead.

'Libera me, domine, de morte eterna...'

Cozanet heard Lafontaine's order to the firing squad to present their muskets, saw and heard the cocking of the weapons.

'Apprêtez armes!'

'Ah, fuck it,' said Kerouac.

Cozanet's last sight was of three children, two boys and a girl, in the centre of the front row, their expressions at once sad and curious, their presence so reminiscent of his own lost family. The three children were staring directly at him. He repaid them with a smile, then heard Lafontaine give the order to open fire.

'Feu!'

Georges Cozanet smiled no more and heard no more.

EPILOGUE

France had a new government. The feverish excitement of the fall of the Bastille had given way within a few years to the unmitigated horrors of the guillotine, but the Terror in turn had faded into memory as a reaction against its excesses set in. Now the National Convention had been dissolved, the Committee of Public Safety had met for the last time, a new constitution had been inaugurated, and the newly inaugurated Directory ruled the fledgling republic. Five men were now entrusted with the powers once exercised by the Bourbon kings and took on the responsibility of continuing the seemingly interminable war against France's formidable array of enemies. On a day early in Frimaire that would once have fallen in the old month of December, with a blizzard lashing the windows of the Luxembourg Palace and thick snow carpeting the streets of Paris, Philippe Kermorvant sat across a paper-strewn table from one of them, an expensively dressed man with dark, unruly hair, a prominent nose and a broad, thin-lipped mouth.

'Philippe Kermorvant, Vicomte de Saint-Victor,' said General Lazare Carnot in a slightly bored tone of voice. 'My cousin Leonore extols your virtues most generously.'

Philippe was aware that Leonore had been writing regularly on his behalf to her eminent relative, a connection by way of Carnot's maternal line, but neither of them had really expected there to be a positive outcome. The summons that had come to the Chateau de Brechelean three weeks earlier came as a shock to them both.

'I do not deserve her acclaim, sir, nor her intercession with you.'

Carnot looked at him levelly.

'Well, Captain, you're right in that. Her relationship to me is tolerably distant and wouldn't have got you through the door of this building, let alone into this room and onto that chair. But I find your story intriguing. I wished to meet you to see what kind of metal you were cast from. To see what kind of man the son of Verité was.'

Philippe found Carnot impressive. The general was businesslike, did not waste words, and rarely failed to look his visitor directly in the eye. He had a formidable reputation as the man who had organised France's revolutionary armies, performing the miracle of turning an untrained rabble into a fighting force formidable enough to take on and defeat one formidable enemy after another. In the opinion of many, Lazare Carnot was the man who had saved the Republic and the French Revolution. And for such a man, only plain speaking would do.

'I am as you see me, sir.'

'Hmm. And how am I expected to see a man who has an English mother? A man who is cousin to their spymaster, Wilden, who we know was in Brittany in the summer during the affair of Quiberon? The files are full of suspicions of you, Captain. Admiral Fidelin was particularly strident on the subject, hence your dismissal last year from command in the Marine Nationale.'

'By your leave, General, Admiral Fidelin was a traitor himself, seeking to divert suspicion on to me to conceal his own guilt.'

Carnot raised an eyebrow.

'Perhaps so, Citizen, perhaps so, although never proved in his case just as it never was in yours. All entirely academic, however, since Fidelin has died of fever in the Indies. You didn't know that? Convenient for you. Convenient for him, too, as far as death can ever be convenient. Removed from suspicion, removed from rumours and whispers that were getting louder by the day. So one of your enemies has left the stage, Captain, but you have others. The most notable, I think, would be Citizen Antoine Heinrich of Rennes, who was most strident in his denunciation of you before his unfortunate demise at my cousin's hands.'

'General Carnot, I have made legal depositions concerning the true nature of Citizen Heinrich's dealings—'

'Which I have read. Such an unsavoury tale, and so unlike all the other papers that pass across my desk. The perversions a man's lust may drive him to... But whatever the man's predilections, Captain, the essential fact of the case is that he lies dead in a vault, and I also have sworn depositions from several reputable witnesses testifying to the honourable nature of your dealings with him.' Carnot picked up a small bundle of papers and waved it. 'From the Basque Ugarte, various respectable citizens of Rennes, Concarneau and the Batavian Republic, all in addition to a particularly forceful plea on your behalf by a certain Scot, a British officer and thus an enemy of France, who nonetheless takes the trouble to write to me, a sworn enemy of his country. An incomprehensible name, but his sentiments are clear enough.'

Thorfinn Rendall. It could be no one else. The crippled soldier of Orkney had acted on the debt he owed Philippe

Kermorvant, just as Philippe had acted on the debt he owed Rendall. But to take the risk of writing to one of the most senior figures in the government of his national enemy showed a degree of courage as astonishing as that which had ruined his body on the battlefield.

'Of course,' said Carnot, 'there are still friends of Citizen Heinrich in positions of authority, members of our new Council of Five Hundred and so forth. Friends of the late Admiral Fidelin, too. But I place no weight on such things, Captain. I am interested only in the present, not in the prejudices of the dead. My concern is solely for the best interests of France, and the Republic is in sore need of men who know how to fight and command at sea. I have considered the evidence before me and I have considered *you*, Captain.' Carnot sat back in his chair, a decision seemingly made.

'Very well,' said Carnot, 'I have more important matters to consider, and I have given you enough of my time, Monsieur le Vicomte. So, then. Admiral Truguet is Minister of Marine since Thermidor. I will write to him on behalf of the Directory of the French Republic. I will instruct him that when a suitable vacancy occurs in the Marine Nationale, he is to commission you to a command with the restored rank of *captaine de vaisseau*. You may pass on the good news to my cousin, along with my acknowledgement of her passionate advocacy on your behalf. And, naturally, pass on my warm congratulations to her upon her marriage. You, too, of course, Citizen. The Vicomtesse de Saint-Victor... that little cousin Leonore should have grown so high! But the title suits her, I think. Good day to you, Monsieur le Vicomte, Captain Philippe Kermorvant, and *bon chance*.'

HISTORICAL NOTE AND ACKNOWLEDGEMENTS

The Quiberon expedition of 1795 is a calamitous but relatively little-known episode in the French Revolutionary wars, despite providing the backdrop for individual books in C. S. Forester's Hornblower series and the Poldark canon by Winston Graham. Although the pre-existing royalist rebellions in the Vendée and the so-called *Chouanerrie* in Brittany spluttered on intermittently for a few more years, the expedition was the last serious royalist attempt to overthrow the French Republic. Yet despite significant British support, notably the deployment of a squadron under Sir John Borlase Warren, and the cover provided by Lord Bridport's fleet, the expedition was doomed almost from the outset. There were strong mutual suspicion and distrust between the *emigrés*, chiefly aristocrats who had gone into exile during the early stages of the revolution, and the Chouans, who had remained in Brittany throughout and run far greater risks in consequence. Such avoidable mistakes as the insistence on the Chouans adopting red uniforms and British boots, and learning proper drill, only served rapidly to exacerbate the native Bretons' disillusionment with the arrogant *emigrés*, while the recruitment of former republican prisoners into the royalist army was a cast-iron guarantee of disaster. All of these tensions and mistakes were exacerbated by the division of the royalist command between the Comtes de Puisaye, who had built up extensive contacts among the Chouans but was no soldier and was suspected for his previous republican sympathies, and Hervilly, an experienced but (as it turned out) overly cautious military veteran. This episode remains controversial in France, and as Lord Wilden predicts in Chapter Twenty-Nine, down the years some French writers have sought to blame the British for the fatal decision; *plus ça change*. But the evidence proves otherwise, so my hypothesis that Pitt and another minister (with Lord Wilden standing as a proxy in my story for the actual 'culprit', William Windham, the Secretary at War) deliberately arranged a divided command is purely dramatic licence.

Cornwallis's retreat and the Battle of Groix (also known by other names, such as the Battle of Lorient) have again been recounted as accurately as a fictional narrative will allow, based on a range of primary and secondary sources including the original logbooks of several of the British ships. The reasons why Admiral Villaret de Joyeuse broke off the action with Cornwallis and missed a golden opportunity to destroy an entire squadron of the Royal Navy remain unclear, although it is difficult to escape the conclusion drawn by Captain Sir Erasmus Gower in this story, namely that Villaret and his officers, deceived by the ingenious theatricals performed by Captain Robert Stopford of the scouting frigate *Phaeton*, convinced themselves that Lord Bridport's fleet was much nearer than it actually was. On the British side, though, Bridport was a notoriously difficult and quarrelsome individual, and as he proved in the Battle of Groix, he too lacked the quality of fearless decisiveness that might have led to the destruction of the French Brest fleet.

Of those encountered by the principal protagonists of the story, the Heinrichs, father and son, are based very loosely indeed on Christophe Bourcard of Nantes and formerly of Basle, who set out the privateer *Adelaide* from the former town in 1798 and whose activities are described by R. P. Crowhurst in *The Mariner's Mirror* for 2013. William Pitt, Lord Bridport, Sir John Borlase Warren, the Comtes de Puisaye and Hervilly and many other characters encountered by Lord Wilden are all real historical figures who played very similar parts in history to those I have assigned to them, but I have taken a few liberties with my treatment of all of them and even more with more minor characters. For example, the nonagenarian governor of Pendennis Castle mentioned as entertaining Lord Wilden in Chapter Eight was General Felix Buckley, but although he was the governor in 1795 and remained so until his death at ninety-nine, he was actually a mere stripling of seventy at the time when this story is set. Lord Hugh Seymour was almost certainly less charismatic than I have made him, although he was certainly as well connected and innovative; he went on to command the naval forces in the West Indies and led the capture of Surinam in 1800. General Lazare Hoche, little more than a year older than Napoleon Bonaparte, had a career that might have equalled or surpassed that of his Corsican contemporary. Originally a common soldier who was no more than a corporal at the outbreak of the revolution in 1789, he was a general by 1793 at the age of twenty-five. Hoche won several battles in the Rhineland, successfully suppressed the royalist revolts in Brittany and the Vendée, and commanded the army sent to invade Ireland in 1796, when bad weather thwarted an expedition that forms one of the great 'might have beens' of Irish and, indeed, European history. Briefly war minister in 1797, Hoche was in command of the Army of the Rhine when he died of tuberculosis at the age of twenty-nine. His name was inscribed on the Arc de Triomphe, and a statue commemorating his victory in the campaign of 1795, the subject of this book, stands in Quiberon.

Aside from these real historical figures, Colonel Georges Cozanet is an invented character combining elements of several Chouan leaders who served in the vicious French civil wars of the 1790s, notably François de Charette, Georges Cadoudal and Rene Augustin de Chalus. I have also taken some liberties with the sequence of events: for example, the successful royalist attack on Fort Sans-Culotte took place after the requiems for Louis XVII rather than before, while I have omitted the desultory operations that took place at Quiberon and in the offshore islands through to the autumn of 1795 when the British finally abandoned all efforts in the area, despite the fact that the Comte d'Artois had finally made a long overdue landing in France to try to rally the royalist forces. Probably my most egregious deviation from the historical record, though, has been to send a privateer to sea under the French flag in the summer of 1795. In reality, the French Republic declared a moratorium on privateering from 1794 until late 1795 in order to ensure the navy was properly manned and, above all, to provide resources for a projected French invasion of the British Isles.

The combined Anglo–Russian fleet of 1795–7, of which the fictitious Captain Komarov's command *Drakon* forms a part, is something of a historical curiosity, but a Russian squadron came to Britain in the summer of 1795 to form part of Admiral Adam Duncan's command, the North Sea Fleet, during its operations primarily against the fleet of the French satellite state, the Batavian Republic. The circumstances of that republic's creation, mentioned in this story, did indeed include probably the only occasion in history when a navy, trapped in a frozen sea, surrendered to cavalry.

The isles of Orkney and the great natural harbour of Scapa Flow, which play a prominent part in this book, became renowned in naval history in different wars fought in a later century. They played relatively little part in the French Revolutionary and Napoleonic wars, although a Martello Tower and battery were built at Hackness on the island of Hoy in 1815 to protect what had by then become an important assembly haven for convoys going to and from Russia against French and American privateers. I hope readers will have found some interest in my descriptions of one of the world's most famous naval harbours long before it entered the national consciousness and the pages of the history books. I have incurred many debts during my visits to Orkney over the last ten years or so, not least to the staffs of the Orkney Library and Archive, Stromness Museum, the new Scapa Flow Museum on Hoy and its curator, Nick Hewitt, and the Orkney Museum in Tankerness House, Kirkwall. Thanks too to all those whose hospitality and friendship we have enjoyed in the islands. I must also thank Peter Buckman, agent extraordinaire, and Kit Nevile, my ever-patient editor at Canelo, for their unstinting support and encouragement. Wendy made this book, like all my previous ones, infinitely better than it might have been, and not just because of her persistent and insistent championing of Leonore. As ever, my principal thanks are to her.

Finally, anyone who has read all my previous novels (and if you have, please accept my deepest sympathies) will know that I wrote a series based on a seventeenth-century naval officer named Matthew Quinton, whose Dutch wife, Cornelia, had a twin brother called Cornelis. Over a dozen novels later, and quite late in the writing of this one, I stumbled across the startling coincidence that the far from fictitious fourth lieutenant of HMS *Sans Pareil*, aboard which several chapters of this story are set, was named Cornelius Quinton. Unsurprisingly I decided to squeeze him in as a character, albeit only fleetingly. After all, and to paraphrase the satirical magazine *Private Eye*, I wonder if they were by any chance related?